SABBATICAL

CURRICULUM VITAE
BOOK 2

KATRINA JACKSON

SPRING

CHAPTER ONE

"We don't need another poorly attended conference," Leonard Hsu said, trying to hide his aggravation. "Sorry, symposium," he added sarcastically, effectively sidestepping Susan Beard's only real contribution to this committee.

Toni glanced at the other woman, her index finger in the air, a triumphant smile dying on her lips. Susan never missed an opportunity to suggest a symposium at their meetings. She'd been at the university for almost a decade and was still searching for a way to create a "signature annual event" — one that would look good in her merit file but require very little work for most of the year. Leonard had caught onto her very quickly, and every meeting, his ability to hide his disgust at her self-serving search for one more event frayed ever thinner.

As a person, Toni found the drama between Leonard and Sue riveting, some of the best entertainment of the month. She also happened to agree with Leonard. The last thing her calendar needed was one more conference or symposium clogging up the last few weeks of spring semester. But as chair of the President's Advisory Council on Belonging and Inclusion, she had to pretend to be diplomatic or, at the very least, stop the argument that had been brewing all academic year.

Preston Marks beat her to it. "What about an essay contest?"

Margery Pham sighed, and internally, Toni sighed right along with her. Externally, Toni smiled in Preston's direction.

"Preston, this is the end of your first year at the university, right?" Toni hated asking questions she already knew the answer to, but sometimes she had to walk people — students and colleagues alike — through a lesson from A to Z.

"Yes," he said, sitting up straight in his chair, beaming at her.

She smiled, feeling a sense of warmth that was only tainted at the edges by a deep exhaustion she hoped he never felt but knew he probably would. Preston reminded Toni of Deja during her first year. The ones who came straight out of grad school always had a certain naïve optimism that was as inspiring as it was heartbreaking. They always thought they were on the verge of changing the world. It was devastating watching reality hit them hard and change them. Whether it beat them down or taught them that selling out was much better than sticking to your morals, at least in the short term — no matter which road they chose — it was painful to witness.

Toni couldn't remember being so green. She didn't think she'd ever been naïvely optimistic. She'd walked out of grad school with a prestigious two-year post-doctoral fellowship, but when it had nearly killed her with microaggressions and over-work, she'd expected it. And when she'd left her last institution because her old department wouldn't grant her tenure, a part of her had expected that as well. What other outcome could she imagine after reporting the chair of the department for sexual harassment and racial discrimination? Especially when the College had brushed her complaint under the rug? If there had ever been a time when Toni hadn't felt rubbed raw by her job, she couldn't remember it.

"Do you assign a lot of writing in your classes?" she asked Preston.

"Oh, yes," he said, beaming at her across the table. "It's so important that students get to practice writing and get ample feedback and guidance at the same time."

Someone in the room groaned. A few of the senior faculty shifted uncomfortably in their seats. She couldn't help but wonder where all this enthusiasm went. Did it start to fade after day one or the first year? In her official and unofficial roles as a mentor to junior faculty, Toni spent an uncomfortable amount of time fighting bitterness as she watched the university sap the energy from her younger colleagues. She tried to sit as a bulwark against it, but even she knew that most of her efforts were only a temporary solution to systemic problems — systemic problems no one with any real power seemed willing to address. Thankfully, Toni had learned early in her career how to push her own emotions aside to get the work done — because the work was what mattered.

"I agree," Toni said, smiling patiently at Preston. "But if you can, imagine the students you've had this year writing an essay on the importance of diversity on this campus." She took a breath and consulted her notes. "Let's be generous and imagine that they have a one-month turnaround from our prompt going out and submission. Imagine the state of those drafts. Imagine the time it will take to give them the feedback and guidance they need before presenting at a symposium of some sort. Imagine doing that right in the middle of spring semester."

On the other side of the table, Susan had started at her favorite word and then shrunk back as Toni kept speaking.

"How much time would it take them to write it?" she asked

Preston. "How much time would it take us to review them, deliberate, and decide on a winner?"

Even though there were people in the room who believed otherwise, Toni derived no pleasure from watching Preston deflate as she spoke. Unlike some of her colleagues, she didn't find it entertaining to watch people she respected shrink in on themselves. But she did think it was her job to be honest and set boundaries younger colleagues could not, would not, or didn't even know were possible. Even when she was not mentoring, she modeled what she hoped was good behavior. And taking on more needless busywork was *not* good behavior.

"I see," Preston muttered, sitting back in his chair with a frown. "Sorry."

"Don't apologize," she said, still smiling warmly at him. He gave her a half-hearted smile, and then Toni turned to look around the small conference table. "Look, we don't have to make any decisions today. In fact, it would be foolish if we did."

She made meaningful eye contact with the members of a committee she'd been conned into chairing for the last two years. These weren't her people per se, but one of the problems with Toni's personality was that everyone, after a while, became one of her people. It was a trait she'd inherited from her grandmother; they both had big, soft hearts and sharp tongues. Toni had loved this trait in her grandmother, but over the years, she'd come to believe that, for her, it was a liability.

"Anyway, it's the end of finals week. Spring semester is almost over," Toni said, thrusting her fists into the air in victory. "We're almost free."

Leonard made a tiny fist bump motion that made Toni smile.

"I suggest," Toni said sagely, "that you all take the summer and forget all this nonsense. Rest. Take a vacation. Binge-watch a Swedish crime drama. Plant a garden. Do literally anything else. Don't worry about this event. Chances are we'll come back in the fall, and the provost will have changed direction on Student Belonging Week anyway. Why don't we just wait and worry about it then?"

"Not we," Leonard interjected.

"What?"

He grinned at her across the length of the conference table. "*We'll* come back in the fall, but *you* will be on sabbatical."

At that last word, the table erupted into something that couldn't be described as anything other than a titter. The only word that inspired more interest at a university than 'tenure' was 'sabbatical.' If tenure was the thing that convinced you to buy into the system, then the sabbatical was the thing that made you stay even when you wanted to leave.

Usually, sabbatical came right after tenure, but Toni hadn't been at the university long enough to apply. But now, her time had finally come. For so many semesters over the last five years, Toni had worried she'd never see this day. She was so happy that she beamed as she looked around the room one more time. "I forgot," she admitted in an uncharacteristically gentle voice.

"How could you forget?" Leonard asked bombastically. "Your sabbatical is the best part of all this." He gestured around the nondescript conference room they'd been meeting in for months. Most of the people in the room had been at the university longer than Preston, so they knew that Leonard's enthusiasm had little to do with Toni's sabbatical and more to do with his.

Leonard had been the chair of the Classics Department four years ago. He'd left for his sabbatical a tired, stooped, and angry man. A few graduate students had placed a bet on the likelihood Leonard would return from his sabbatical or just say fuck it and email his resignation. Toni had seriously considered getting in on that action. She could have made an easy hundred dollars because everyone knew Leonard hated his department, the university, and their small town with the fire of a thousand suns. In fact, the only thing that had stopped him from quitting was that sabbatical; he'd earned it and a prestigious grant to co-lead an archeological dig in Ethiopia. He returned a year later, tanned, smiling, and married to an Ethiopian scholar with an application for a spousal hire locked and loaded for submission. He'd returned from his sabbatical a changed man.

Leonard and Desta Hsu were the fairy tale overworked academics told themselves as they revised their sabbatical applications. The Hsus were the promise of what a sabbatical could be. Toni wasn't among the cohort of colleagues who needed that kind of inspiration, but she appreciated Leonard's enthusiasm all the same.

"It's been a long semester," she reminded him. "But in any case, you're right. I won't be here in the fall, so whatever the Dean has in store for you, Margery will guide you to success."

Toni nodded in Margery's direction. The other woman beamed at the table. Of all the junior scholars who'd flocked to Toni over the years, Margery was the most self-assured. She'd come to the university much like Toni, with a few bad years at another university under her belt and a healthy dose of cynicism dripping from her words like sarcasm burned to ash. But, also like Toni, Margery had a fire burning under her to do what needed to be done. As soon as Toni's application for sabbatical had been approved, she'd invited Margery for coffee, ready to convince her to take over this committee she had never wanted, but of which she was protective. And then she'd found that Margery had been waiting for the opportunity. Passing the baton to Margery now gave Toni that elusive feeling of a weight being lifted from her shoulders. And apparently, she wasn't the only one who approved of the committee's new chair.

"Excellent," Leonard said with a bright smile and an eager

nod. The only person on the committee more opposed to Susan's symposia ideas than him was Margery.

"I'm happy to leave you in very capable hands," Toni said with genuine excitement. "But before I go, I would like to remind you all of one simple fact." Most of the people around the table leaned in, but none more so than Margery. "In your contracts, service is no more than twenty percent of your allocation of effort. Do not give *any* of your committee work more time than that. Please."

Toni watched as Preston, in particular, took this in. She gave this simple bit of advice every semester, more times than she could count. She kept hoping for the day when her audience would nod sagely, even dismissively, because they knew this already, but each time she said it, she watched as people seemed to learn it all over again, and it made her chest clench. But no one knew more than Toni that she couldn't save everyone, and she couldn't make her colleagues prioritize their well-being before they were ready.

"I think we're done for the semester," she said. "Happy grading and enjoy your summer."

Her colleagues murmured their goodbyes and stood, rushing from the room.

Toni remained in her seat until they were all gone, one step closer to the start of her sabbatical.

It didn't feel real just yet.

EVERY SEMESTER, someone teaching an intro class assigned their students to find a professor in their major for an interview, and every semester, Toni set a hard cap of no more than three. And at every interview, the student asked why she'd chosen this job.

It was such an expected question that Toni had a small coterie of answers that ranged from joking to very professional and serious, depending on how well she knew the student and the tone of the interview thus far. All of the answers were true, but none of them were completely honest. Because if someone were to ask Toni right now why she'd decided to become a professor, she would have said it was for the physical environment.

Toni loved being on university campuses; she'd never met one she didn't like. As she left her final committee meeting of the academic year, she heaved her leather satchel bag onto her shoulder and began to stroll across campus to her office, enjoying all the sights and sounds and even smells she normally missed as she rushed to her various classes and back.

She was always rushing, if not downright running, to get where she needed to be during the semester. If she wasn't late for class, she was late for a meeting. If she wasn't power-walking across campus to pick up a book at the library, she was sprinting in the opposite direction for a student presentation. Always, always, always in a hurry.

But that rush cost her the beauty of a leisurely stroll through the university oval in spring. She missed sitting on a bench on the east campus, watching the leaves turn yellow. She didn't have the privilege to bundle up in her warmest coat and watch the first snowfall from the observation deck in the science building. Toni loved the wonder of campus, but she so rarely got to enjoy it because if her students spotted her out on a walk or sitting on a bench, they assumed she was holding impromptu office hours. If they spotted her sitting still, they — like her mother — considered her calendar open for more work. And god forbid some administrator spotted her gazing at the sky before her evening class or reading a novel by the lake near the commuter parking lot because they, too, would stop to discuss her committee assignments, mentorship programs she was a part of, mentorship programs they wanted her to join, or her potential future as an associate dean. Which is all to say that during the semester, Toni never got to enjoy the campus.

To be Black, female, and tenured was to be forever visible, always in service, never at peace.

But there were moments like today, usually right at the end of spring semester, when Toni got the chance to enjoy campus. When her classes were done and students were elsewhere, celebrating the end of the semester in the most irresponsible way possible, Toni often strolled through the south oval. She tilted her head back and let the sun warm her face. She took in a deep breath and, for once, enjoyed the smell of the willow trees framing the campus pond. Without the stench of cigarette smoke, vape pens, or exhaust fumes from people desperately searching for parking, Toni could finally detect the smell of moss and hydrangeas. Without the crowd, Toni could hear the ducks honking quietly to one another and birds chirping in the trees. Moments like this almost made all the hassle of the academic year feel worth it.

Almost.

"You look happy."

Toni startled at the sound of Mike's voice as he fell into step by her side. Her eyes darted around, wondering where he'd come from, but Mike had a way of just popping up when Toni least expected him. For the past year, at least, Mike seemed inescapable. She turned around in the faculty dining area to find him paying for her lunch. She looked across the auditorium during the Arts & Sciences Council, and there was Mike, waving his hand and gesturing toward the empty seat next to him. And that didn't even count all the dinners at Alejandro's house, where it always seemed to be Mike who opened the door for her.

At some point, she'd gotten used to his presence.

"As it happens, I am," she said with a shrug.

"Last final?"

"Nope."

"Done grading?"

She smiled. "Lord, I wish."

Out of the corner of her eye, Toni saw Mike turn to her. She watched him watch her — with a little more intensity than was necessary, she thought — and waited for his next question.

She nodded her head at the path through the south lawn.

They walked in a companionable silence that surprised her. Normally, Mike was so damn chatty that Toni had started tuning out his words, especially when he started talking about equations and experiments. But she didn't stop listening to him completely because somewhere along the way, Toni had decided that she liked the tone of Mike's voice. It wasn't too deep or rumbly or too high. Once, Toni had even thought Mike had the kind of voice she wouldn't mind falling asleep to, but she wouldn't volunteer that information to anyone, especially not him.

Still, silence was nice as well.

Although, it was only quiet between them. As they headed toward main campus, the sounds of student life returned. The hackeysack club was practicing barefoot in the grass, and Mike waved at the group as they passed. A few feet away, one of the fraternities had set up turntables for a last-minute raffle to raise money for...something. The sign was too small for Toni to see, and there was no need to strain her eyesight when she still had fifty final reflections to read.

As they passed the queer student theater group practicing monologues from a play Toni couldn't recognize, she thought this was part of the job she also loved. It was all part of the ritual of saying goodbye to her students; some for the summer, some for good.

"You just had your last committee meeting," Mike said out of the blue. He clapped his hands together and smiled triumphantly in her direction. He looked so happy it was infectious.

Finally, she turned to him, the smile on her face so big and wide. "As of five minutes ago, I am no longer the chair of the President's Advisory Council on Bullshit and Incoherence."

Mike laughed. "I thought it was called the President's Acting Committee for Tokens and Future Administrators."

Toni shook her head and laughed with him. "That was the committee before this one."

"What's the difference?"

"I have no fucking idea," Toni said. "Something about the Board of Regents mandate or whatever. All that matters is that for the next year, it's not my job to care."

"Because you're officially on sabbatical," Mike said happily.

Toni stopped walking and turned in his direction.

He mirrored her stance, his smile faltering at the edges as they came face-to-face. He ran his fingers through his hair and ducked his head.

She peered up at him. Something about the way he looked right now made her brain stumble in confusion. In this moment, Mike's happiness about her sabbatical far exceeded her own. Toni was too tired to be happy. Too tired to be excited about the future. Too tired to figure out a nice way to ask what the hell had gotten into him.

But her brain was not too tired to notice that something was different about him. Was the beard new? Thicker? Was his jaw sharper? Was he taller? The semester brain fog clouded Toni's ability to think but not, apparently, her body's ability to react —

hardening nipples, wet warmth between her legs — which made her wonder what had gotten into her.

Had she eaten lunch? When was her last sip of water? Clearly, she was delirious.

She turned away and wiped at her sweaty upper lip. It was a hot day, of course.

"Technically, my sabbatical doesn't start until August," she said, stepping from the gravel path through the lawn onto the concrete. Mike easily kept pace with his much longer legs. "And I still have final exams from my intro class to go over and grades to submit, but if this university burns down in the next fifteen months, that is none of my business."

"It's not," Mike replied seriously.

Toni glanced at him quickly. "Where are you coming from?"

He rolled his eyes. "Final presentations. Every semester, I sit through a week of some of the worst group presentations I've ever seen, just waiting for a sinkhole to swallow me up. I tell myself I'm never going to assign them again, and then I do. It's like I love pain. I don't know what's wrong with me."

Toni chuckled. "Nothing's wrong with you. You just hate reading student papers."

He groaned. "I sure as fuck do. The way science majors write gives me a headache. I have a stack of quizzes from my intro course, and then I am completely free."

"I'm jealous," Toni deadpanned.

"Bullshit."

She giggled. Actually giggled. And then her steps slowed as they neared the southwest corner of the Student Union. Mike's office was in Schlessinger Hall in the opposite direction to Toni's building.

Mike pulled ahead of her and then turned when he realized she was no longer by his side. He lifted an eyebrow at her and frowned.

"Isn't your office that way?" Toni asked, pointing to her left.

"It is."

She frowned at him, refusing to ask another question. Probably because she knew the answer.

Mike waited for a few seconds before smiling and playfully rolling his eyes. "I'm walking you to your office," he said.

"Are you?"

"Obviously."

"Obvious to whom?"

"Me. Let's go. You've still got so much grading to do." He turned halfway toward her building and blinked at her.

Okay, dehydration or no, Toni thought there was definitely something going on with him and her. Her first step toward him was shaky, and Mike moved quickly, his hands reaching out as if he'd catch her if she fell. But she didn't. They resumed their walk, but this time, Toni couldn't stand the companionable silence for some reason.

"Summer plans?" she asked in a tight, high voice.

"Rest. Research. Running?"

"Sounds boring. I approve."

"Good," Mike said. He opened his mouth as if he wanted to say something else. Toni found herself ready to lean in his direction, but she kept it together, and in the end, he seemed to reconsider whatever he'd been about to say anyway. "What about you?" he asked, glancing away. "Are you starting your sabbatical work this summer?"

"Fuck no. I'm not cracking open a single book or downloading any articles. As soon as grades are in, I'm going to sleep too much, hang out with my cat, and start tackling all the home renovation projects I've been putting off for the last two years."

"Sounds fun," Mike deadpanned.

"Sounds boring," she corrected. "And that's exactly what I want."

She could see him looking at her from the corner of her eye, but she didn't look at him this time.

"You deserve that," Mike said softly.

"I know," Toni replied triumphantly.

Mike laughed before looking forward again. "Are you coming to the Multicultural Graduation tonight?"

"Of course, I am."

Now Toni did shift in his direction, but it was his turn to ignore her attention. Well, he tried to. As Toni glared at him, she watched his neck and cheek turn red while the corner of his smile lifted, exposing a shallow dent of a dimple she'd never seen before.

Never seen before but liked immediately.

"Of course, I'm going," she said again.

He turned to her. "Just checking. Some of us are getting together for drinks after at that new indie brewery."

"What new brewery?"

Mike squinted down at her. "How do you not know about this? It's right by your house."

"It is?!"

They arrived at the stairway that led up to Mark Hall. Toni stopped and watched as Mike climbed a few steps up, stopped, and turned, frowning down at her. He shrugged. "You need to get out more."

Toni hated when people said that. She couldn't even remember how many times someone had lobbed the accusation that she studied too hard or worked too much at her. But it stung that much more in this moment, and she didn't know why. "Who has time to get out?" she spat back.

He shook his head mournfully. "Great point." Toni was

shocked at Mike's easy acquiescence. "That's why you should come out with us."

"I'll think about it."

"You always say that."

"I don't."

Mike scoffed. "Okay." He turned away and continued up the steps.

Toni started after him, feeling uncomfortable about it even as she endeavored to move faster, trying to catch up with his long stride.

"Deja and Alejandro are going," he said nonchalantly once she'd caught up with him.

"I said I'll think about it." Toni didn't want to give him the impression that she was running after him — even though she was — so she breezed past him up the steps. She'd planned to waltz right into the building and leave him behind, but Mike jogged up and reached around her to pull the door open.

Toni took a deep sigh as she walked into Mark Hall with a little less pep in her step. She stomped across the vestibule on the main floor, Mike hovering at her heels, to the stairs. She stopped at the bottom step and turned to find Mike standing close. Too close?

"Marie will be there too," he said as if there hadn't been a break in their conversation. "Maybe. She's hard to pin down sometimes."

"I'll think about it," Toni said for the third time.

Mike nodded, and his eyes dipped to her collarbone, no lower. "Think about it for real," he said in a husky voice. "Don't just like say you'll think about it while planning what sweatpants you want to change into as soon as you get home."

Toni's mouth fell open, and her face started to heat in shock. "I would never," she lied with a straight face.

Mike licked his lips. "I know you," he said, his eyes

lingering on her mouth as his gaze moved up her face to finally make eye contact. A heated eye contact that made her heart race.

Her breaths shortened. Her entire body was warm, excited, aroused.

Over the last two years, she and Mike had shared so many seemingly inconsequential conversations. Ever since Deja had started dating Alejandro, they'd been thrown together at meetings and dinner dates and drinks. And even before that, Mike had been familiar to her as one of the few faculty of color at the university, but he was simply someone who existed at her periphery, never quite real.

Except now he was real, and something about this moment was different. She and Mike stared at one another, and Toni felt like there was static building at the back of her head. She just didn't know what it all meant.

Mike cleared his throat but didn't look away. "Your first drink is on me."

"You don't have to—"

"I know," he said. "Your first drink is on me."

Air rushed from Toni's mouth, and she nodded. "Okay."

He nodded in return, trying to keep the grin on his lips from bursting into a full-fledged smile. "I'm going to head out. See you at the graduation?"

Some tiny part of Toni hated the fact that he had to frame that as a question. That somewhere along the way, Mike had decided that Toni was so unreliable that her attendance at an event she had singlehandedly led for three years was up in the air. "I'll be there."

The smile erupted on his mouth for a quick second before he reined it in. "Great. Sure. See you then." He stepped away, backing into the rotunda, his eyes still trained on her.

"Okay," she breathed because she felt the need to say something, anything.

"Okay," he said, a deep smile on his face.

For whatever reason, that one word brought Toni up short. She nodded and watched as Mike turned away, covering his smile with his right hand. "Okay," he said again, although this time, Toni thought he was speaking to himself. Reassuring himself.

And somehow, that reassured her as well.

CHAPTER TWO

There was a knot right in the center of Toni's back.

For the past two years, she'd been going to a masseuse at least once a month to work out the bundle of tense and stressed muscles over and over again. She kept hoping that one of those visits would get rid of it for real, but every three to four weeks, she was back on that massage table, letting a woman with the strongest hands Toni had ever seen or felt manipulate her body into rest and relaxation. One of her quiet sabbatical hopes was that her monthly massages would stop being absolutely crucial to her future mobility and become enjoyable moments of self-care, but she wouldn't admit that to anyone; she could barely admit it to herself.

But it had been barely a week since her last massage, and she could already feel her back tensing. She'd sat at her desk for an hour trying to focus on the driest student reflections she'd ever read before she noticed her shoulders rising toward her ears and then called it a day. At home, she stripped, climbed into the shower, turned the water as hot as she could stand, and set her showerhead to pulsating. She didn't worry about the water spraying her hairline; it was almost time to take out her braids anyway. All that mattered was the degree of relief she could get. There would always be an old set of braids ready to take down and a fresh set ready for installation. Toni could count on those two things with the same certainty as the volley of grade appeal emails at the end of a semester.

When she finished washing her body and climbed out of the shower, she felt lost for a second. When she'd bought this house three years ago, she'd planned to slowly renovate it as time and money allowed. It was perfectly livable, but Toni had a vision for how to make this house her home. Unfortunately, even as her home reno savings account grew, her free time shrunk. When she wasn't teaching, she was in an endless stream of meetings. When she wasn't on campus, she was falling asleep on her couch with a stack of essays in her lap. And when she wasn't working...well, she was always working. The demands of her job were never-ending, and every time she stepped out of the baby pink shower-tub combo from the Nineties or sweated her ass off in her claustrophobic kitchen, all she could think about were the renovation plans gathering dust in her brain.

She wrapped her towel around her damp body with a sigh and padded across the bathroom to the matching baby pink sink to wash her face. She worked the cleanser into her skin in slow, methodical circles with her fingertips, giving herself a massage she hoped would stave off wrinkles from stress. Hopefully. While she cleansed her skin for the recommended two minutes, she stared at her blurry reflection in the steamy mirror above the sink — the mirror she was so damn ready to change, the replacement was already in the basement — and tried not to let the list of all the things she had to do, wanted to do, and had been planning to do overtake her.

When she'd bought this house, life had seemed full of possibilities, and it still was, but without the time to achieve any of her goals, possibility felt like a burden. She'd bought her new bathroom mirror a year ago, but what was the point of changing the mirror before she painted the room? And why paint if there was a chance she might move a wall in her closet to make just a little more room in her bedroom? And what if she found a contractor who could reconfigure the space like she wanted and had to move the mirror in the end? What if? What if? What if?

She rinsed her face, brushed her teeth, and then made her way into the bedroom, the list of possible renovations multiplying. She had rolls of sample wallpaper in the basement as well and a new California king bed in an online cart at a local furniture store. She'd been planning to buy the bed for four months, but every time she thought she was ready, she changed her mind. She worried her new bed would feel out of place — all big and brand-new — in this old room. And then she worried that it would be too big for just her.

She walked to the dresser, stepping over the squeaky floorboard in the middle of the room, and closed her eyes. She grabbed the bottle of lotion on top of the dresser and sat at the foot of her bed to moisturize her skin.

"Just a couple more weeks," she muttered under her breath. Just a couple more weeks until summer, and after that, she could rest.

She'd earned this break. She deserved this break. She sometimes had to remind herself that she deserved rest just as much as the faculty she mentored.

When a faculty member was eligible for a sabbatical, it wasn't an automatic process — which was something Toni had been arguing with the Provost about for the last six months. Like everything else in academia, applying for a sabbatical was needlessly bureaucratic and tedious. First, there was the decision on if the professor wanted one semester off or two. This should have been an easy calculation, but two semesters triggered a financial conversation about everything from outside funding to pay rate to retirement contributions. Then there was the application process itself. Faculty needed to submit a three-to-five-page narrative about their proposed research activities, which wouldn't have been so terrible, except the committee that reviewed sabbatical requests usually had no expertise in some — if not all — of the proposed research, so who were they to judge? The Provost had not appreciated the sincerity in Toni's voice when she'd posed that question, but she was right, and she wouldn't take it back. And then there were letters of support to collect, CVs to update, and, if necessary, grant applications to throw together to prove research activity. Toni had known people to spend months agonizing over their applications only to be crushed by rejection.

Toni had thrown hers together last fall over a glass of wine. It was all a lie, anyway. Anyone who believed that Toni was going to spend the next year in libraries or conducting participant interviews or applying for grants didn't know her at all. The goal of her sabbatical was to rest. That was it, and that was more than enough.

But first, she needed to get through these last few spring semester events.

When her skin was gleaming from her chest to her toes, Toni walked naked into her walk-in closet — the only part of the master bedroom that she loved almost completely. She smoothed the last of her lotion into her hands as she considered the outfit possibilities.

One of Toni's mentors once described the end of spring semester as a campus-wide existential crisis. Suddenly departments remembered they had budgets to spend and viability to prove. Most students wanted to end the year with a bang, even if the rest of their time had been a sad whimper; this was doubly true of graduates. The number of events was staggering and, for someone like Toni, who seemed to be on every committee, endless. Besides her final exams and the last-minute departmental and college committee meetings, there were all the student-centered events to which she could never say no. There were the student conferences, the award ceremonies, the spring play and musical, the art shows, and on and on and on. The last few weeks had been running Toni ragged. But every spring ended with the graduations. Tonight was the Multicultural Graduation for students of color — which merged primarily because of a lack of funding for the individual graduation ceremonies. Toni had spent a few years organizing the event but passed it on to Alejandro a couple of years ago. Still, whenever she saw the call for faculty participants, she replied. Allegedly, all these events made the rest of the year worth it, but she was so tired that this year made her question that assessment.

About the only thing that *might* make this all worth it was the chance to have a cute little sartorial moment.

She stood in front of the dresses hanging together, organized by length, shifting them left and right and back again, waiting for one to inspire her. Normally this was an easy choice; she grabbed the first dress that wasn't too tight or low-cut, threw on a pair of flat strappy sandals, and was out the door in a heartbeat. But for some reason, today, she spent a little more time looking at her options.

And thinking of Mike.

"CAN you two pretend to be adults?" Mike asked Alejandro and Deja.

They were gathered in the small atrium of Nedderberger Hall behind the auditorium. As Multicultural Graduation advisor, Mike had been running between the auditorium to help students set up before their families arrived and the atrium to supervise the faculty; he was having a much harder time with the latter group.

"Come on," he grumbled. "What if the kids see you?" He looked around. No one else seemed to be worried or even interested in the fact that Deja and Alejandro had started making out nearly as soon as they arrived.

They were so engrossed in one another that Mike would have been believably certain that they hadn't heard him except for the fact that Deja's head flinched in his direction. Unfortunately, Alejandro cupped her face and pulled her mouth back to his.

"Unprofessional pendejo," Mike muttered, turning away.

"Do I have to wear a stole?" Marie called to him. "And if I do, can I choose any one?"

"Yes and no," Mike said in an exasperated tone. "AAPI faculty wear the red stoles. You know this. You're the ASA faculty advisor!"

"I know, but the red clashes with my suit," she said, gesturing toward her two-piece butter-yellow outfit and the light floral dress shirt underneath. Mike had to give it to her; she did look good. "Can I wear this one?" she asked, holding his stole in the air.

She didn't look that good. "Are you Salvadoran?"

Marie lifted her eyebrows and had the nerve to smile at him. "I could be."

"That's mine."

"Are you Salvadoran?"

Mike groaned. He wished he was back in the ballroom with the students, but they were off changing for the ceremony. "I'm literally the only Salvadoreño on this entire campus. I checked."

Marie rolled her eyes. "Okay, what about this one?"

"No. Wear the stole you're assigned." He threw his hands up in exasperation and then gestured toward Alejandro and Deja. "You're my friends. You're supposed to want to make this easy for me. Why are you not doing that?"

Marie nodded slowly. "Have you considered getting new friends?"

"Every day, but options are limited."

"Don't I know it," Marie nodded, fingering another stole that matched her outfit better than her own.

"I'll be your friend, Mike."

Mike closed his eyes and sighed silently. He'd recognize George Morales's voice anywhere because he'd been hearing it damn near every day all year. Some days it seemed like George was his shadow; wherever he was, there was George, trying desperately to force a friendship Mike didn't have the time, energy, or interest for, especially not when he was trying to become Toni's shadow. He didn't know how he'd found himself in this situation, but he didn't like it.

Okay, technically, he did know. Mike had attended George's job talk — something he always did with the Latinx candidates, although the added benefit was that George's interview was for a position in Toni's department, and Toni was the head of the search committee. He'd cleared his schedule so he could attend every candidate event the committee invited him to — job talks, teaching demonstrations, lunches, and dinners. Anything to spend a little more time in Toni's presence. And what had he gotten in return? George. For the last year, the other man had followed Mike from one university event to another, committee to committee. And, of course, when Toni rotated off the faculty senate, George had jumped at the chance to replace her.

When he'd brought the issue to Alejandro, his friend had

laughed for at least five minutes because he was a fucking traitor. They all were. Every single person he called a friend on
this campus. Next year, he planned to leave it to one of them to
plan the Multicultural Graduation. Maybe then, they'd see the
bullshit he had to put up with every year. But that was next
year. This was now.

Marie was smiling smugly. He mouthed the words, "I hate
you," and turned around, smiling at the other man. He might
have been annoying, but at least he was wearing the correct
stole and not making out with one of the other faculty.
"Thanks, Jorge. Did we order a stole for you?" Mike asked,
squinting at the quality of the fabric, which was much better
than the ones the Office of Multicultural Affairs could afford.

"I brought my own," George said excitedly. "I had it
specially made in college," he said, pointing out the Mexican
flag on one side and a German flag on the other.

"Great. We're going to line up soon. We're just waiting for
a few more people to show up."

"Cool. Do you need any help?"

"No, no. Everything's taken care of." Mike gave George his
best fake smile and started to turn away. He knew from
previous experience not to engage George in too much small
talk unless he wanted to get stuck. He did not have time to get
stuck.

"You're late!" Marie yelled.

"Bullshit!" Toni yelled back. "I am always right on time."

At the sound of her voice, Mike's entire body seemed to
freeze at attention. His eyes lifted over George's head,
searching for Toni and then finding her framed by the afternoon light coming through the double doors that led out into
the main hall. Mike was speechless.

"Oh, someone let the girls out to play," Deja called. Mike
flinched and turned, surprised to see her face apart from

Alejandro's. "I guess the semester is really over," she laughed as Alejandro practically wrapped his arms around her waist.

Toni smiled at them as if they were an adoring audience — which Mike was, just to be clear — and then she bent over dramatically to shake her breasts at her friends.

"You alright, Mike?" Alejandro asked in an unnecessarily loud voice.

Mike scowled at his friend out of the corner of his eye. But he didn't linger in his ire. In a heartbeat, his gaze was back on Toni, taking her in. She was wearing a mustard yellow dress that accentuated all the brown tones in her dark skin. The cut of the dress also highlighted every one of her curves, even the ones that didn't normally keep him up at night, hard and needy. His eyes moved hungrily over her body in that dress, the cap sleeves and peek of her shoulders, the cinched waist and the round of her hips, even the hem fluttering around her thighs. He'd never seen this dress before because he would have remembered it. Not that he'd seen her entire wardrobe or anything, he just had a good eye for Toni and, apparently, everything she wore. Okay, and apparently, how whatever she wore made him feel. But then she twirled around to show off the dress, and Mike's mouth went dry.

He couldn't look away.

Unfortunately, she hardly even glanced in his direction.

Mike understood how Toni saw him probably better than she did herself. As far as Toni was concerned, Mike was a child, not because he was that much younger than her — five years was not that much — but because Toni considered most of the faculty of color on campus to be her kids. Toni was the person the deans called in to help new faculty adjust to campus, being in such a white town in a white county in a white region. The fact that she was Arts & Sciences faculty never stopped deans from the Business and Education colleges from calling on her to give advice on faculty lines, tenure processes, or recruitment tactics. Toni had the kind of sway on campus that some people envied, but not anyone with principles because they knew that the kind of sway Toni had only came with more responsibilities, nothing else. It didn't guarantee her more money, more time off, not even a smaller teaching load.

Maybe seeing them all as her wayward kids made advocating for them easier for her, but just because Toni saw him as a baby didn't stop him from seeing her as a woman and wanting her like he had from the moment they met.

She probably didn't remember. No, scratch that; Mike knew Toni didn't remember their first meeting five years ago. He'd dropped into her job talk because even when she was interviewing for the job, she'd already been a legend. Toni had been an albatross in the applicant pool. She was older, more experienced, wider published, and far more accomplished than the other candidates. All of that made her an attractive candidate, but some people on the search committee were worried about her. Everyone on the hiring committee could do the math. Toni had been on the cusp of applying for tenure at her current university, and the only reason to apply for a new job at that stage was as a negotiating tactic, out of fear one wouldn't get tenure, or a deep desire to escape a bad situation. She was the talk of the search committee, and Mike spent weeks soaking up the chatter about her. Her job talk was the best attended of the on-campus interviews, which said a lot about her standing on its own. He'd shown up to her talk very curious and left a little in love.

And over the last five years, a little in love had blossomed into pathetically infatuated. And the worst part about it wasn't that everyone knew how he felt about it; it was that everyone *but her* knew.

He ran his hand through his hair, turning away to the rest

of the faculty, and cleared his throat. "Alright, let's line up," he called.

"There's bottled water on the stage," Alejandro offered.

"Shut up," Mike spat, wiping a hand over the back of his neck where the skin was hot to the touch.

CHAPTER THREE

Toni's personal motto was that if you've been to one graduation, you've been to 'em all. Sure, sometimes there was spring rain or an early summer sun beating down, or a muggy humidity. And sometimes, as faculty, you got to slip onto the stage to give a particularly special student their diploma or hood, while other times, you used your hair to hide your earbuds while you listened to a cozy mystery on audiobook. The details might change, but the broad strokes so rarely did. Attending these kinds of events was a service, one of the many things faculty were expected to do as no more than twenty percent of their job responsibilities. For someone like Toni, however, service could easily swell to forty or fifty percent, so she chose her assignments carefully. And the graduations, however boring or repetitive, were requests she found difficult to deny. She might attend up to four graduation ceremonies a year, but for the students, each one was special, unique, and important, and Multicultural Grad was high on their lists. So, no matter how tired she was or how terrible the semester had been, she never failed to put on her kente cloth stole, smile, and resolve to do more than just bear it.

And this had been a particularly exhausting year — they said the year before sabbatical always was.

For months, she'd been running on too little sleep, far too much coffee, and anger, but her students didn't need to know all that. After the ceremony, they'd excitedly introduce her to their parents. She'd find the kindest words she could for each student because, at the end of it all, no parent cared about all the late papers or absences that had almost stood in the way of this moment. And when it was all said and done, Toni didn't care either. She took pictures and pretended that this semester — in combination with all of them — hadn't come close to shattering her. And in a few years, when they remembered the best bits of their college experience, hopefully, they would remember her — because the thing they never tell young faculty is that you will remember most of your students because, more semesters than not, they will be the reason you stayed.

As Marie and George Morales encouraged students to line up in alphabetical order for the procession into the small auditorium, Toni watched contentedly. She remembered all the work it took to make this event come together on a shoestring budget. She didn't envy Mike in this moment, but she did try to remember when he'd taken over the event. She thought for sure that was something Alejandro would have told her, but she couldn't recall that conversation. Or maybe it was an email? Either way, she had to give Mike his props; he was doing much better leading the Multicultural Graduation than she had. The event was still exactly the same; the difference, she noted, was that Mike was so much better than her at delegating.

While Mike ran through the list of graduates, Alejandro helped the last few family members to their seats inside the auditorium, and Deja coordinated the student MCs to go over the schedule of events one more time. When Toni ran this event, she was often literally running from one corner of the auditorium to the next, one mishap to another, putting out fires she hadn't set.

All her life, Toni had struggled to trust anyone to meet her standards, so she just always did it herself. But Mike...

"Ready?"

Toni jumped at the sound of Mike's voice close at her left side. His minty breath was icy-warm over her bare shoulder. Goosebumps she couldn't explain and had never felt before erupted on her arm. Her face started to warm. Toni didn't know what exactly had caused this response. Maybe it wasn't because he was close so much as that she could smell his cologne, and it was warm, peppery, and made her think of liquid gold and smoke. Or maybe it was the air conditioning. Either way, Toni swallowed that response and lifted her chin with a smirk. "I'm always ready."

One of the strange things Toni learned while teaching was the different silences of life; the silence of a thirty-student small lecture course that hadn't done *all* the reading was markedly different from a one-hundred-and-fifty-person intro course that hadn't done *any* of the reading. The silence of someone who wanted to say something but, for whatever reason, was stopping themselves was...distinct, and this was the second time she'd heard this silence from Mike in a single day. She turned her head, and they came face-to-face.

His eyes were big and brown, ringed by short, dark, straight eyelashes. Very ordinary. Nothing to write home about or gush about to her girls over drinks. And still, those goosebumps spread over her chest, and other parts of her body seemed to wake up from the semester-long hibernation.

Mike took in a slow intake of breath that he held for three

beats — Toni counted, her eyes on his lips — before sighing and backing away quickly. Whatever he'd been about to say, he'd decided against sharing it with her again.

Toni shivered at the loss of Mike's warmth, soft breath, and nearness. She thought about turning around to look into his eyes because that would tell her a lot. But she couldn't do that.

Wouldn't do that.

"Ready," Mike said, his voice a shaking whisper as he stepped beside her behind the rest of the faculty.

Toni nodded, too shaken to speak, a first in a very long time.

The deejay at the head of the room said something Toni didn't catch because so much of her attention was on Mike while the rest of her focus was tangling in confusion.

"Uh... Not to like interrupt y'all or nothing, but I got a shift at Burrito Bonanza at six-thirty," Jamaal Hicks leaned forward to say.

They both turned to look behind them.

"I didn't forget," Mike said apologetically. "We'll be outta here in time. Did you get a shape up?"

"Oh, that's sharp," Toni said.

Jamaal blushed and ducked his head. "There's a new dude at the barber college."

"Oh, yeah?" she and Mike said at the same time.

Jamaal shrugged and shuffled his feet. Not that Toni was particularly interested in her students' dating lives, but she did note that Jamaal's refusal to look either of them in the eyes let her know that whoever this new dude was, he was not inconsequential. "Sometimes he comes to the BB after his classes end at seven."

"Got it," Mike said happily. He cupped Toni's elbow gently and turned her around.

Toni giggled at Jamaal's crush until she locked eyes with Deja.

Deja's eyes darted between Toni's smiling face and her arm, or rather, where Mike was holding her arm. It wasn't Deja's shock or Marie's smug smirk, or even Alejandro's equally smug grin behind them that affected her. It was that Mike didn't let her go.

And that she didn't want him to anyway.

———

TECHNICALLY, the Multicultural Graduation was scheduled to last from four to five-thirty in the evening, but it always ran longer.

Mike's digital calendar was a masterpiece, every class color-coded, with coordinating colors to subtly differentiate between preparation time, instruction, extracurricular events, and grading. He was so organized that every fall semester, he taught an all-university time management course through the Faculty Instruction Center that some department chairs made mandatory for all new hires. The best advice Mike offered his students — colleagues — about time management was to be honest about how long tasks actually took and to plan for events, like the Multicultural Grad, that had a life of their own. That was why as soon as he'd left Toni at her office, he'd rushed home to shower and change before arriving at Nedderberger Hall to start setting up. He had a trunk full of decorations he'd bought because the graduation budget only stretched so far. He made the students decorate the room, though. He was on hand for anyone who needed help tying a tie or practicing their speech, or dealing with any technical issues — and by dealing with, he just meant calling campus operations.

And because he knew the event had a tendency to drag at the end, he set an alarm for five-twenty-five to start herding everyone toward the door. But before that, he also reminded them to eat the desserts they'd (over)paid for; otherwise, campus catering would throw everything away. His students were sick of his stories about when he was a student worker in campus food service, but he didn't mind telling them about it one more time before they left campus because, above all else, Mike did not believe in wasting food.

But he also didn't believe in rushing them off if he didn't absolutely have to, and invariably five-thirty came and went. Some students, like Jamaal, rushed off to work. Other students went out to dinner with their families. But for the ones who didn't have family or whose family couldn't afford to visit, Mike hung around. Of all the things Mike had to offer them at this late stage of their college careers, bearing witness to their accomplishments was such a small thing.

A few years ago, the graduates had wanted to hang out and reminisce on the lawn in front of the building. Toni had stayed after them, and so, of course, Mike had hung around as well. He threw his jacket down so she didn't get grass stains on her dress. He tried not to stare at her as the sun set behind her head. That was the night he'd realized that his schoolboy crush on Toni wasn't likely to go away anytime soon, if at all.

Alejandro slid next to Mike at the dessert table. "I'm glad you finally graduated from covert pining to blatant, pathetic infatuation. It's not creepy at all." He grabbed the last two snickerdoodles and bit into a cookie with a smug smile.

"You're so goddamn annoying now that you're with Deja," Mike said, irritation dripping from every syllable.

"I'm gonna tell her you said that."

"Good."

"And then she's gonna tell Toni you said that," he said, chuckling to himself.

Mike rolled his eyes and turned away from the other man. He was just about to yell out to the students hanging around that there were a few more lemon bars when the Multicultural Student Union vice president and president-elect for next year, Bianca Tranh, snatched them up. She folded them carefully inside a napkin and put them in her backpack. Before Mike could suggest it, she also grabbed the last few bottles of water and smiled up from her haul. A burst of pride bloomed in Mike's chest.

"See you next year, Dr. Hernandez. Have a good summer, Profé," Bianca trilled as she headed toward the door.

Mike and Alejandro waved her goodbye.

"You know what's wild?" Alejandro said as soon as she was out of earshot.

Mike rolled his eyes again and refused to answer. Alejandro kept talking anyway.

"I've had Bianca in half a dozen classes, and the thing she's going to remember most is you telling her about food waste on college campuses."

"You say that like it's a bad thing," Mike replied. "Are you jealous?"

"I'm gonna tell Toni you're staring at her."

"Shut up."

"Are you two fighting?" Marie asked.

Mike and Alejandro jumped at her voice and sudden appearance at their side. Instinctually, Mike looked for Toni in the crowd, his heart racing at the possibility that she might have heard Alejandro's last sentence.

"Oh, you're talking about Toni," Marie said with a knowing nod.

Alejandro choked on his sip of lemonade and started coughing-laughing.

"Do you want the last brownie?" Mike asked Marie in a panic.

"Not really. Toni loves brownies, though."

Mike knew that. He also knew that the only dessert she liked from campus catering was an apple tart that was too expensive for this event; otherwise, he would have ordered it. A whole tray of overpriced tarts just for her. But he couldn't tell Marie that, and Alejandro didn't need to be told, so he decided to say nothing.

"Smooth," Marie laughed. "We all going to the brewery?"

"Me and Deja are down," Alejandro said.

Marie turned to Mike, and he nodded. "I invited Toni."

"Of course you did," Alejandro muttered under his breath.

It took every ounce of Mike's restraint not to respond to that *and* to ignore Alejandro's smug smile, which he could see clear as day out of the corner of his eye.

"I invited her like two weeks ago," Marie said, rolling her eyes.

"You did? She seemed like she didn't know what I was talking about."

"Of course she did. The closer she gets to her sabbatical, the more she refuses to put anything on her calendar. Deja and I tried to schedule a lunch to celebrate her year off, and she said no. Just 'no.' Not 'maybe later' or 'after grades are in,' just 'no.'"

"Really?" Alejandro asked. "That doesn't sound like Toni."

"That's what I said. And *she* said, 'you know Toni on contract.' Apparently, sabbatical Toni is interested in giving her digital calendar a break. So far, sabbatical Toni is annoying as hell."

Mike's gaze shifted to the woman at hand. She was standing in the middle of the room, talking to a kid Mike didn't know by sight, but he did recognize Toni's warm smile at the student's parents. He'd had that conversation more times than he could count, felt the apprehension of taking thanks for helping a student survive, thrive, and graduate, from smiling parents or guardians or older siblings or close friends tearfully recounting everything that student had weathered to arrive at this moment. He'd had to fight back tears and exhausted yawns. And more than once, he'd shuffled from one foot to another, trying to mask the end-of-semester aches and pains that were becoming more frequent and worsening in the years since he'd gotten tenure.

"She needs a break," Mike said, watching as Toni subtly slipped her left foot from her heel, just enough to stretch the ball of her foot, it looked like. "She looks tired."

"And you are fucking whipped," Alejandro said, shoving the second cookie into his mouth whole.

Marie, frustratingly, nodded in agreement before taking a bite of one of the last brownies.

CHAPTER FOUR

Toni pulled into her driveway and pressed the button on the garage door opener clipped to the sunshield in her car, and… nothing happened. She pressed it again. And then again and again and again.

"You raggedy bitch," she groaned. The motor on her garage door opener had been acting up for the last six months. Some days it worked. Some days it didn't. Some days it opened smoothly. Some days the door made this noise that sounded something like an amateur musician trying to emulate a Carlos Santana breakdown but failing epically.

The point was that her garage, like so many other parts of her house, was vying for top of the shit list in her brain. She sighed in frustration.

Homeownership was central to the cult of academia.

Both times she was on the job market and visited for the on-campus stage of the interview, homeownership was a topic the committee returned to every time there was a lull in the conversation, a supposed enticement to get her to accept a position they hadn't offered. The prices of homes that were supposed to be affordable, even though they didn't know the state of her finances, and neighborhoods with the best school districts, even though she didn't have any kids, were the approved talking points she endured when what she'd really wanted to know was if there was a Black beauty salon in town and if there was a place to get bean pies within a fifty-mile radius. Unfortunately, none of the white people on the hiring committees ever seemed to know those things. Even after she'd accepted her current position, homeownership was the small talk crutch preferred by other faculty who didn't know her well and didn't want to bother trying.

That's why she'd ignored everyone's advice when it came time to buy her house. She knew exactly what she wanted. She didn't want to live in the suburbs. Toni grew up in the suburbs; she knew what that life was like and had no desire to go back there. She wanted the option to walk to work on a lovely fall day, at least two bedrooms, a good-sized backyard, at least one and a half baths, and a basement that wasn't a disaster zone. To keep all of this inside her very modest budget, Toni had settled on a livable fixer-upper in a neighborhood just beyond off-campus student housing, and she'd found it.

For the past three years, Toni had been aggressively saving while getting a feel for her house. For the past two years, she'd been compiling a list of all the things that needed to be renovated, and every few months, she tried to order that list based on urgency. The problem was that she had to keep shuffling that list because things like her garage door opener refused to wait their turn.

Toni's house was her constant project, which would have been fine if she had the time to devote to it, but she didn't. Although now, she was only days away from having the time she craved. She had a stack of DIY books and an open line of credit at the local hardware store. As soon as summer break was officially underway, the house work would commence. She didn't want to do any research. She'd turned down every invitation to give a conference keynote or chair a conference panel. If it didn't involve a hammer, she wasn't interested.

"Just a few more days," she muttered to herself. Unfortunately, it seemed like every day until then was going to be a goddamn struggle.

She put her car in park and turned it off, muttering under her breath as she climbed out.

"Should we park on the street?" Deja called from the passenger seat of Alejandro's car.

"Yeah. One of you can slide in behind me. Sorry, my garage door is acting up."

"Don't worry about it," Deja said. Toni watched as Alejandro pulled along the curb in front of her house while Mike eased his SUV into her driveway. He stopped just before his bumper met hers.

Mike's driver's side window slid down, and he bent his left arm over the door. "Am I good?"

Toni was tired. That was the only reason she could come up with to explain whatever the fuck happened in her gut when Mike smiled up at her and asked her that question in a voice that was deeper and silkier than she'd ever known it to be. All day he'd been surprising the hell out of her, and she didn't understand what was going on.

"Uh, yeah. Yes," Toni wheezed. "You're good. Fine. You did a great job parking...your car...in my—" She couldn't stop talking. Nothing she was saying made any sense, but somehow everything she was saying sounded like sexual innuendo to her own ears. Mike bunched his eyebrows at her babbling. She turned toward the street and took a deep breath as he turned his car off.

"Hey," Marie called, forcing Toni to turn back to Mike's

car. Her friend was leaning over Mike — to his annoyance — and snapping out of the window at Toni — to her annoyance. "You're malfunctioning. Have you eaten today?"

"Are you hungry?" Mike asked. His eyebrows were still bunched, but they moved subtly to convey worry rather than confusion.

There were lots of questions cycloning around in her brain, and pretty much all of them wanted to know when the fuck Mike's voice had started sounding like that and he'd started looking at her like this. "I'm fine," she said blandly rather than ask anything risky. He squinted at her in disbelief.

Toni turned away, closed her eyes, and lifted her face up to the sun. She just needed a moment to catch her breath. Still, she could feel Mike's gaze on her.

When she opened her eyes, Deja and Alejandro were standing on the curb. He'd wrapped his arms around her from behind and was kissing his way up her shoulder.

"Is all that really necessary?" Marie called to them before slamming Mike's car door.

Toni turned to smile at her friend but made eye contact with Mike instead. He was watching her with a look of concern. He made her heart race, so she thought it was best to keep turning until she found herself looking at her front door; that blanched the warm but confusing feelings in her gut in an instant.

The goal had been to paint the front door a bright color. She'd thought it would be an easy DIY project, something she could do immediately after she moved in to make this house her home. She was wrong. Toni hadn't thought herself to be indecisive, but this house had taught her differently. The permanence of her house — knowing that she was setting down roots here — broke something in her brain. Suddenly every decision was so much more consequential because it could be. She could paint, she could drill holes in walls, and change the flooring. She could do whatever she wanted because this house was hers. And at the end of the day, it wasn't just that she didn't have time to do all the things she wanted; it was that she didn't know exactly what she wanted.

Every time she looked at her boring brown front door, it made her think of all the easy DIY projects that should have been easy but weren't.

"You alright?" Mike's breath brushed her shoulder and made her shiver.

She turned to look at him and once again came face-to-face, eye-to-eye with this man she thought she knew but clearly did not.

"I'm fine," she said because saying otherwise was to open a door she simply did not have the time to close, let alone paint.

Most people took Toni at her word for reasons that had more to do with them than her. They were also doing 'fine' and didn't press in hopes that she would return the favor. They didn't care. They needed her to be strong for them, not because it did her much good. And it did not do her much good, to be clear.

But Mike did not accept the lie Toni had become so comfortable telling. Mike saw through her. "What can I do to help?" he asked in a soft whisper only she heard.

Toni gasped, her lips parting on the desire to say…something. Something she knew she shouldn't say to someone she worked with, someone who had become part of her life — on and off-campus — someone who was so many things she liked… would have liked if only he weren't so close.

His eyes moved down, his gaze shifting to her mouth. And now it was his turn to open his mouth. Toni watched as his tongue darted out to taste the curve of his bottom lip, and she wanted to taste it herself. She even moved forward the tiniest fraction to get closer to him, that lip, his tongue.

"We need to get there before all the tables go. Let's roll," Marie said.

Marie's timely push disturbed the gentle air between her and Mike. "Um, actually—" she said, turning toward the street.

"Absolutely not!" Deja yelled preemptively, pointing an accusatory finger in Toni's direction with a matching frown on her face.

"What?" Toni asked, that knot tightening in the middle of her back.

Deja shook her head vehemently. "You are not wiggling your way out of this. You're going to come have a too-expensive pint of probably shitty craft beer brewed by a dude named Sven or what-the-fuck-ever. I will not allow it."

Toni was speechless. Out of the corner of her eyes, she saw Marie raise her hand and sighed in relief. Toni gestured in her direction, teaching muscle memory taking over.

"A cute little lesbian couple owns the brewery, actually. They wear a lot of denim but are really nice."

Toni smiled in smug relief.

"Oh," Deja said, frowning dejectedly. "I didn't know that." Alejandro ran his hands up and down her arms to soothe her. "Okay, but everything else I said still stands."

Marie's interlude was enough time for Toni to come up with a good answer to the accusation that she wanted to get out of their plans. Just because she did didn't mean she needed Deja to call her out on it. "I need to feed my cat before I go. That's all I was going to say," she lied.

"Oh," Deja said again. "Sorry. I was just nervous because you're, you know—"

"Antisocial now that your sabbatical is coming," Alejandro added supportively. "But no worries. We'll meet you there."

"Great," Toni deadpanned.

"Mike'll stay with you, though," Alejandro added.

"Excuse me?!" Toni spluttered.

"Sounds like a plan," Marie said, already turning away.

"I don't mind," Mike said eagerly.

"I don't need an escort," Toni grumbled.

"Do you know where we're going?" Deja asked.

Toni should have been too old to be petulant, but where there was a will, there was a way. She crossed her arms in front of her chest and rolled her eyes as her only response.

"Thought so." Deja waved annoyingly. "Mike does. He can *escort* you. See y'all soon!"

Toni glared at the side of her friend's face as she and Alejandro followed Marie down the street.

"You raggedy bitch," she muttered under her breath.

"I won't tell Deja you said that," Mike whispered, his breath tickling the sharp edge of her chin.

Toni swallowed and tried to make her voice sound stronger than her wobbly knees. "Tell her. I don't care." But since Deja was halfway down the street by now, her defiance didn't feel nearly so good. She sighed. "Anyway, come on. This shouldn't take long."

She turned on the balls of her feet and began to stomp toward her front door. The gratifying clip of her heels on the paving stone of her front walkway helped ease the clash of feelings of the last few minutes.

Unfortunately, the echo of Mike's footfalls behind her only undid her all over again, one step after another. And as her grandmother often said, Toni got a little too big for her britches.

One second, she was on sure ground; the next had her heel missing the paving stone by a fraction of an inch. She yelped and flailed her arms to her side, reaching for something and coming up with nothing but air. Toni's mind raced with fear and annoyance. She didn't have time for a sprained ankle or worse. She had health insurance, of course, but she refused to give over even a second of her sabbatical to recovery from an injury.

But then Mike's arms wrapped around her waist. One second, she was falling, and the next, she was tucked against his surprisingly broad chest.

She was safe.

"I've got you," he said, his chest rumbling against her back.

"Shit," she ground out.

Shitshitshitshitshit.

MIKE WAS NOT ALEJANDRO.

For years, he'd watched his friend flit around Deja, existing at the fringes of her work life, waiting patiently for the day when she would look at him just a little bit differently than all the times before. Okay, in that way, he and Alejandro were pathetically similar.

What he could not relate to was the way Alejandro had seemed to keep his cool once she did let him in. The day Toni finally let him in, Mike would not be nearly so chill. Why bother? What would be the point of wanting her so deeply and then hiding it when — if — she ever looked at him with even a fraction of that same attention? He had been pretending for so long.

And as the weeks and months and years wore on, it had become harder than he expected to put the mask back on, especially when Toni wore a dress like this, and she fit perfectly in his arms like he knew she would.

It was hard as fuck to let her go. But he did. And then he

had to shove his hands into his pockets and ball them into fists for a few moments while Toni unlocked her front door.

As soon as she pushed the door open, however, Mike's selfish attention was interrupted by a loud yowl that operated like a record scratch in his brain.

Toni sighed and stepped inside. "It's not that deep, you greedy monster," she said with a frustrated sigh.

Mike stepped up to the threshold and finally saw the cat he'd heard a lot about but never seen before — not even a picture. Actually, he didn't even know her cat's name. The cat sat on the other side of the foyer at the top of a single step and yowled at Toni again.

She ignored him this time and turned on the light in the foyer. Mike watched as Toni kicked off her left shoe haphazardly. But she pulled the right one off carefully and lifted it up, squinting at the heel to check the damage.

"Alright?" Mike asked.

"Hmm?" Toni said before looking up at him, her eyes widening in surprise.

There was nothing like the woman of his dreams forgetting he existed to shock Mike into cold reality. It barely fazed him anymore.

"Oh, it's fine. Just a scuff. I can get it fixed."

Toni's cat yowled and sauntered down into the foyer.

"Don't even think about it," Toni hissed. She dropped her shoe and scooped her cat into her arms. "Take your shoes off if you want to come inside," she called, not even bothering to look back at him.

This was not the invitation Mike had spent years dreaming about, but it would do. He stepped into Toni's house for the very first time feeling like he was entering hallowed ground. He carefully closed the door behind him, gently turning the lock, treating her house the way he wanted to treat her.

Mike had heard so many stories about her house — all the renovation projects she'd been planning and the various frustrations that came with them — hoarding the details of her life in ways he was too embarrassed to admit. In his dreams, the first time he entered Toni's house was in the midst of a passionate kiss, her fingers fumbling with a keyring while he preoccupied himself with unhooking her bra. A better scenario but not one that lent itself to a thorough perusal.

Not of her house, at least.

So he kicked off his dress shoes and stepped into Toni's living room, a small smile forming on his lips.

If asked to describe Toni in a word, Mike would have called her 'vibrant,' and her living room was exactly as he would have expected. There was something to see everywhere he laid his eyes, and he had to force himself to go about his investigation methodically.

The room was large and airy, with high ceilings. There was a window that took up most of the far wall. The curtains were shut, but Mike assumed it looked out onto her backyard. The walls were painted a light, unassuming gray, which could have been boring except for all the eclectic artwork hanging on them. But the star of the show, so to speak, was the overstuffed beige sectional sofa nestled into the far corner. Mike could imagine Toni sinking into the cushions after a long day, and that, too, made him smile. He also noticed the loose threads and claw marks on the couch, reminding him of every time Toni rushed out of a meeting, saying she had to rush home to feed her cat before he clawed her furniture to pieces. He'd always thought she was bullshitting, but clearly, she'd lost that battle a time or two.

There was a bookshelf along the close wall that he turned to just as Toni's frustrated voice pulled his attention away.

"Are you serious right now? Come back here, you little—"

Mike turned around just in time to see Toni's cat dart through the dining room. He ran into the living room and up a cat tree in the corner next to the tv unit. Toni followed behind her cat and stood at the entrance to the living room, glaring at her pet with arms crossed in front of her chest.

"What's up?" Mike asked.

"What's up is that this little bastard was yelling at me but doesn't want to eat now." Toni was replying to his question, but her gaze was focused on her cat. For his part, the cat was resolutely ignoring her to groom the hind leg he'd shoved into the air.

"Do you need me to do...something?" he asked carefully.

Toni rolled her eyes with a sigh. "No, it's fine. He'll probably eat as soon as we leave. Let me just go to the bathroom real quick, and we can go."

"Okay," Mike called as Toni stomped up a flight of carpeted stairs. "No rush."

She grumbled something he didn't hear.

He tried not to watch her ass, but just before she disappeared upstairs, he let his eyes wander over the beautiful, plump curve of her butt.

When she was gone, Mike turned to Toni's cat. He'd moved to groom the other leg. Mike crossed the living room slowly, the cat's eyes on him as he approached, not that that stopped his grooming. He lifted his hand slowly, whispering soft words in Spanish to the cat. He listened carefully for the low growl that would tell him he needed to retreat, but it never came. And when he began to scratch the crown of the cat's head, what he got instead was a contented, rumbling purr.

"If only your mama could be this easy," Mike breathed sadly.

CHAPTER FIVE

Spring, as it happened, was Mike's favorite season. There was something about new life that always made him feel most alive. When the freezing winter wind and icy-snowy slush gave way to wet earth, occasional rainstorms, and sporadic sunny days so bright he had to spend every moment he could outside, he was happy. The only part about the end of spring semester that he hated was that the end of spring always followed closely after. By the time graduation rolled around, it was usually too hot to be inside in a suit, let alone outside, but this year, spring seemed to be holding on with all its might.

As he walked down the street with Toni, the air was warm enough that they didn't need jackets but still cool enough that Mike had become distracted by the goosebumps pebbling the delicate skin of her arm. He tried to keep an eye on the path in front of them to make sure they were heading in the right direction while also watching her steps, braced just in case she tripped in those heels again. But he made sure not to let his attention move to her chest; one glimpse of her hard nipples pushing through the fabric of her dress was enough to make his mouth dry. He didn't want to know what another glimpse would do.

"Is it on Maine?" she asked.

"No," he said and then cleared his throat.

She'd been trying to guess where the brewery was ever since they'd left her house. Mike thought she was frustrated to not know something, which was a very Toni thing to be mad about.

"Is it in that weird plaza on Chestnut and Second?"

"No. What weird plaza?"

"What do you mean, what weird plaza? It's like some outlet mall but only for health and fitness shops. They were putting a smoothie place in last time I drove by, but all the buildings had some weird brick façade, so the whole place looks like a bootleg English village."

Mike laughed and shook his head. "I didn't know. I've never been there."

"Oh, you must live in the suburbs with the rest of the bougie people?" Toni had a way of making the most judgmental things sound even worse, but she always said it with a smile on her face, and the smile was more than enough to appease Mike. Besides, the people who lived in the suburbs were bougie. And house-poor.

"Absolutely not," he said. "Everyone's been trying to get me to buy a house since I went up for tenure. We only have so much free time, and I refuse to spend it shoveling snow or mowing a lawn. I got a condo on the north side of campus. Near that nature preserve," he offered, trying not to make it sound like an invitation even though it was.

Toni frowned in his direction.

Mike had been trying to keep his eyes mostly forward, but now that he had her attention, he couldn't resist turning to look at her head-on. The sidewalks in Toni's neighborhood were narrow, crowded on one side by large bushes that partially blocked the houses from the sidewalk. The overhang was probably inconvenient as hell for a regular stroll, but if he and Toni wanted to walk side-by-side — and Toni absolutely did — it pushed them together, their bodies crowding the free space between the foliage and the curb. And Mike could not be mad about that.

"I would have thought you'd buy a house," she said, somehow managing to judge him for not doing what she expected right after she'd judged him with her expectations.

"I want to spend my free time doing exactly what I want, not completing a long list of HOA demands."

Toni huffed out a laugh with a knowing nod. It surely wasn't the first time Toni had ever laughed at something Mike said — whether it was a joke or not — but it was different this time. Mike *wanted* it to be different this time. With the sun streaming down on them, especially on Toni's perfectly sculpted inky eyebrows and the pout of her lips, Mike tried not to hope for too much when *this* could be enough to placate him for a few months or years.

"I like it," she said, glancing in his direction.

Of course, Mike's brain morphed that sentence into "I like you," but that was a private delusion. "Like what?"

"Taking care of my house and planning renovations." She shrugged, and for maybe the first time in all the time he'd known Toni, he saw a flash of vulnerability on her face. "All the projects help me to stop thinking." She said the word 'stop' with extra emphasis, lifting her hands in front of her, palms toward the ground, tamping down on the air as if she could push her responsibilities away, even if only for a few minutes. The small movement made Mike feel something he so rarely did for Toni — pity. "I just never have enough time." That pity was overshadowed by an all-too-familiar desire. He wanted to help Toni; he just didn't know how.

No, that was an oversimplification. Mike wanted to help his students and some of his colleagues, and old people at the grocery store who couldn't reach the bottle of juice on the high shelf. What Mike wanted to give Toni was so much more.

"Is that why you're planning to do nothing but home renovations on your sabbatical?"

"Absolutely. I just want a year where I don't have to think," she said, lighting up at her answer. Her luminescence didn't come from the sun this time; this was what Toni looked like when she was actually really happy.

He opened his mouth to say something, but they came to a corner, and Mike looked up at the intersection in confusion. He was supposed to be leading Toni to the brewery, but for a few seconds, he'd been so focused on her that he'd lost the thread of their journey. He cleared his throat and tried not to peer too hard at the sign across the street.

"Are you lost?" Toni teased.

He smiled and shook his head. "Not anymore. This way." He put his hand on her elbow without thinking. And it was only because they were so close that Mike felt the way Toni shivered at his touch. And because Mike felt as if this moment *was* different than all the others, he moved his hand from her elbow to the small of her back, and he left it there as they walked the last two blocks to their destination.

TONI THOUGHT she would combust as they walked the last couple of blocks to the bar. The last block alone felt long as a country mile, and Mike's hand lingered at the small of her back the whole way, not possessive but not inconsequential either.

His touch was light enough not to be oppressive but substantial enough that it made her sweat in parts of her body that had been uninterested in men for a while. His touch kept her close enough that by the time they arrived at their destination, Toni had become very acquainted with the scent of Mike's cologne, and her pussy approved.

When Mike finally led her into what at first glance looked like an empty, partially paved parking lot, Toni was mostly relieved that now they had some space to move apart. They didn't take advantage of it, but there was space, so that was something.

On second glance, she noticed the squat square building in the center of the lot. There were a couple of metal table and chair sets, already filled with people Toni vaguely recognized from work. She looked away from them immediately; the last thing she wanted was for a colleague she didn't recognize to take this opportunity to talk to her about work. Her friends were already pushing it.

She spotted Deja and Alejandro just to the right of the entranceway. They were standing — as they so often were these days — with Deja's arm wrapped around Alejandro's waist and his around her shoulders. They each had a small mason jar of beer in their free hands. Marie was standing in front of them, speaking animatedly, her own beer sloshing in a jar as her hands moved.

Deja was the first to see them coming, and she carefully waved her beer in their direction.

Toni rolled her eyes in greeting. "Why have you brought me to a shack in the middle of the woods?"

"It's not a shack," Marie said.

"Oh, girl," Deja interjected. "Yes, it is. It's a very nice shack, though."

Marie rolled her eyes and turned to Toni. "Fine, but we're

definitely not in the woods. I can see a CVS through those trees. Anyway, the owners are into reclaimed buildings, tiny houses and shit like that. I think most stuff in here is recycled. It's very hipster. I like it."

Toni and Deja looked at Marie, but it was Toni who spoke. "Are you out here making other friends?"

Marie smirked. "I can't spend all my time with straight people. It's depressing."

"I know you didn't mean that to hurt, but it did," Deja said, prompting Alejandro to kiss her on the forehead.

"I'm unmoved," Toni said haughtily. "Just as long as your new friends aren't assholes."

"You're the only asshole I hang out with."

"I better be." Toni smiled triumphantly.

"She's not an asshole," Mike muttered under his breath as his fingers dug into her waist.

She turned in his direction and watched his bicep harden as he lifted his free hand to his head to run the fingers through his hair.

Toni didn't need anyone to defend her — she was so often the person defending others — but it had been so long since anyone had extended her this courtesy, and it took her breath away.

She turned back to Marie and plastered a tight smile onto her face. "The beer better be worth it. And I'm not sitting out here in the sun."

"Don't worry, you don't have to," Marie said as if she'd been expecting Toni to make this exact objection.

"We reserved a table," Deja said, waving them inside.

Mike's fingers dug into her flesh for a brief second before he let her go. Toni walked out of his hold easily but also reluctantly.

It was only because of her keen hearing that she heard Alejandro whisper.

"You alright?" he asked Mike.

She turned to see Mike quickly looking away before shrugging at his friend. "Yeah, I'm fine. Why?"

Alejandro's face went red with suppressed laughter. "No reason."

But Toni could see by the flush spreading over Mike's cheek that he didn't believe his friend. And neither did she.

CHAPTER SIX

Mike had been to Butches Brew once after some particularly frustrating meeting that had been so bad someone had suggested they have drinks to decompress. It was easy for that one drink to turn to...more, which was why Mike had had his one drink and then three glasses of water before he drove home at a respectable hour, refusing to give too much of his free time to work bullshit. He remembered the beer had been good, though, and had always been planning to come back when the semester was over.

Unfortunately, when he stepped into the bar, it looked like he and half the Arts & Sciences faculty had made the exact same plan. Normally, that was the kind of tidbit that would make him swear off a location. If this outing hadn't been his idea, he might have turned right around and texted Alejandro from the parking lot. It wouldn't have been the first time. Mike loved his job, and he could at least tolerate most of his colleagues, but he did not want to spend more time with them than was absolutely necessary. But he would go anywhere to spend even a few minutes in Toni's presence, so he ducked through the slightly too-small door and walked inside, his eyes adjusting to the dim light, searching for her in the crowd.

He and Alejandro followed the women across the room to a booth near the bar. Out of the corner of his eye, Mike recognized too many people. He plastered a friendly but empty smile on his face, but he did not stop. Today was not the day to get drawn into a conversation about next year's enrollments or student evaluation averages. He didn't care most days, but with his hand still tingling from all the time it had rested along the gorgeous curve of her lower back, he really did not give a shit about anything from work right now. Not even a fraction of a shit.

Marie and Deja slid into one side of the booth, and Toni slid into the other. Mike pushed Alejandro out of the way to slip onto the bench next to Toni.

"Really?" Alejandro muttered. Mike didn't bother to respond.

Alejandro grabbed a free chair from a nearby table and sat at the head of their booth. He glared in Mike's direction. Mike smiled back, but then his jaw tightened as Toni shifted in her seat and her arm brushed his. He turned away from Alejandro and made eye contact with Deja, who smiled at him and lifted her eyebrows before shifting her eyes quickly in Toni's direction.

Mike rolled his eyes with a loud sigh.

"What's up?" Toni asked.

"Nothing. What do you want to drink?" He didn't pretend to be speaking to anyone else besides her.

Toni looked across the table at Marie and Deja, just like Mike expected her to. She always did this. Whenever he wanted to focus on her — whenever *anyone* wanted to focus on her — she tried to redirect their attention elsewhere to anyone else. Selflessness was a thing he loved about her, even as it exasperated the shit out of him. Clearly, Mike didn't mind playing the long game with Toni, but tonight he found himself uncharacteristically impatient. He didn't give in to her and look across the table. He didn't let her force him to pretend as if he cared about anyone else's drink order.

Besides, "We already have drinks," Deja said. Mike could hear the smirk in her voice.

"And I'm pretty sure he's only talking to you," Marie added with a soft giggle.

Mike rolled his eyes again. This was another thing he was used to, the inside joke of this group. Now that Alejandro and Deja were together, Mike sometimes thought there was a spotlight on him — and the way he felt about Toni — that everyone could see but her.

"What do you want to drink?" he asked again, although this time he leaned forward to whisper his question, making sure that there was no mistake on Toni's part about who he was speaking to. "I told you your first drink was on me."

He watched her throat bob and her eyelashes flutter. He stifled a groan when her mouth parted, and her tongue swiped along her lips; slow, insistent, sexy. Her head turned, and she took another shallow breath. "I'm..."

His gaze was intent on her lips as they moved. He was ready for whatever she had to say, but when nothing came next, he lifted his eyes to hers. He smiled, realizing that he had made Toni speechless. They'd never be even, but it was nice to give back just a little of all she'd given him over the years.

He thought about leaning forward just an inch or two more, close enough to smell her perfume again. Close enough to kiss her, if only he was brave enough.

"What do you want to drink, Antonia?" he asked again.

She couldn't hide the shiver that moved through her body. "I'll take something light or amber. I'm not picky," she said, and then added a quick "please," to the end of her sentence. And then her tongue swiped across her lips again.

Mike couldn't help it, and his tongue moved across his own mouth this time. He nodded and grunted before sliding out of the booth. He blinked, not really seeing the room around him because all he could see was Toni, her lips, and her tongue.

"Hey, I'll take another beer," Alejandro called after him.

"Get it yourself," Mike called back.

Somehow, the Butches Brew seemed even more packed than just a few moments ago. The crowd was barely big enough to fill one of his large lecture courses, but in this small structure, it was oppressive and annoying. Worst of all, navigating through the crowd meant it took longer to get to the bar and back to Toni.

As soon as he made it to the reclaimed slab of wood that looked like a slice out of a dead tree, Alejandro's hand clapped down on his left shoulder. Mike sighed in audible annoyance.

"So, is tonight the night?" Alejandro yelled almost directly into Mike's ear.

Mike tried to shove him away with his shoulder while motioning to get the bartender's attention. "I don't know what you're talking about."

"Yeah, you do."

"No, I don't. Can I get two glasses of pilsner?"

"Make that three," Alejandro added, placing his empty glass on the bar.

"He's paying for his own beer," Mike said.

The bartender grabbed the empty glass and turned away without a word.

"You need me to keep Deja away from Toni? Clear the way?"

Mike pressed his back teeth together but didn't speak, which was probably the exact response Alejandro wanted.

"I can't do anything about Marie, though." He laughed. "I can try, but..." Mike felt Alejandro's shrug rather than saw it.

"I don't know what you're talking about," Mike said again.

Alejandro chuckled. "You sure about that?"

"Yes."

Alejandro shrugged again. "Okay. Then you probably don't care that Steve Titjens just took your seat."

Mike whipped around in an instant. Alejandro moved out of the way, leaning against the bar casually because this was all fun and games for him. It wasn't for Mike. His eyes narrowed at the blond man sitting next to Toni. Fucking Steve Titjens. For the past year, he always seemed to find the other man hovering around Toni's orbit, invading her space and Mike's.

"Este maje es un pesado," Mike muttered under his breath.

Alejandro's laughter was more than unappreciated. "Bet you know what I'm talking about now."

CHAPTER SEVEN

Steve Titjens had a crush on Toni. She knew it. Hell, half the Political Science department knew it. They also knew that she was not interested. Well, everyone except him.

Toni blamed Deja and Alejandro.

Ever since those two had gone public with their relationship, people all over the university had taken it as a sign that it was their chance to shoot their shot with...well, anyone. According to one of Toni's friends who worked in Human Resources, between the mass of paperwork from people registering new relationships and dissolving them nearly as quickly, scheduling mediations, and sending out the volley of memos essentially meant to remind everyone that they were not Deja or Alejandro and to take their dating lives off-campus, the last two years had been a nightmare.

As a rule, Toni did not believe in office entanglements. In grad school, she'd dated a guy in her cohort, and for a while, their relationship had seemed like a dream. They went on dates to the local art house movie theater and had late-night meet-ups in the library to read for class or grade stacks of student papers.

She'd imagined their relationship as a fairy tale; coming back to reality had nearly shattered her.

Toni still remembered the sinking feeling in her gut when the man she thought was the love of her life stood in front of their class and read out a paper abstract that wasn't suspiciously like her dissertation proposal; it *was* her dissertation proposal. It took a year and a half of official complaints and laying bare five years of her intellectual life to prove that his work was actually hers. It was an emotionally expensive lesson she never forgot.

But that betrayal was years ago and not actually why Toni was only pretending to listen to Steve tell her about his summer travel plans — even though she didn't ask and didn't care — it was the aftermath. Somehow, fighting for the right to her idea made her the bad guy. It was her fault her ex had been reprimanded by the university for plagiarism. Her fault his advisor dropped him for ethical concerns. *Her fault* he'd had to transfer universities. Not his. Toni's. And long after he left, it was Toni who bore the brunt of his friends' anger. The relationship was one thing, but whenever someone she worked with asked her out on a date, her brain skipped over that date and painted a vivid picture of all the ways it could — and surely would — end. Toni never wanted to tiptoe around someone else's possible reprisals in her work life ever again.

Right now, Steve was reminding her of why she had set those professional boundaries. She started to wish she hadn't come out tonight. And as soon as that thought formed in her brain, Toni reached for her purse. She was forty — a grown ass woman — and if there was one thing age, independence, and a steady paycheck afforded her, it was the ability to just leave when she was ready to go.

She turned to Steve, ready to wish him good luck on...whatever the hell he was doing in Costa Rica this summer when Mike placed a mason jar in front of her.

Her eyes traveled from his hand cupping the glass, up his arm, to his face. He leaned forward between her and Steve — completely blocking the other man from view. There was a look on his face she couldn't quite name but could feel in her chest. It was a mixture of frustration and knowing, as if he could see right through her.

"Do you want to dance?" he asked in the deep voice that had been rattling her on and off all day.

"What?"

He tipped his head to one side toward the center of the room, an almost clear space she guessed could pass for a dance floor if she squinted.

"Um... I don't—" she started.

"We'll watch your drink and your purse," Deja said, pulling Toni's wallet right out of her hand.

"We'll what?" Alejandro asked.

"Shut up," Deja muttered under her breath. "Go dance. Don't you love Etta James?"

As soon as Deja said her name, Toni heard the opening strings of Etta's rendition of "Stormy Weather," one of her favorites, begin to blare from unseen speakers.

"You do," Mike said. "Love Etta, I mean. So come dance with me." His eyebrows bunched together as his warm gaze seared into her.

Toni could have said no — she was still a grown ass woman — but she didn't want to. And that was the thing about adulthood and her sabbatical; Toni wanted to live a life, even if only for a few months, where she only did things that intrigued her, that made her happy, that felt good. She wanted to rediscover things she loved, and dancing to an Etta James song was a thing Toni had always, *always* loved.

She took Mike's hand, still wet from her sweating glass of beer, and let him pull her to her feet. Vaguely, she heard Steve's weak protest that they had been in the middle of a conversation, but his feelings were none of her business. She had her own feelings to worry about, like the gooey warmth that spread through her as Mike's hand once again landed on the small of her back.

He felt even better the second time around.

<hr>

TONI HAD BEEN on the verge of leaving. He knew how she was. As soon as university meetings ended, Toni's figure was a blur out the door. When they went out for dinner with colleagues, Toni always managed to pay her bill in cash and be unlocking her car before anyone else had even figured out the tip. She was better when it was just the five of them; sometimes, she would hang around for dessert or a leisurely walk to the parking lot as a group. Mike cherished those moments, and he wasn't going to let Steve fucking Titjens get in the way of their night out.

"Does this place have a jukebox?" she asked, craning her neck to look around the room.

"Huh?"

Toni leaned closer to him and raised her voice. He'd heard her, but he leaned forward so she could whisper in his ear, so her lips could brush against his earlobe.

"I said, does this bar have a jukebox? I can't believe someone is playing Etta. That's not really the vibe of this place."

Mike shifted his head and grinned at her. Out of her line of sight, he self-consciously tapped the cell phone in his back pocket. He'd paid the bartender twenty dollars to connect to the Bluetooth speaker for the length of a single song. It was extortion, but she was worth it. "Um, I'm not sure," he lied. "Come here."

At those last two words, Toni seemed to realize where they were, and she looked around shyly. Shy was not a word Mike would normally use to describe Toni, but he enjoyed this new facet of her.

"No one slow dances anymore," she said, balling her hands into fists. She shook her head slowly and frowned.

He moved a hand to her hip and pulled her gently toward him. "When has Antonia Ward ever cared about what everyone else is doing?"

Her mouth quirked into a smile for a brief second before she bit it back. "This place is so damn small. There's not enough room to dance."

"It's a good thing we don't need much space." Mike dug his fingers into her soft waist again and pulled a little harder. One step, and then two, and she was pressed against him. He began to shuffle his feet, leading her with the press of his hips while he held her close.

Her fists pressed against his chest, and her body was tense, but her feet moved in rhythm with his. "Where'd you learn how to dance?"

The chorus began. Etta's voice was low and pleading. Toni's breath was tickling his beard, and every second, she relaxed just a little bit more in his hold. He moved his hands to her back, one palm pressed flat against her spine, the other low, dangerously close to the upper curve of her ass, but he wasn't nearly that brave. Besides, he knew Toni would hate that, especially in front of so many of their colleagues.

All he wanted was to hold her close enough to finally get her to understand that he didn't want to be *just* her colleague.

When her palms were finally pressed flat against his chest,

their legs had intertwined, her head was tilted back, and their gazes finally locked.

"Answer my question," she whispered. He led her in a slow sway, careful and controlled. Toni's eyes lit up as they moved, and he smiled. "Who taught you how to dance?"

"My father." He leaned forward, and his lips skimmed across her cheek in the barest touch. "I was tall and awkward and had acne, so my dad taught me how to dance to boost my courage for the homecoming dance in middle school."

In the dim bar, Toni's big, dark eyes were like shimmering pools, soaking up every speck of light. Mike's chest was tight with familiar emotions.

"Cute story."

"It's one of my favorites."

"Now I feel like I should tell you something."

"You don't have to," Mike said, even though there was a yawning pit in his soul that had always been hungry for as much information about Toni as was humanly possible to know.

"I know I don't have to," she said, "but my mother always said one good turn deserves another."

Mike nodded and then stepped quickly to the right, spinning them in a tight, fast circle.

Her laughter was like bells, and now it was her turn to dig her fingernails into his shirt. He could feel his groin tighten at the sharp pain of her holding onto him.

"Is that what you meant?" he laughed.

"No," she giggled. "It was better."

During the spin, one of her braids fell from behind her ear. He moved the hand from her waist and carefully touched the braid, letting the pads of two fingers just feel the texture. He heard her breath hitch as he caressed her hair. And then his knuckles grazed her cheek as he moved the braid back into place.

Toni let out a shuddering breath and sank into his body.

Mike's fingers caressed her cheek and down her jaw. His thumb moved across her chin, but his gaze was focused squarely on the lush pout of her mouth.

"Did you hear about Susan Grammar?" Toni spluttered.

He blinked a few times in quick succession. "From the Business College?"

Toni nodded. "Apparently, she was trying to do the secret admirer thing with Nnamdi Johnson, and he was *not* happy about that."

"What?"

"Mmhmm. There's probably going to be another HR memo before we're off contract."

"Um, okay. Why are you telling me this?"

She shrugged awkwardly in his arms. "Just...you know, general information. The next woman you try these moves on might not be as understanding as me." She was giving him her fake laugh and tight, faker smile.

That last sentence made Mike stumble. "Toni, what do you—"

The Etta James song ended before he could finish that sentence. Mike lifted his head and stared across the room at the bartender. She tapped her watch and turned away.

"Welp, that was nice while it lasted," Toni said, pulling away.

"One more song," he said.

"Huh?"

"Give me one more song," he begged. "One more dance."

"Why?"

Mike sighed and pulled his phone out of his pocket. He unlocked it and showed her the Etta James Greatest Hits playlist open on his phone. "Because I'm not testing out my good moves on you to use on someone else."

"I—" She squinted at him. Mike recognized this look on her face. There were a number of people at their university who shrank away from this kind of attention from Toni. But Mike was probably the only person besides Steve, maybe, who'd been waiting — longing, even — to have Toni scrutinize him so completely.

"What are you saying?" she asked.

He sighed and pulled her back against him. The music on the Bluetooth speaker wasn't really right for a slow dance, but he didn't care. "I'm saying, Antonia Ward, that I just want to spend some time with you when we're not working, but only if you want that too."

"Oh," she said. And it was only because they were standing so close that he caught that soft exhalation.

"So, do you want to keep dancing?" he asked, his heart lodged in his throat.

SHE USED TO LOVE DANCING.

In grad school, Toni and her old roommate used to go out every Thursday night to the gay club downtown for Black music night. They would dance until sweat had broken down every bit of makeup on their faces and their feet ached. Toni used to dance herself ragged before walking home as the sun was lifting into the sky. She didn't need alcohol or drugs, just the music. On the dance floor, she could let herself be mediocre and happy instead of twice as good and miserable.

But she didn't let Mike hold onto her and turn her offbeat around the makeshift dancefloor to recapture something she'd lost all those years ago. Toni let Mike hold her and rock her because, for the first time since he'd walked her across campus, Mike was the only person she could see.

She'd always thought of Mike as 'Alejandro's little friend,' but as he moved against her, he became someone new in her eyes. She just wasn't sure who he was yet.

CHAPTER EIGHT

"I can't believe I never knew you were a good dancer all these years," she said in a voice thick with...something.

Mike smoothed his palm up her back. "That's because you never asked. All you had to do was ask."

"Apparently so," Toni breathed. She leaned back to look at him. This had the fortunate but unfortunate effect of pressing her breasts against his chest. He gulped and inched his hips back, just in case she felt how much he liked holding her this way.

He couldn't remember the last time he'd been out dancing, but some things were etched in his DNA, and so to distract himself from the flutter of her confused eyelashes and the press of her body, he spun in a fast circle again, ripping a peal of laughter from Toni that made his mouth go dry and threatened to make his dick harden. He wanted to hear it again.

Once he'd verified that the path was clear, he pushed at her soft waist and used their joined hands to spin her before pulling her against his body again.

He'd never seen Toni quite like this. Even in the dim room,

her face was bright with glee, and her red lips were parted as she panted. He could have avoided her heaving breasts if he'd been willing to try, but since he wasn't, he made sure his glance was quick.

"Behave," Toni said. But it was the way she said that word that intrigued him. She wrapped those two syllables in something sultry that made his fingers flex into her flesh for a moment.

And then she gasped.

"Hey, hate to break it to you two, but everyone's watching you."

Mike scowled at Alejandro, who, as usual, wasn't fazed by it at all. "Go away," Mike groaned.

"I'm just trying to help." He pushed Mike's beer into his reluctantly free hand.

"Who's watching my purse?" Toni asked, and they both turned to see their now-empty table; even Steve had moved on. Mike, of course, scanned the bar looking for the other man, one arm still possessively draped around Toni's waist.

"Still me," Deja said, handing over Toni's purse and glass of beer. "So, Mike...where'd you learn how to dance? And can you teach Alejandro?"

Of course, Deja was the only person who could make Alejandro splutter. "I can dance," he said defensively.

"Oh, for sure, but not like that."

Toni giggled and took a sip of her drink.

"It's getting hot and crowded in here. We're going to go outside. You coming?" Deja asked.

"Or do you want to dance some more?" Alejandro teased.

Mike actually did want to keep dancing with Toni, and Alejandro certainly knew it. He glared at his friend, who seemed the tiniest bit fazed right now.

"Definitely," Toni said, unknowingly deciding for both of them.

Mike noted the moment Toni walked out of his grasp to fall into step beside Deja, and he hated it. And even worse, Alejandro noticed it as well.

"Drink up. You look thirsty," Alejandro teased.

"Fuck you," Mike mouthed back as they followed the two women toward the exit.

The cool air hit Mike's face in a rush. The bar had been so dark that he was surprised to find that it was still relatively light out. He'd become so used to leaving campus in full dark after his late classes or some student activity that he was shocked for a moment at the fact that the semester was over. Almost over. He still had one stack of essays to grade, and then he would be done. But summer break was close enough to taste. Almost as close as Toni's mouth had just been.

"So, what are we doing this summer?" Marie asked when they joined her. She was leaning against a planter full of flowers just to the side of the entrance, casually sipping the last of another glass of beer.

"We're heading to Costa Rica and Brazil," Deja cried happily.

Mike sighed inwardly. Toni and Marie were not nearly as polite.

"Girl, we know. It's all you two have been talking about for months," Toni said.

"Y'all don't have to hate," Deja said, sounding offended.

"Yes, I do, actually," Marie said. "Not all of us are going to big-name conferences on a beach and then traveling around Brazil on an actual vacation. *Some* of us are going to fucking Wisconsin for a month-long 'professional development' retreat." Marie put those two words in air quotes like she had been all year. Mike didn't know exactly what she was objecting to, but he nodded in solidarity.

"Where in Wisconsin?" Toni asked.

Mike didn't care, but he took advantage of her quick question to look in her direction. He'd planned for it to be a quick glance, but it was not. Because Toni was beautiful. Not that that was brand-new information or anything; it's just sometimes, once or twice a semester, Mike would look in her direction, and she would be perfectly framed by the sun or an overhead track light or the glare from a projector screen, and he would see her anew. This was one of those moments.

Her skin was glowing with a soft sheen from the close bar and their dancing. That's what got him in the end, knowing that her skin was heated because of him. Because their bodies had moved together in perfect, slow sync. Because he had surprised her with his dance moves and his words, and for a brief moment, he'd seen a look in her eyes that made him think, hope, dream that his years-long crush wasn't all in vain.

"Milwaukee. I would have declined if it were somewhere else, but I have a friend from grad school who teaches there," Marie said. "Mike, didn't you go to school in Milwaukee?"

There was a moment of silence that, to be fair, Mike did register; he just forgot to respond until Toni turned in his direction.

She was *so damn beautiful*, even when she was looking at him like he had two heads, and then — he thought — as if she could finally see all the emotions he always thought he'd done a poor job of hiding.

"Mike," Alejandro coughed. "Get it together."

That pulled Mike out of the moment only because *of all the people* who could tell him to 'get it together,' Alejandro was not on that list.

"Really?" Mike seethed.

Alejandro laughed and pulled Deja into his side as if to say, 'Checkmate.'

"I hate you," Mike mouthed.

Alejandro kissed Deja's forehead but didn't respond. He didn't need to. Mike wanted to punch him, at least.

"What?" he asked Marie in an exasperated huff.

Marie huffed back a laugh. "I said, didn't you go to school in Milwaukee?"

"Oh. Yeah. I hated it. The food is good, though."

"Fuuuck," Marie groaned.

"Way to go, Mr. Rogers," Toni hissed at him.

"What?" Mike whined.

"Hello, fellow professors. How are we doing tonight?"

Everyone groaned at Justin Michel's greeting. Generally speaking, Justin was very nice but corny as hell.

"Kill me," Mike muttered at the same time as Toni mumbled, "End me," under her breath. They just happened to turn to one another and made eye contact. Mike smiled, and this time Toni smiled back.

"What's up, Justin?" Deja said happily, even though everyone, even Alejandro, frowned slightly in her direction.

"Have you heard the good news?"

"Is the good news that this long ass semester is over?" Alejandro asked.

Justin chuckled amiably. "That, *and...*" He reached into his pocket and pulled out a small rectangular sheet of paper. "A union is coming."

Justin might have been corny, but his news was met with a flurry of activity.

Marie snatched the flyer from his hand. "Holy shit, really?"

"*Really*," he said. "Obviously, we need to keep this hush-hush right now, but—"

"There's a meeting next week," Marie announced, reading from the flyer. Deja was reading over her shoulder.

"Does the administration know?" Toni asked.

Justin shrugged. "We think they've heard some rumors but nothing concrete. We can't keep it secret forever, but for right now," he said, snatching the flyer from Marie's hand and handing it to Toni, "feel free to take a picture if you need it. For obvious reasons, I'm going to take this."

Toni grabbed the flyer and scowled at Justin. Mike took his phone from his pocket and snapped a quick picture of the flyer for relevant details.

"Are you running this info session?" Toni asked.

"Oh no, I'm not a leadership kind of person. We have an organizing rep from the Union of American Teachers and Professors coming to answer our questions and talk us through the process if we decide to unionize."

"Which we better," Marie added.

"Democracy and all that," Justin said breezily. "I assume I'll see you all there."

"Obviously," Alejandro said.

"You'd be surprised," Justin said with a sunny smile. He reached for the flyer in Toni's hand, but he didn't snatch it as he had with Marie. Smart man. Toni glared at him for a few silent seconds before handing it over.

"What's that supposed to mean?" Toni asked.

"If you come to the meeting, you'll be surprised. Anyway, I think that's enough work for me. It's time for a beer. Bye." He spun in a half-circle and then strode toward the front door.

"He's weird, right? It's not just me?" Mike asked.

"Not at all. Very weird," Alejandro said.

"Aw, I like him," Deja said.

"What exactly do you like about him?" Toni asked.

"He clearly would have been a serial killer in an alternate

universe, but in this one, he's using his charisma for good," Marie replied.

"Charisma?" Mike asked.

"Um, that's not the vibe I get," Deja said, looking confused.

"It's not?" Alejandro added.

"Anyway," Mike said, tapping at his cell phone to airdrop a copy of the flyer to everyone. "So, I'll see you all next week then, I guess."

Deja smiled at him. "You say that like we won't see you at half a dozen graduation events between now and that meeting."

Toni groaned. "God, don't remind me."

"Okay," Deja said. "You can just be surprised by all those calendar alerts on your phone."

Marie laughed, but Alejandro and Mike tried to hide their smiles.

"I need new friends," Toni groaned, downing the last of her glass of beer.

"Do you want another?" Mike asked.

"God, yes," Toni said, already heading toward the door.

Mike fell into step behind her, avoiding Alejandro's mocking smile the entire way.

CHAPTER NINE

"Oh my god," Toni screamed, looking at her watch, "it's almost midnight!"

"Yeah?" Marie said, dancing in her seat.

"This is way past my bedtime."

"Me too," Alejandro said around a yawn. "Are you ready to go yet?"

Deja was squirming on his lap, dancing to the music. An hour ago, Alejandro had looked very excited about her sitting on him, but now he looked as if he might pass out any second and was too tired to hide it. Toni could relate.

"Aw, really?" Deja cooed. "So early?"

"It's almost midnight," Alejandro said, echoing Toni. "How are you not falling asleep right now?"

Deja laughed. "I accidentally had an espresso before the Multicultural Grad."

"How do you accidentally drink an espresso?" Toni cried, sounding like someone who monitored her caffeine intake very closely because she did. She had to. She yawned.

Deja, on the other hand, shrugged like someone who was

more than five years her junior and hadn't yet felt the ravages of time that was life after thirty-five. "I'm so hungry, though. Don't you want chicken and waffles from that new diner downtown?"

"God, yes," Marie replied.

"If it means we can leave and get our order to-go, absolutely," Alejandro said, gently pushing Deja to her feet.

Toni was right behind her, with Mike and Marie following her lead. It still took an ungodly amount of time for them to get out of the bar. Tabs had to be settled — not Toni's since Mike had intercepted all of her drink orders all night. They had to navigate their way from their table, wading through the crowd even though it had thinned considerably in the past few hours.

But once they made it outside, Toni took a breath of fresh air and a new surge of energy coursed through her veins. Not much, just enough for the short walk home. Deja and Marie led the way back to Toni's house with a curious — and for Toni, almost infuriating — pep in their steps. Alejandro trudged behind them while she and Mike brought up the rear.

All Toni wanted to do was lock her front door and fall into bed. She was so tired there was a chance she might not even take off her makeup. But with every other step, her left arm brushed Mike's, and a delicious frisson of electricity shot through her veins and undercut all the exhaustion.

"Alright, who's riding with whom?" Deja asked when Toni's house mercifully came into view.

Her voice was a little too loud for Toni's neighborhood, and she shushed her friend with a loud hiss. "I'm going to bed."

"Boo," Deja whispered.

"How much did you have to drink tonight?" Alejandro said.

It was dark on her street, but Toni could still see Deja's shadow leaning against her boyfriend, and she smiled despite herself. "At least one more beer than I should have. If you don't eat all your waffles, I will."

Toni heard Alejandro sigh indulgently. "What's new?" he deadpanned. "Mike, you coming?"

"Um... I'm not hungry. I don't really eat after ten."

"Why?" Marie asked incredulously.

He shrugged, and his shoulder knocked Toni's. "I don't know, I just don't. But Marie, I can drive you to pick up something."

"No, it's okay," Deja said a little too quickly. "Marie can come with us. She lives closer to Alejandro anyway, and we're staying at his tonight."

"I don't mind," Mike said.

"No, it's cool," Deja said, grabbing Marie by the wrist and turning toward Alejandro's car.

The move instantly made Toni suspicious. *Something* was going on in Deja's espresso-and-booze-wired brain.

"What's going on?" Toni asked.

"Who knows?" Alejandro yawned. "But we'll take Marie to get food and then home. It's no big deal." His car lights flashed as he unlocked his car, clearly ready to leave.

"And you can make sure Toni gets in okay, Mike," Deja said easily.

"I live here," Toni said, pointing at her house. "I'm in and okay."

"That's a long walk to your front door, and your heels are pretty high. Watch out for her, Mike. Let's go." Before Toni could even fix her mouth to say...something, Deja and Marie had already rushed into Alejandro's car, giggling like schoolgirls.

Toni squinted at the car as the engine roared to life — also too goddamn loud for her quiet neighborhood — and then it eased into the dark, empty street.

It was only when the rear lights lit up at the stop sign on the corner that Toni stopped glaring at Alejandro's retreating car and remembered that Mike was still standing next to her, silent as a mouse. Her pulse started to race, eating away the recent flash of annoyance at her friends.

"So, where do we find new friends?" Mike asked in a soft voice. For a second, Toni thought his voice seemed to tremble, but she was so tired she decided not to trust herself.

"God, I wish I knew," she breathed nervously.

"Um, come on. I'll walk you to your door. That way, when Deja asks, I won't have to lie."

"You think she'll ask?"

"You think she won't?" There was something teasing in his voice.

Toni sighed in resignation. "Come on, then."

THE STONE PATH to Toni's front door was lit on either side by small lanterns Mike hadn't noticed before — probably because he was too busy trying and failing not to stare at her hips. But he noticed them now — mostly because he was so focused on her steps, making sure each one landed correctly, ready to catch her in the event that she stumbled again — and he appreciated the extra illumination they gave to get the job done.

It didn't hurt that even her ankles looked sexy in those shoes.

On her front step, Toni turned carefully around to face him. He stopped just under the arc of light from the lamp above her door and smiled. Her eyes dipped to his mouth, and Mike was too tired to stop the groan from rumbling loudly in his throat.

Fuck.

Toni licked her own lips. "Um...thanks," she mumbled.

"Anytime."

Her lipstick was still perfectly in place somehow, and she licked her lips again. She crossed her arms over her chest, and Mike's gaze moved to her cleavage. He only had so much restraint, and he'd probably used the last of his reserves hours ago. This day had been hours and hours of time in Toni's company, close to her, touching her enough that it would take more than a day to reconstruct his defenses. But right now, he had none.

"Mike," she said.

He swallowed at the way she said his name; tired and dry, but husky. It wasn't hard to imagine that she might sound something like this after sex, and his groin began to tighten at the thought. He shoved his fists in his pants pockets and took a half-step back. "Toni," he replied in a voice tight with exhaustion and need.

She shook her head and dropped her arms. "Nothing."

Toni didn't give up. Mike didn't like that she was doing so now. "Ask me," he ground out, his voice, like his restraint, stripped raw.

Toni gulped loudly. "There's something different about you," she whispered.

He turned his head and looked down her street before looking back to her and shaking his head.

"The first time I saw you, you were wearing this tight purple suit with a black tank top underneath. It was low-cut," he said, tracing the fingers of his right hand across his own chest. "Not low enough to be unprofessional, but it was sexy as fuck to me. I knew from the moment we met that you were the smartest person in the room, even if you sometimes have to pretend otherwise."

"Purple suit...?" Toni breathed.

"There's nothing different about me, Antonia. I've wanted you since the first moment I saw you. The only thing that seems to be different is you just realized it."

"What?"

"Goodnight, Toni."

"What?"

"I'll see you next week at convocation."

And with that, Mike turned and walked down the path to her driveway. He unlocked his car and stepped inside. His heart rate was running a thousand miles a minute. He was panting so hard he'd started to sweat. But when he looked up, he could still see Toni with her back pressed against the front door, her mouth wide open in shock.

He gripped his steering wheel and watched her. He wanted nothing more than to stomp back up the path, hustle Toni inside her house, and figure out exactly what it took to wipe that perfect lipstick off her face. But he was exhausted, and so was she.

And when he finally undressed Toni, he wanted them both to be wide awake.

It took a few moments, but eventually, Toni shook her head and turned around. She tried to open the door, but it was still locked. She shook her head again and then started digging in her purse. She pulled her keys out and then let herself inside.

He counted to twenty, making sure she had enough time to lock the door behind her, and then he started his car and slowly backed out of her driveway.

CHAPTER TEN

Technically, the semester was over. For real. Toni's grades were submitted. Her end-of-semester reports had been uploaded to her department. The last letters of recommendation for grad students had been submitted. She'd spent the morning closely monitoring her inbox for student grievances, changing scores when necessary, and sending overly detailed responses when not before finally scheduling her out-of-office message to start sending at eight tomorrow morning.

The only thing left to do was convocation.

"I absolutely hate this bullshit," Deja said. "Where is Marie?"

"Not here because she's smart, and they don't ask junior faculty to volunteer until their second year."

"Why not?"

"It's policy. A policy *you* benefitted from for two years, actually," Toni reminded her friend.

"You can't shame me. This sucks. We should be paid for this."

"We are," Toni laughed, gesturing toward the too-sweet

punch and stale university catering cookies that were definitely left over from previous events.

"Ghetto," Deja said.

"Very. Are your grades in?"

"Girl, yes! As soon as we're done here, I'm going home to start packing."

"You don't leave for a few more days."

"And?"

Toni laughed. "Good point. You two deserve to get away."

"Yes, we do."

"Just don't come back here pregnant," Toni whispered.

"Oh my god, I would never," Deja said and then back-tracked with a slight grimace. "Okay, maybe I would. We're going to an all-inclusive resort in Brazil, and once those drinks hit..."

"Dear Lord," Toni interjected. "I don't need to know any of this."

"I'm just saying that if I didn't have very good birth control, there would be at least one big-headed Alejandro in the campus nursery already."

"You have the big head in your relationship. You do know that, right?"

"Bitch!" Deja shrieked and then looked around at the other faculty. She remembered where they were and lowered her voice. "Anyway, we are not at the baby stage of our relationship yet. So don't worry, I will come back happy, relaxed, and still childless."

"Hallelujah, amen. The end is nigh," Gladys said.

Deja and Toni turned to see their favorite campus administrator walking into the room. "How you doin', Miss Gladys?" Toni called.

"I'm almost free, so I'm almost doing great."

"Are you really retiring?" Deja asked.

"I sure am. Me and the hubby have been paying off a holiday home in the Sea Islands for twenty years. Made the last payment last month, put our house here on the market three months ago, and we are under contract as of yesterday. By the time they announce my last day, I will be halfway home."

"That's amazing," Toni said.

"God is good all the time. Now you two, hear this. I gave this place thirty mostly good years of my life. I've been planning this day for five years. And do you know what happened when I put in my resignation letter?"

"They offered you more money than you know what to do with to stay for five more years?" Deja asked, still so beautifully, naïvely optimistic.

Gladys laughed. "Honey, no. They thanked me for my service and told me they're not going to institute a search for my replacement. They're just going to give my duties to someone else. Someone who certainly didn't ask for more work and won't be compensated for it. So you remember this when it's your time. They don't care about me, you, or the next one. When it's your time to go, go, and don't worry about anybody else's comfort or happiness but your own."

"Okay, let's line up," Dean Chung called as she walked into the room.

"Damn," Deja whispered.

"Truth hurts," Gladys whispered back.

"YOU COULD BE LESS OBVIOUS," Alejandro said.

"And you could shut up," Mike replied. He craned his neck again, trying to look down the hallway opposite to the one he and Alejandro had used to line up at the auditorium entrance. The campus-wide graduation was not Mike's favorite event, but like the faculty senate meetings and some college-wide diversity events, it was one of the few places he was usually guaranteed to see Toni. So even though he hated the three-hour-long event where faculty mostly just sat in their hot ass robes and stoles, he didn't mind it enough to skip. And since Toni would be on sabbatical next year, this would be his last for a while.

"They're coming," Mike said, turning toward Alejandro. "Be cool."

"This is pathetic. You're better than this."

"Did I ask you?"

Alejandro sighed and turned toward the hallway.

"What are you doing?"

"Not acting weird. You look cute," he called, and Mike knew just by the tone of his voice that he was speaking to Deja.

It was Mike's turn to roll his eyes.

"Thank you," Deja trilled, followed by the sound of her heels as she sped up to rush into Alejandro's arms.

"God, give it a rest." At the sound of Toni's voice, Mike turned to find her shaking her head at their friends. She rolled her eyes and turned away, right in his direction.

They hadn't seen each other since that night on her front porch. That was four days ago. Four days and eight hours. Not that Mike was counting. But when they finally made eye contact, those four days could have been a blink of an eye.

"Good morning," he said with a smile.

She tried to bite back her own smile. "Morning. Grades in?"

"Yup. You?" Mike asked, leaning against the wall, trying to feign a kind of nonchalance he didn't feel.

"Two days ago," Toni said, smiling big enough to show all of her front teeth. It was a proud but adorable smile he didn't think he'd seen before.

"Two days? How the hell did you manage that?" Sharon Fein yelled from the front of the line.

Mike sighed. He'd forgotten there were other people around just that quick.

Toni turned to Sharon. "Most of my students turned in their final papers the last week of classes and did a self-assessment finals week. I had a week's head start on the rest of you."

"Damn," Deja muttered. "That's a great idea."

"You could switch out the self-assessment for a peer review, probably?" Alejandro asked. Mike knew the other man well enough that he could practically see the wheels turning in his brain.

Toni shrugged. "Yeah, that could work too. All that matters is that while you all were looking at stacks of blue books and ten-plus-page papers, I had one class of short-answer exams and one-page write-ups for the rest." She took a dramatic pause to smile smugly at them. "Double-spaced," she finally added.

Most of the faculty lined up in the hallway groaned — including Deja. Mike, however, ducked his head to hide his own proud smile.

"Alright, everyone, let's go. If this is your first time, all you have to do is follow the procession and sit. Easy-peasy. Let's go!" Of all the deans who could've run faculty procession, Dean Chung was always Mike's favorite. She didn't want to be here anymore than the regular faculty. Some people liked to pretend as if these near-mandatory events were actually voluntary spaces for friendly socializing. Not Dean Chung. She wanted to get in, do the job, and get home to record this event on her CV before heading out of town for a week-long vacation with her wife. Mike respected that.

Toni and Deja didn't seem to appreciate Dean Chung's practicality. Mike watched them roll their eyes at one another as they lined up on the other side of the hallway.

Alejandro tapped Mike's right shoulder. "Come on," he whispered before darting across the hall.

"Seriously?" Toni whined as Alejandro slipped between her and Deja, kissing his girlfriend on the cheek.

"Get a room," Mike said even as he ducked behind Toni, careful not to let any part of his body touch hers, no matter how badly he wanted that.

Still, he watched as her head turned, and she looked at him over her shoulder quickly before facing forward again.

Dean Chung and Gladys strolled down the long hallway, counting them. Behind them, Gladys moved two people from their line to the other to replace Mike and Alejandro. The four of them were silent as the two women walked forward again. Deja giggled once they were out of earshot.

"Here we go," Dean Chung called down the hall.

A few seconds later, they were marching forward out into the main auditorium.

Maybe it was because the semester was over. Maybe it was because he hadn't had a single grade complaint this semester. Or maybe it was because, now that he was in line behind her, Mike could smell Toni's perfume, the same perfume he'd been smelling on her skin since the day they met. Maybe it was all of the above and also all the years he'd been infatuated with her that made Mike lean forward to bring his mouth close to her ear. "You look beautiful, by the way."

And he was close enough that he felt her shiver in response.

TONI WAS OPPOSED to university-wide events and avoided them whenever she could. There were some people in her position who hated being segregated in diversity and multicultural work, and they absolutely used the word 'segregation' to voice that disdain. Toni did not consider herself to be in community with those people, and she let them have the university-wide events that gave them the exposure they craved. She preferred to shepherd her students at the smaller, lower-profile activities anyway. Unfortunately, no one else in her department wanted to be on graduation duty, so she took one for the team, so to speak.

Normally this was an event she just had to endure — sometimes alone and sometimes with Deja and Alejandro — before she could be free of these people for a merciful ten weeks of summer. But with Mike at her back as they walked out into the stadium and sitting to her left throughout the ceremony, she did more than endure it; she might have even liked it.

But Mike was distracting. Halfway through the ceremony, one of her favorite students had waved at her from the line. He was almost on stage. Toni had forgotten his request to have her give him his diploma. She'd had to shimmy by Mike to rush on stage. And as she shimmied back to her seat, Mike's steadying hand had landed on her back, that one touch distracting her all over again.

And even though he made sure not to touch her, not even an accidental brush of their legs, she could still feel the weight of his hand on her back and hip as they marched out of the auditorium. Back in the dressing room, she took off her loaner robe and stole and then brushed her own hand across her back where his had been.

"What are you getting up to now?" Deja asked.

Toni threw her purse over her shoulder and snatched up her garments. "No plans. You?"

Deja shrugged and turned toward the door, with Toni following close behind. "Think we're gonna get lunch with Mike. Wanna come?"

Toni was thankful that Deja was looking away because she could feel her face heating at his name, and she fanned herself. "Um...where y'all going?" she asked, trying to act disinterested.

Clearly, she failed.

Deja whipped around, a wild smile on her face. Toni prepared herself for whatever Deja had heard in her voice, but the other woman simply turned away with a knowing smirk. "There's this new diner that just opened up near the hospital."

"The hospital?"

"I know. Weird location, but according to the reviews, the pancakes are worth the trek."

"Oh, interesting."

"Very. So you coming?"

"What's up?" Alejandro asked, grabbing Deja's regalia from her with one hand while snaking his free arm around her waist.

"I'm trying to convince Toni to come to lunch with us," Deja said.

"Oh, yeah? The Sunrise Café is supposed to be amazing," he offered, barely taking his eyes off Deja. "Best pancakes in the state."

"That's a big claim," Toni said.

"I've been there," Mike interjected.

Toni's head turned at the sound of his voice. Her body didn't even give her time to think about it. As soon as he started speaking, she was looking at him, drinking him in, watching his lips move, and then abruptly turning away because her thoughts had made a sharp turn to filthy.

Mike kept up the conversation, blissfully unaware of what she'd just been thinking. "Their pancakes are okay. Definitely better than their waffles," he said with a shrug.

"See?" Deja trilled.

"But I would recommend their omelets, and their biscuits are amazing."

"How many times have you been there?" Alejandro asked, the 'without me' very evident in his tone.

"A few. I like eating out for breakfast, and you don't leave the house before ten these days. So, are you coming?" he asked, turning his attention fully to Toni.

She couldn't return his gaze. She didn't trust herself at the moment, but she could see him looking at her in her peripheral vision, watching her.

"Um...okay," she breathed. "I love omelets."

"I know," Mike said, carefully plucking Toni's regalia from her hands.

CHAPTER ELEVEN

"Wait, so this place is new? Like built in this century?" Toni asked in disbelief.

"They're clearly going for a retro vibe," Deja said.

"Ya think? I swear the local dive bar in my hometown doesn't even have a jukebox anymore. Where the hell did they find that?"

"eBay," the *very* perky waitress who seemed to appear in front of them out of nowhere trilled. "My sisters and I furnished the entire dining room by thrifting."

"Really?" Toni gasped.

"Ugh," Alejandro said.

The waitress took both responses in stride. "Don't worry, we had everything professionally cleaned and repaired, but yeah! This place was a labor of love."

"Why?" Deja asked, as unsure about this location as Alejandro.

Once again, the waitress's response indicated that she — and presumably her sisters — had prepared themselves for this question. "We grew up here. Before the hospital was built, this whole area used to be a family farm. Our family's farm for four generations. This diner is an almost-exact replica of the diner my grandparents used to run here."

"Almost?" Toni asked, very curious.

The woman beamed at her. "The original diner was attached to the butcher's cold room. We thought people wouldn't appreciate that level of authenticity." Her eyes flickered playfully around the group. "Besides, we get our meat from an organic farm twenty miles away. Table for four?"

"Uh..."

"Yep," Mike said excitedly.

"You're a historian. How are you not excited about this?" Toni asked Alejandro as they settled into their booth.

It was a good question, but Toni was struggling to concentrate on Alejandro for an answer because, once again, Mike was sitting on her side of the booth, but this one was much smaller than the one at the brewery. When Mike slid along the bench to sit beside her, she felt as if his body was practically covering her right side, and there was nothing either of them could do about it. Every time one person moved, they touched the other. When Toni opened her menu, their arms didn't just brush; it was as if the hair on their forearms started to braid together. And that only made her squirm in her seat all the more.

"Actually, it's because I'm a historian that I'm not a fan. If the four of us had been alive when their grandparents owned this diner, we wouldn't have been able to enter through the front door."

They all sat in silence at that, eyes shifting away from one another and around the diner, seeing it with new eyes.

"That really brought the mood all the way down," Toni said.

"Sorry, but this is how I think."

Toni nodded and shrugged. "Oh, I get it. It's my job every

semester to watch as all our brand-new majors who come here thinking they can change the world by getting into politics suddenly realize all the problems with that train of thought. I'm not affected, not really. I still want my Jim Crow omelet, but now I'm going to be a little sad if I like it."

"Toni," Deja hissed.

"Deja?" Toni hissed back, uncowed.

"What about you, Mike?" Alejandro asked.

"What about me?" he retorted, looking around the table, only briefly letting his gaze touch Toni's face.

"How close to the dark ages would your field be in the Fifties?"

"What is your field?" Toni asked, her eyebrows and mouth bunched as she realized that this was a very basic thing she somehow didn't know about him.

So much of the way faculty learned to relate to one another was through departmental designations. In some ways, it made social interactions easier. If you were in the same building, like Toni, Deja, and Alejandro, you could always chitchat about the ancient HVAC system. If you were on similar committees, complaining about meetings was always a safe space. Years of tedious conversations mostly made it easy to figure out where everyone fit in the campus ecosystem geographically, intellectually, and politically.

The problem with Mike was that he was in the School of Natural Sciences, which housed a number of science departments. And somehow, over all the years they'd worked together — and even over the last two years as their social circles merged because of Deja and Alejandro's relationship — Toni had never once asked which unit specifically was his. But to be fair, he'd also never spent an entire evening looking at and touching her as if her skin was made of the softest velvet.

All of a sudden, Toni was curious about Mike, and the

impromptu question made sure that her newfound curiosity had not gone unnoticed.

When Mike turned to her and finally let his gaze linger on her face, their booth felt even smaller than before. "Physics," he said simply.

Well, the word was simple, but his voice sounded deeper, richer, warmer to Toni's ears, and in the small space of this booth, no one missed when she swiped at the sweat on her top lip and turned back to her menu as if it was full of breaking news. But they were all nice enough not to mention it.

Yet.

Deja caught Toni's eye and smirked.

Toni rolled her eyes.

Mike, however, moved on. "The Fifties were actually a revolutionary time in my field. Everyone was racist, but the scientific developments were amazing."

"Oh, fun," Deja said and then elbowed a snickering Alejandro in the side.

"Sorry," he whispered.

"Can I get y'all anything to drink?"

"Coffee," they replied in unison.

The waitress smiled. "Hospital or university?"

"University," Alejandro said.

She nodded. "Got it. I'll be right back with a full pot."

"She's nice." Deja beamed at Alejandro.

"She's probably trying to make up for the Jim Crow omelets," he muttered under his breath.

Toni couldn't stop herself — she started laughing and kept laughing, her body brushing Mike's with every gasping breath.

"I'M SO FULL. My first afternoon nap of the summer is about to be amazing."

"You can't nap, we have to pack," Deja said.

"We don't leave for a week," Alejandro said, covering his yawn with a big hand.

"A week is not a lot of time. Have you seen your closet?"

"What's that supposed to mean?"

Mike and Toni were already lagging behind their friends, but as soon as Deja put her hands on her hips, they both instinctively slowed their steps and let a little more distance build between them.

Mike's gaze darted to the right to see Toni out of the corner of his eye.

"So...what are you doing for the rest of the day?"

"Huh? Oh." She shrugged. "Nothing. Well, nothing much." She lifted her arm and started tapping at her smartwatch.

Mike turned his head and followed her movements. He wasn't trying to spy or anything, but he was definitely interested.

"Only thing on today's agenda is to take my library books back and relax. Maybe I'll even take a nap. God, that sounds boring." She frowned and seemed to shrink in on herself.

He hated when Toni frowned. Unfortunately, on campus, she frowned more than she smiled. He once went nearly a year without seeing her even grin. And even though Alejandro had been getting on his nerves recently, ever since he'd started dating Deja, Mike had seen Toni smile more times than he even knew what to do with.

Still, Mike thought there was beauty even in Toni's frustrated frowns. Like the soft wrinkles on the left corner of her mouth and in between her eyes or the way her bottom lip always seemed thicker than her top. As far as he was concerned, it was impossible to mar Toni's physical beauty because there was so much more below the surface.

"It's your sabbatical," he reminded her. "It can be as boring as you want it to be, Toni."

This was familiar advice. He gave it to students and faculty alike. The impulse to stuff the summer break with more was attractive — in some fields, even expected — but Mike knew better. A single day of rest wasn't enough. Ten weeks of rest sometimes wasn't enough. He knew Toni knew this, but when she turned to him with big, grateful eyes, he realized something he hadn't before. Toni was the person most faculty of color went to for good, practical advice, and she gave it freely. Unfortunately, she didn't seem to save any of it for herself.

"You deserve to relax, Toni. This summer and next year. If all you want to do is nap, then do that."

"Nah, I've got a house full of renovations, remember?"

They'd reached their cars, parked side by side. Toni's thumb slid over the button on her car handle to unlock it.

It would have been so easy to let her climb into her car and drive away, but he didn't. Instead, he followed Toni into the space between their cars and put his hand over hers, caressing her thumb with his until she let go of the handle and let him slide his fingers between hers.

"Mike?" she breathed.

She wasn't a little drunk or hungover, but she said his name the way she had that night on her doorstep. He placed his free hand on her hip and squeezed, eliciting a delicious squeak of surprise from her lips.

He turned her slowly around and then pressed her back against her car door, taking a quick moment to let his gaze move over her body. She was wearing another dress, a beige knit thing that didn't just hug her curves but exaggerated them. His body's reaction grew exponentially.

And when she groaned, he let the last of his control slip and crushed his body against hers.

"Oh god," Toni said, squirming against him. She wrapped her arms around his and pulled him close. Her eyes went big with surprise at her own actions.

There was no way to hide his growing erection from her. After all these years, Toni finally knew at least a little of how he felt about her. But just in case she was unsure, he cupped her face gently and slowly lowered his mouth to hers.

If he were being honest with himself, Mike had always dreamed about kissing Toni as a prelude. Kissing her was a thing that, in his mind, came before *everything* else he wanted to do to her. But when his lips were actually pressing against hers, prying them apart so he could slip his tongue into the warmth of her mouth, and their tongues met for the first time, he realized that he had been selling this moment short.

This kiss didn't have to be the prelude to anything to consume him entirely.

Their tongues tangled together, lips pressing forward and retreating, pulling back again and then coming together hungrier than before.

Mike slid his hands down her back and finally cupped the swell of her ass after years of waking up hard and sweating just thinking about it.

She groaned, and he crushed his lips to hers, wanting to taste that and the bitter remnants of her coffee all at the same time.

It was when he was just about to pull her up his body by the grip on her backside that he knew they should stop. If he spread her legs around his waist, there wasn't a law in the world that was going to stop him from fucking her right then. And he figured Toni might not approve of that at noon on a Friday afternoon.

He ripped his mouth from Toni's painfully.

"What the fuck?" she breathed, shocked but smiling. She sounded sleepy or tipsy, but her face looked utterly relaxed.

He smiled proudly because he'd done that to her.

"Don't look so smug," she said, resting her forehead against his chest while she caught her breath.

Mike swallowed a groan and bent forward to bury his face in her hair for a few charged seconds that did nothing to ease the tension in his pants. They held one another for a few moments, forgetting the rest of the world until a shrill beacon ripped through their peace. They jumped apart and watched as an ambulance raced past them.

"Damn hospital," she breathed.

"Yeah," he said, mostly because he couldn't think of anything else to say.

"So, you weren't lying," she said.

He squinted at her, trying to understand her words when all he really wanted was to hold her. "What do you mean?"

"About...me? I thought you were lying."

It was maybe only because Mike was so attuned to so many shifts in the tone of Toni's voice that he heard something new there, something wobbly and unsure.

"I don't lie, Toni," he said gruffly. He hated her even thinking that was a possibility.

She laughed and rolled her eyes. "Everybody lies. Even just a little bit."

Mike shook his head. "Not me. I'd rather say nothing than lie." He stared deep into her eyes.

"Oh," she breathed, a small smile lifting the corners of her mouth.

Mike didn't want to leave, but he understood that the timing had to be right; he'd waited too damn long for anything less. Besides, overwhelming Toni was a surefire way not to get the only thing he wanted. Her. So, he leaned down to brush his mouth across the top of her left cheek and then turned to walk to his car.

"Enjoy your nap, Toni," he called.

He was halfway home before he realized he hadn't noticed Alejandro and Deja leave.

CHAPTER TWELVE

I saw you and Mike making out!!!

Toni was halfway to the library when she got that text message from Deja, but she didn't respond until she made it home. She didn't think Deja was sitting around waiting for a text back, but if she was, she was probably frustrated at Toni's three-word response.

No you didn't.

But maybe she had been waiting around because she texted back a little too quickly for Toni's liking.

I have eyes and Alejandro just made me get an eye exam. I know what I saw!

There was *a lot* Toni wanted to say in response to that message. Many questions she wanted to ask. Top of the list was why Alejandro had to make Deja get an eye exam. Deja was set to turn in her tenure packet in the fall, and it was a damn good packet as far as Toni was concerned; and not just because she had gone over every file — every page of every file — with Deja, including five rounds of revisions on each of her narratives — teaching, research, and service. Deja had been running herself ragged for months trying to get it all done, so actually, Toni decided she could shelve that question about the eye exam; she'd answered it all by herself.

Toni was much more confident than Deja about her prospects for tenure. Deja was the best faculty member the Sociology department had hired in over a decade, according to campus gossip. Unless her senior colleagues planned to burn every strategic plan they'd written in the past five years — with Deja's input — and disappear into irrelevancy, Toni thought they would be foolish not to make sure she made it over this last hurdle. But Toni knew all too well that nothing was certain, so she wouldn't begrudge her friend her anxiety.

Besides, Toni had a penchant for focusing on everyone else's shit and trying to fix everyone else's problems rather than keeping her eyes on her own plate; this was one of the reasons she was so excited to disconnect from work over her sabbatical. It was finally time to see to her own needs.

Fine, I'll tell you what happened between me and Mike if you tell me everything you know about him!
I'm fine with you pumping Alejandro for intel.
Thx

WHILE TONI WAITED for Deja's response, she turned the air conditioning up and rushed up the stairs to her bedroom. It was a hot day, only made hotter by that goddamn kiss. Even just thinking about it made her entire body start to warm again. She placed her phone on top of the dresser before leaving a trail of clothes on the way to the bathroom. She needed a cold shower. The coldest she could stand. But the sound of an incoming text message called her back. She jogged back to the bed and was happy to see another message from Deja.

Happy to do that kind of reconnaissance!

Toni's face bunched into a ball. "Ew," she typed back and dumped the phone back on the bed. When she turned around, she found her cat sitting silently in the doorway, watching her with his penetrating yellow eyes.

"What?" she said, hands on her hips. "Stop looking at me like that."

The thing about Paw Robeson was that he had been an ungrateful, judgy roommate since the day she adopted him ten years before. She hadn't even wanted a cat. She'd just wanted to volunteer at a local shelter on the weekends as a post-break-up release. She hadn't wanted to notice the big bushy black cat that no one seemed to want, but she had. And for the next three hours of her volunteer shift, that cat had glared through the bars, seemingly daring anyone to get close to his cage. Something about his glare had touched Toni. She'd also felt a keen sense of injustice at the cat's position, especially when one of the older volunteers had explained that it was his color and age that would likely keep him from finding a home.

When she was little, Toni's grandmother used to call her Goody, as in Goody Two-Shoes, because Toni had an almost pathological sense of right. And that was how she'd left the volunteer event with a cat in a secondhand cat carrier, adoption papers she promptly lost, and a pamphlet about how to best care for a cat for complete beginners.

Toni didn't even like cats!

But over the years, Paw had become her best friend. Her mooching ass roommate who cost her an arm and a leg each year in specialty cat food, thought every piece of soft furniture in the house was a scratching post, and cuddled against her stomach whenever she cried herself to sleep.

"Do you want a treat?" she asked in irritation.

He started at his second favorite word and stretched his forelegs out in front of him.

"Greedy bastard," she said before stepping over him to jog downstairs to the kitchen.

Paw was hot on her heels. He could move fast when properly motivated.

AN HOUR LATER, Toni threw a t-shirt over her clean, naked body. Once she'd cooled down, she decided to have a little spa day and shave her thighs — since she'd skipped that out of time and necessity — trim the hair covering her mound and exfoliate the hell out of her body from her neck to the bottom of her feet. Of all the ways to mark the end of the semester, taking care of her skin was one of the best.

As she left the bathroom, the list of DIY projects begged for attention. At the top of the list was her home office. It was actually a conversion of a sad, small spare room she used for storage into a fully functional office, and the list of things she needed to do to prep that room alone was a mile long.

But then she glanced at her bed, and her reno plans started to evaporate. There was a buzzing feeling in the pit of her stomach, some insistent voice at the back of her mind that made her think she needed to *do* something because there were so many things that needed doing. But she also wanted to take a nap. Or rather, Mike had told her she deserved to rest, and she couldn't get his words, his mouth, or his hands off her mind.

She glanced from the door to her bed again, but this time she imagined Mike between her sheets. So unlike her. But then she heard the echo of Mike's voice. *"Enjoy your nap, Toni."* Goosebumps erupted all over her body, and the bed won the battle.

There would be plenty of time to pry up the old carpet and measure her walls for wallpaper later.

On her way to bed, she took a detour to the dresser inside her walk-in closet and crouched down to pull the bottom drawer open where she kept her sex toys; some of them, at least. Toni usually preferred a good clitoral sucker to get her to a quick orgasm because her schedule rarely allowed for more, but today she wanted something else. She was celebrating the end of the semester and her sabbatical, after all.

Her fingers glided over her favorite black vibrating spongy dildo. It had looked good in the package, but it felt even better inside her. It was a modest length and width, but this toy was all about the curved head that hit her g-spot and gave just the perfect amount of pressure. On the right setting, this toy would wind her slowly to a soft reverberating orgasm that wouldn't rock her world but would relax her muscles. But today Toni wanted amazing, so she grabbed her favorite clitoral sucker and practically skipped her way back to bed with both toys, a rare treat.

It was full light outside, but she yawned as she walked to her bed, pulled back the covers, and crawled inside. Toni had a lot of strategies for stress release, and she gave advice to the faculty she mentored freely. She jogged, she swam, she cooked, hell, she lifted weights when she needed to work through some real suppressed aggression. But she also used to dance and fuck. She didn't do either of those things much anymore; in their place, she made room in her schedule to talk to a therapist virtually, and masturbated once a day. For the past couple of years, as the list of her responsibilities grew and her body slowed, some weeks, she only had time for quick orgasms that *technically* got the job done but never left her satisfied.

But she had time today.

Toni loved touching herself. She loved getting acquainted with her own body, marking the changes, and reminding herself that she didn't have to assign a value to any of them. Her body was beautiful and whole as it was. She enjoyed the feeling of her skin, especially now that it was freshly exfoliated. And when her fingertips moved over a patch of hair in the crease of her thigh, she sighed in resignation because somehow she hadn't shaved her legs as thoroughly as she thought. But nothing could make Toni hate her body; she was too old for that. And nothing could stop the electric sensations that pulsed through her gut as her fingers skimmed over the curly hair at the top of her mound, circling her clit, moving through her soft lips, and then teasing her opening. She liked making herself wet enough that she could easily slip her dildo into her opening with only her arousal.

She hadn't had a regular sexual partner in too long to count, so she'd become that for herself. She wished she had known in her twenties how good it could be to be with herself in this way, to trust that she would always get off because she knew exactly what she needed.

One hand moved her dildo slowly in and out of her opening; the other traveled over her torso, charting a path around her soft belly in playful circles and then finally across her chest to tease the soft skin under her breasts.

When she was short on time, she usually covered her clit

with her toy, rolled her nipples between her fingers, and focused on getting herself off as fast as humanly possible. But Toni didn't plan to be short on time anytime in the next fifteen months, so she teased herself, alternating her touches between light and hard as she moved her dildo fast and slow.

She lost track of time. She couldn't even remember the last time that had happened. That alone made a small smile spread on her lips. And then an orgasm crested over her, pulling her mouth open and a gasp from her throat. She shuddered and sank into her mattress, the promise of another harder orgasm lifting her already heightened mood.

She kicked the covers from her body and lifted her left leg into the air. She crouched forward, bending herself into the perfect angle to fuck herself exactly the way she liked.

Still, she avoided her nipples, knowing it would get her off faster than she wanted.

She licked her dry lips and flicked her wrist faster.

And faster.

And faster.

Toni liked to think of her orgasms as an inflating balloon. Sometimes she was just working to get it nice and full, so she could ride the wave of a slow, measured, deflating release. When time was short, she was working for the pop, rushing toward a completion that left all the pieces of her drifting to the ground, limp and ready to go about the rest of her day or fall to sleep, whatever the case may be.

Today, however, Toni wanted to float. She wanted to make herself come as long and as hard as she could manage and then revel in the lightness of it all.

One mini orgasm gave her a lovely microdose of joy, and she laughed as the next hit harder, each release stronger than the last. Half an hour later, Toni's body was covered in sweat, soaking her t-shirt and the sheet beneath her. Her muscles were exhausted, but she reached for the clitoral sucker, sure she had one more orgasm in her.

And she was right.

When that very last release washed over her, Toni was euphoric as she drifted off to sleep with Mike's face emblazoned behind her eyes.

CHAPTER THIRTEEN

"Sir, can you get a job? Can you put a load of laundry in the washer? Can you vacuum? Can you do something?"

Toni threw these questions at Paw Robeson each time she passed him. Every time she happened to see him lounging on the couch, watching her as she carried boxes of books and paints back and forth to the garage and back again, she thought of a new chore he could be doing. Paw Robeson was unfazed. But this was their thing — he did nothing, and she spoke to him like he was a person.

When she was done clearing some of the detritus from her soon-to-be office, Toni plopped down on the couch next to her cat. "So, what's new?" she asked him.

Paw Robeson stared at her for a few silent seconds before stretching his forelegs and then climbing into her lap. His claws dug through her thin leggings.

"Thanks for the reminder that I need to clip your claws," she muttered while using her hand to brush his fur.

He curled into a ball and closed his eyes, purring while she scratched him behind the ears.

"I'll count this toward your share of the utilities for this month."

Like a lot of academics, Toni usually thought of summer break as the time to do all the work she couldn't fit into the academic year. That was all well and good to fill up the lines of her CV, but it meant she never walked into the fall semester feeling rested. Even though she always counseled junior faculty to rest during summer, she so rarely did. So it was fitting that she spent the first actual day of summer doing work of a different sort.

Rest was a thing she was apparently going to have to work at.

With Paw Robeson already asleep on her lap, Toni thought she might drift off and join him, so of course, her phone rang at the exact moment that her eyelids were beginning to droop. It took a bit of work, but she was able to maneuver herself onto her back and stretch across to the coffee table for her phone.

"What?" she whispered by way of hello.

"Oh, she has an attitude," Deja teased.

"She has chores to do and a cat snoozing on her lap."

"And a crush, apparently," Deja said.

"I will hang up on you," Toni said in an empty threat.

"Sure you will," Deja laughed.

"Shut up," she whispered.

"Okay, if that's what you want. I guess I'll just keep all the intel I've been pulling out of Alejandro to myself."

Toni sat up too fast — a move Paw Robeson did not approve of. He flailed and dug his claws into her leg. "Ah, shit," she hissed. She dropped her phone on the cushion beside her and helped Paw dislodge his claws from her pants. Once he was free, he darted away without a second glance.

"You better spill," she said when she picked her phone up again.

Deja was cackling into the phone. "Thought you'd say that."

Toni glared at the phone and bit her lips shut to stop from saying something she wouldn't mean in a few minutes.

"Okay, so basically, according to Ale, Mike has had a crush on you for years. He was married briefly in grad school. Dates sporadically but not seriously. I think it's because he's been waiting for you, but Alejandro said it's because he's a workaholic." There was a brief pregnant pause before Deja trilled, "Like you. Anyway, Alejandro says he's a good man. That means nothing because men can't tell when other men are good, but if anyone can, it's probably him. And actually, I agree. Mike's great. He also has very big feet. That last part is coming from me, not Alejandro."

Deja whispered that last sentence, and Toni rolled her eyes. "I'm telling your man you said that shit."

"Bitch!"

"Bitch," Toni replied. "Anyway, it took you two days to find that out? Really?"

"Ugh," Deja groaned. "Of course not, but I had a plagiarism case pop up after final grades were in, and that took up all day yesterday. I'm still pissed."

"What happened?"

"Basically, one of my students contested their final grade, and I had to review their final exam because my TA graded it, and it didn't feel right. Copied and pasted it online and literally found half that shit on Reddit. So then I had to spend like an hour writing one of those long ass letters to the Dean of Students. Ghetto."

"Ugh, sorry about that. Why didn't the online plagiarism system catch it?"

"Great fucking question! I had to also send an email to ITS asking that exact question. If they're going to make us require students to submit their essays online — even though *some of us* prefer grading physical papers — the least they can do is make sure all the widgets and shit they overpay for work."

"I predict you get a written response, shocked but unhelpful, in mid-July."

"July? Oh, sabbatical has made someone optimistic..." Deja laughed.

Finally, Toni laughed. "I guess so. Anything else?"

"Not really. I tried to find out what Mike does for fun and about his family, but Alejandro wouldn't give me anything. He said something about you discovering that when you finally went on a date with him."

"A date!"

"Oh, girl, shut up and let that man take you out. No, don't—"

Deja's voice cut off, and it was Alejandro's laughter that filled her ear now. "Yeah, let Mike take you out. Money is *no* object."

"I don't know what you're talking about," Toni said.

Alejandro's laughter was annoying to Toni, but she guessed she could understand why Deja loved it. "He's a good guy. He likes you. He has no kids. He can cook."

"He can cook?" Toni asked.

But Deja's voice faintly came over the line. "Do you know what size shoe he wears?"

"What?" Alejandro asked.

"Oh my god, I'm hanging up now." Toni didn't bother waiting to see if Alejandro heard her before she tapped her phone screen and tossed her phone back on the coffee table. She sighed and looked around her living room. It was a mess. All of Paw's toys were strewn around the room, the art prints she still needed to get framed and hang were stacked in a corner, and the dust. God. All the dust.

She sighed again and was about to stand when Paw came sauntering back into the living room with a peeved cry. Toni leaned back in her seat and tapped her lap. He didn't run because that would be beneath him, but he eventually jumped elegantly from the floor onto her thighs. He patted at her legs, his claws sometimes piercing her leggings and digging into her skin. But soon enough, he'd curled back into that same soft, furry ball, somehow drifting almost immediately back to sleep.

Toni watched him with a forced fascination. If she was focusing on her cat, she wouldn't have to think about Mike and the crumbs Deja and Alejandro had given her about him.

"SO SHE ASKED ABOUT ME?" Mike said, loud enough for his cell phone to pick up.

He was fresh out of the shower and working his way through the beauty routine his younger sister insisted he follow. A routine he couldn't shirk since she was a dermatologist, and whenever they FaceTimed each other, she always seemed to know when he hadn't been wearing his sunscreen regularly.

"Yes," Alejandro said, sounding annoyed.

"What did she ask?"

He could practically hear Alejandro's shrug. "I don't know, just about you. She asked Deja whatever she knew about you, and Deja, adorably, asked what I knew about you." Alejandro said this word jumble like it made sense. It did not.

"And what did you tell her?"

There was the sound of Alejandro's shrug again. "I don't know. You're not a serial killer. You have good credit. You once met the Harlem Globetrotters in Vegas."

Mike was sure he was having a stroke. "Next time I see you, I'm going to kill you."

"Oh, for sure. Anyway, you're coming to the meeting tonight, right?"

"Of course. Toni's going to be there, right?"

"Oh, I'd love to tell you, but you just threatened my life, so I'm not gonna do that."

Mike had moved on from his skin to his hair. He needed a haircut, but he didn't have the time for an appointment yet. "Alejandro."

"Michael?" For the past two years, Alejandro had been nothing but smug every time Toni came up in conversation. The rational part of his brain could understand that this was payback. He'd spent years teasing Alejandro just like this, but it was so much more fun when he was giving rather than receiving.

"I'm sorry," Mike ground out.

"What'd you say?" Alejandro asked, barely controlling his laughter.

Mike's fist wrapped around the handle of the comb in his hand. "I said, I'm sorry."

"For what?" Alejandro asked, openly laughing now.

"Baboso," Mike muttered under his breath. "I'm sorry for teasing you before you got with Deja. I realize now that it was insensitive of me."

"It sure the fuck was. I'm glad you learned your lesson."

"If you don't tell me if Toni is coming tonight, that won't be the last thing I have to apologize to you for."

Alejandro laughed for at least a full minute before Mike hung up on him.

CHAPTER FOURTEEN

The Union of American Teachers and Professors was one of the country's biggest and best-known academic unions. Toni had a few friends in the union at other campuses but not anyone at schools in the region. The UATP had been struggling for decades to get a foothold at schools in the Midwest because of twenty-year-old anti-union legislation that had made it harder — if not impossible — for students, faculty, and staff to unionize.

That was almost certainly why they were meeting at a bar off-off-campus. It was also the first Sunday after the end of the semester; what better way to emphasize that this was not a university-sponsored event?

Normally Toni didn't believe in work meetings on the weekend, but since this technically wasn't a work meeting and technically their university needed to unionize thirty years ago, she'd made an exception. But she promised herself this would be the last work exception until after her sabbatical.

The Stax Bookstore and Bar had opened the year before, but Toni had never been. She rarely came to this part of town, and she rarely ate out these days — too tired to even call in an order.

But The Stax was new to her, and she'd dressed up for the occasion.

Certainly not because Mike would be there.

Probably not.

Anyway, she'd been dying to wear the tight red knit skirt that hugged all of her curves and the matching crop top somewhere. She couldn't wear it to work, and all she did was work, and technically, this was not a work event. Ipso facto, she showed up at the union event looking like she was heading out to dinner at an expensive restaurant.

"Hey, girl, hey!" Deja called from across the parking lot.

Toni turned toward the sound of Deja's voice and then easily spotted her across the parking lot.

Deja was wearing a bright yellow short romper and tan platform espadrilles. She was bouncing on the balls of her feet and waving her hands with all her might. Someone was clearly very happy that the semester was over. But Deja was also easy to see because she was flanked by two tall men, Alejandro on one side and Mike on the other.

Toni had known Mike for years, but after their last few encounters, she saw him with brand-new eyes tonight. He was one of the few unmarried straight men on campus, and now that Alejandro was taken, there was a significant contingent of women on campus who'd transferred their interest to him. He also was a bit of a golden boy as far as the administration was concerned. There was only one event she could remember marring his pristine reputation.

Toni had a vivid memory of Mike and some of his undergraduate students picketing outside of the Business College. Business had been slowly colonizing prime campus space for the past five years, and no unit had been unaffected by their expansion. As the university shuffled shrinking departments out of central campus into older buildings on the periphery, Mike and his students had picketed Astronomy's eviction from Schlessinger Hall so the Business faculty could set up a satellite lab. And they'd won. That was probably the first time Toni remembered thinking that maybe Mike wasn't just Alejandro's little friend. But still, he was just...Mike.

Until he wasn't.

As Toni walked slowly across the parking lot toward him — and their friends — she couldn't look away from him. He didn't look away from her. She couldn't see his eyes clearly from this distance, but she could feel Mike's gaze on her body, all over her exposed skin, and she couldn't help but react. By the time they met one another in the center of the parking lot, Toni's nipples were hard, her skin was warm, and her thighs were clenching with a growing desire.

"Come on, curves," Deja said, pulling Toni from the hypnotizing beam of Mike's gaze.

Toni rolled her eyes and smiled at her friend. "Can you *not* objectify me, Ms. Black Feminist Futures Club faculty advisor?"

"First of all, this is an interim position until you're off sabbatical. And second of all, this is how Black women bond."

Toni rolled her eyes again. "Don't give the girls that lecture. I just got them to stop calling each other bitch."

"But—"

Toni shook her head sharply. "You weren't there during the MLK Day brawl that almost was. They need to learn boundaries and mutual respect before they can jump to pejorative-laced banter."

"Fine, Dr. Ward," Deja muttered, also rolling her eyes. "Anyway, no one else is gonna tell them that you were swangin' them hips in this little get-up, but I approve."

"Where's Marie?" Toni sighed.

Alejandro wrapped his arm around Deja's shoulders and pulled her into his side. "She went inside to grab us a table."

Toni nodded.

"Still, we should probably get in there before it gets crowded and we lose a chair. Someone might have to sit on someone else's lap."

"Oh, I'm okay with that," Deja said. "Mike, Alejandro's not nearly as heavy as he looks."

They all laughed at that, even Toni. Deja's phone chirped, and she glanced at the screen. "Marie says to hurry up. Let's go!" She walked swiftly toward the entrance, dragging Alejandro behind her by their joined hands. That left Toni and Mike standing in front of one another, looking awkwardly at the edges of each other's bodies.

"Hi," she said, looking somewhere around his left elbow.

"Hi." His voice was gentle and deep, and it did something to Toni. Many things, actually. The hair on her arms and the back of her neck stood to terrifying attention at that single word. Her core clenched right along with the muscles of her sex. Her mouth went dry.

One word and the blithe, nonchalant acquaintance of all the years before seemed to go up in smoke. Toni would never see Mike the same way again.

"Come on," Deja called before she and Alejandro walked into The Stax's front door.

"Yeah, come on," Alejandro called absentmindedly, not even bothering to look in their direction; his eyes were steadfastly on Deja. Well, her ass.

Toni sighed. "This is why some schools have non-fraternization policies."

Mike laughed. "They'd probably be near unenforceable, though."

"But their hearts would be in the right place," Toni said, smiling at her own joke.

It was a brief smile, though one that froze on her face when Mike's arm snaked around her waist, and he started to lead her forward. He didn't pull her in per se, but now there was so little space between their bodies. His hold was intimate in a way the kiss hadn't been. Not more, not less, just different. And as soon as his forearm touched the bare exposed skin between the hem of her crop top and the waist of her skirt, all she could think about was that kiss.

"Deja's right," he whispered low enough that only she could hear. "This outfit looks amazing on you."

It was a combination of what he said, how he said it, and the fact that his lips brushed the shell of her ear as he did. Toni's legs felt weak and wobbly, and soon enough, she thought her inner thighs would be wet if they kept it up.

Nope, she'd never be able to think of Mike the same way again.

MIKE WAS PLEASANTLY surprised to find the bar so packed. The last time the university tried to unionize, the only people who'd shown up to the first meeting were the janitorial staff, a few people in support staff positions, and a sprinkling of faculty. In the aftermath, the entire janitorial department had been fired because the university decided — completely out of the blue — to subcontract out. That last attempt was such a resounding failure that no one had tried to unionize any part of the school in nearly thirty years. Mike didn't know how many people in this room knew that history, but if this was more than a one-off meeting, he thought they'd find out soon enough. He wasn't the best at estimating percentages, but he guessed at least fifteen percent of the people here would suddenly disappear once they learned exactly what the university would do to impede their efforts.

But that was a problem for another day. Right now, the only thing that mattered was how fucking good Toni looked in that outfit. Mike was having a hard time keeping his eyes — and his hands — off her.

When they found Marie at a round table in the middle of the room, Mike pulled Toni's chair out and then offered her his hand to help her sit. His hand hung in the air between them. He felt everyone watching him, but Toni's reaction was the only one that mattered. She bit back a smile and then took his hand as she lowered into her seat.

"Simp," Alejandro mouthed over the women's heads.

"Fuck you," Mike mouthed in return. "Do you want something to drink?" he asked Toni.

"I do," Alejandro said.

Deja elbowed him in the side but then immediately started petting his stomach. "I didn't mean to hit that hard."

"It's okay, baby."

"Dear god," Marie muttered. "Anyway, I handled that." She raised her hand in the air.

A couple of minutes later, a woman in a button-down shirt and a bow tie sidled up to their table. "Hey, what can I get you?"

"Wait, there's table service?" Mike asked.

"For us," Marie said. "Teri's my friend. We play in a lesbian softball league together."

"You're in a softball league?" Toni asked.

"And you haven't told us about it?" Deja added.

"You two seem to be skipping over the lesbian part."

Toni rolled her eyes. "We could come cheer you on, at least."

"I'll think about that. Can I get a margarita?" Marie asked Teri.

"Sure thing." The waitress turned to the rest of the table, and they all ordered their drinks. Once Teri was gone, Alejandro leaned forward, beckoning them to do the same. Only Mike sighed petulantly, but he didn't care.

"Who do you think is a plant by the administration?"

Only Deja gasped, which Alejandro clearly thought was adorable because he beamed at her and covered her hand on the table.

The rest of the group turned to look around the room, trying to solve the mystery.

"I think it has to be Fitz-Simmons from Geography," Marie said, nodding across the room to a woman sitting at the bar alone, sipping delicately at a martini.

Toni shook her head. "It's gotta be Consuelos. He's chair of his department, but word on the grapevine is he won't win if he decides to run again next year. Also, I know for a fact that he has associate dean aspirations."

"Everybody knows that. Even me," Deja said.

"Who do you think?" Toni asked Mike.

Toni turned in her seat to face him, and their knees knocked together. Her eyelashes fluttered, and her gaze started to shift away, so he pressed his knee purposely against hers this time until she made eye contact.

For a second, there was only Toni at the table — in this room — as far as Mike was concerned. "Johnson-Powell," he said, lifting his hand to point but not looking away.

"Don't be so obvious," Toni hissed, grabbing his hand.

She must have done it without thinking because Mike could count the number of times he and Toni had touched, and they'd all been accidental on her part, not so much on his.

He could see on her face when she realized what she'd

done. He felt when she started to pull away. He turned his hand and let his fingers lightly circle her wrist. Their arms settled on the tops of their thighs under the table.

He waited for Toni to take her hand from his, but she smiled and turned back to their table as if everything was normal. As if his hand wasn't moving slowly up her forearm and then back so their palms could rest together.

Alejandro was watching them with a smirk on his face.

Mike ignored him. "It has to be Derek Johnson-Powell because one—" he lifted his index finger on his free hand as everyone settled their attention on him, "his husband's in the Provost's war council."

"Still can't believe they call it that," Alejandro muttered.

"And two, Derek doesn't just want to be an A-Dean; he's gunning for Dean of Students."

"Wait, for real?" Deja asked.

"Yup," Mike said.

"Where'd you hear that?" Alejandro asked.

"From Derek. We work out together a couple times a month, and he likes to talk. Never shuts up when he's lifting weights, actually. It's annoying as hell, but *someone* is otherwise occupied." He aimed that last barb at Alejandro.

Alejandro rolled his eyes.

"Oh," Marie exclaimed. They followed her gaze across the room to a table where Derek was sitting with a bunch of other faculty from the Physics Department.

"Who were you thinking, babe?" Deja asked while Mike used his index finger to trace circles around Toni's palm.

"Doesn't matter. It's gotta be Derek," Alejandro admitted begrudgingly.

They all nodded silently and then let their attention wander around the room, noting who was there, who wasn't, who was there with someone who was not their legal partner.

And then Teri dropped off their drinks just as the meeting started.

"Good evening!" Justin Michel from the writing program called as he bounded onto the small stage. "What a turnout! We're so excited to see you here!"

"No one should be this excited about anything," Marie muttered, making everyone at their table laugh.

Justin turned in their direction and gave them a wry smile. They all shifted in their seats and pretended to be chastened.

"I won't take up too much time because this is such an important meeting. This is a historic meeting, even. But before I introduce our speaker, I do want to remind you all to think of one another and the people not in this room. Remember, that's what the union is for; not one of us, all of us." That got a round of applause.

Not from Mike or Toni, though. Their fingers had slowly begun to lace together, and rather than pull away, Toni's bony fingers gripped his with a strength that surprised him. He had to duck his head to hide his smile, but when his gaze darted to Toni, she was smiling without a care in the world. He squeezed her hand and turned back to the stage.

"Our guest tonight is a representative of the UATP. She was associate faculty of Political Science at Southern Midwestern Community College, where she, unfortunately, or fortunately, depending on your vantage point, had to leave because of her commitment to university unions. She has real-world and academic experience, she's committed to our fight, and every time I've seen her, she's been a sartorial dream. That clearly doesn't matter to some of you," he said, squinting disapprovingly around the room. He skipped over Mike's table completely, and they all sat up smugly in their seats. "But a good— no, great outfit matters to me. Please welcome Sharon August." Justin started clapping before he had even finished speaking, glaring at the crowd, silently threatening them to follow his lead.

Again, he and Toni refused to even loosen their hold on one another.

The woman who hopped onto the stage wasn't what Mike was expecting. First of all, she looked to be about his age. Mike had just assumed she would be older. Secondly, Justin was right; she was dressed very well in a tight white t-shirt, brown tweed pants rolled up to expose bare ankles, and a pair of suspenders. She capped the outfit off with a pair of camel-colored brogue shoes that Alejandro leaned around Deja to get a closer look at.

"I don't mean to echo Justin's exuberant introduction, but there's just no way around it," Sharon said. "I am so excited to see you all here, no matter how you're dressed."

The room erupted into a gentle rolling laughter before settling back down. Mike *was* listening to Sharon's spiel, but the bulk of his attention was on Toni.

He shifted his head to the right to take her in, shocked to find that Toni had shifted her head to the left to do the same with him.

This was a very important meeting, but Mike would be voting for the union no matter what. So for the rest of the presentation, he simply enjoyed holding Toni's hand.

CHAPTER FIFTEEN

"That was good," Deja whispered excitedly across the table. "I think we have a chance."

Mike and Alejandro glanced at one another. Toni didn't like the look of that, but she'd check in on them later. Right now, she squinted across the table at Marie.

Toni had been on the hiring committee that brought Marie to their university as an instructor. It was ill-advised, but sometimes, she couldn't help but think of Marie as her responsibility, more so even than Deja. Maybe it was because Toni had had to file an official complaint against someone else on the committee for blatant bias against her. Maybe because they'd become friends and not just colleagues. Or maybe it was just because Marie had always been a tough nut to crack. She'd left a prestigious post-doctoral fellowship to be an adjunct for three years and then an instructor for two, all before her file had ended up on Toni's computer. Something had been haunting her at each of her universities, and in all their years of friendship, Toni still didn't know what it was. Marie had never offered up much about her past positions other than how much she hated them, which Toni thought was a given.

"What'd you think?" Toni asked Marie gently.

Marie took the last sip of her drink and slammed her glass on the table much harder than necessary and then flinched, surprising herself at the sound. "Sorry, but what about instructors? And adjuncts?" she asked, looking over Toni's shoulder.

"Oh, shit," Mike muttered under his breath.

She'd let go of his hand under the table, but it had remained close, resting on his knee, touching her when they moved. But at Marie's question, they both put their hands on the table.

For some reason, Marie's response made her feel chastened because she hadn't been paying as close attention as she should have been.

"I didn't think about that," Alejandro said.

Deja sunk down in her chair. "Sorry, Marie."

Marie's eyes moved to Deja's face, and she looked at her quizzically. "Why are you apologizing to me? I'm TT now, but so much of our faculty aren't. In the past five years, we've had more non-tenure track faculty hired than anyone else. Let's say we win, and we get a union. If we don't include adjuncts, and instructors only get to be in the union when they pass their third-year review, that's, what, like..."

"Twenty-eight percent of your faculty who wouldn't be included in the union. And don't forget graduate instructors, who allegedly inhabit some gray area between student and staff." They all turned to find Sharon standing next to Marie, looking down at them with a friendly smile on her face. "It's definitely a conundrum, and there's no good way to fix it."

"Grad students can't be in the union?" Toni asked.

Sharon turned her smile on her. "No. From our experience, including graduate students makes the way that much harder. We recommend that they unionize on their own."

"And adjuncts?" Marie asked.

Sharon turned her attention back to Marie. Her smile shifted to understanding. "In our experience, including adjuncts tends to increase the likelihood that the university will reject us out of hand. We won't even make it to the negotiating table."

"And that's the gray area," Marie said.

"To us, to me," Sharon said, pointing at her chest, "adjuncts are our colleagues. But as I'm sure you all have experienced, there are still some older faculty in some units who believe differently."

Mike nodded, and Toni glanced at him.

"The sciences are notorious for this," he said. "At least once a year, we waste an entire all-program meeting reminding people that the only distinction between adjuncts, instructors, and tenure-track faculty is course load. There used to be someone who treated our adjuncts like graduate TAs. I was so damn happy when he retired."

"Goldfarb," Toni said, nodding.

Mike smiled at her. "Yes, he was terrible. But brilliant."

Toni got lost in his smile for a foolish second, listening as the conversation moved along.

"So, it's not just the administration, then?" Marie asked.

Toni had to tear her eyes away at the sound of her voice. Unlike Deja, Marie wore her emotions all over her sleeve and her face. It seemed impossible for the woman to hide her anger, frustration, or hurt, and Toni heard the sound of impending tears clogging up her voice.

For her part, Sharon took Marie's question in stride. She slipped her hands into her pockets and smiled sadly down at her. "Hey, I wish I could tell you that the administration is going to be your only hurdle, but I don't like to lie. I'm here to help you all organize and hopefully get the union protections you deserve. The only way I can do my job effectively is to be straight up with you. So, no, the administration isn't your only adversary. They aren't even your final boss."

"Who is?" Deja asked.

Sharon shrugged, but her face was tight with her own frustrations. "Apparently, the state is considering legislation that would prohibit union organizing in a host of places, public universities included. They've tried before. They succeeded and failed to varying degrees, and now they're back at it again. The current conservative legislature hates unions, except the ones their parents were in."

"You mean the ones Reagan killed?" Alejandro asked.

"Yep," Sharon said with a smile. "Those. It's just like they hate welfare, except the welfare that helped their grandparents survive the Great Depression." She rolled her eyes in disgust. "Unfortunately, we don't have the luxury to pretend like we live in a world where union busting isn't our reality. All we can do is get ready and stay ready."

"By ejecting the most vulnerable of our colleagues." Marie spat that sentence out with a vehemence that made the entire table stiffen with discomfort.

Sharon seemed unfazed. "What's your name?"

Marie stood from her chair. She was at least five inches shorter than Sharon, but she stood with a kind of slow grace that Toni had noticed in her classroom demonstrations. When she was on top of her shit, Marie had the kind of presence that could fill a room no matter how big and no matter how many students. She might have been average height and bordering on a little too skinny for Toni's liking, but when she wanted to be, Marie was a force. Unfortunately, she didn't seem to understand that about herself, and Toni had been plagued by that since the day they met.

"Marie Lau," she said, putting her hands into her own

pants pockets. "Assistant professor of Ethnic Studies. I was an instructor here for two years before that and an adjunct before that."

If Marie thought she could cow Sharon, she was wrong.

Instead, the other woman lit up.

She reached into her back pocket and pulled out a small silver card case. "We're going to need dedicated people in this fight. People who know more about the ecosystem of a university than just the tenure track. People who can make connections." She peeled a card from the holder and offered it to Marie with a smile on her face. "If you want to get involved, give me a call."

Marie grabbed the card carefully, holding it between two fingers and squinting at it as if she was worried it was radioactive.

"Hey, Sharon." Justin cut into the moment and pulled Sharon's attention away. "Can you come talk to some people?"

"That's what I'm here for." She smiled down at the table and then nodded when she made eye contact with Marie. She turned to walk away but then stopped. "I won't mind you telling me what I'm doing wrong as long as you're willing to help me do it right." And with that, she melted into the crowd.

They watched her leave in silence, but it was Deja who broke the quiet. "She's out of my league, but I would leave Alejandro for her."

"Now, if I said that—" Alejandro started.

"Let it go," Mike muttered, reaching for his drink, his hand stopping when he realized his glass was empty. "Another round?"

"No," Marie said, her attention across the room on Sharon. "I'm tired. And I need to get on the road early tomorrow." Finally, she turned to look at them. "I'll see you guys when I'm back, alright?"

"You need a ride to the airport?" Deja offered.

"Can you volunteer my services like this?" Mike asked.

"Yes," Deja said.

"I'm fine. I'm catching a ride with Holloway. Our flights leave at five."

"In the morning?!" Deja cried.

"Have a good trip," Mike muttered.

"You sure you're okay?" Toni asked carefully.

Marie sighed and then shook her head. "She's probably right, but..." Her voice trailed off, and her gaze softened before hardening again. "She's probably right, but that doesn't mean I have to like it."

"You don't. And we'll figure it out," Toni said because that's what she always said. Toni was the problem solver, even if the problem was big as hell.

"Yeah," Marie sighed and then forced a smile onto her face. "Enjoy Brazil," she said to Deja and Alejandro before turning to Toni. "Enjoy tearing up carpet. And...what are you doing this summer?" she asked Mike.

Mike shrugged and sat back in his chair. He spread his legs, and his right knee bumped Toni's. "Unlike the rest of you, I have no plans. I'm just going to hang around here and relax."

"Here?" Toni asked, her voice rising in shock.

"Here," he replied with a cocky grin she'd never seen before.

***

"OKAY, YOU TWO BE GOOD!" Deja yelled through the passenger window of Alejandro's car as he eased out of the parking lot.

"Shut up!" Toni yelled after her with a friendly sneer.

Deja's laughter mixed with the sound of Alejandro's car

horn, his way of saying goodbye just before he turned the corner and drove off into the night.

Toni cursed her friend under her breath right up until she felt the warmth of Mike's body against her left side and his breath against her ear.

Her own breath hitched.

"You okay to get home?" he asked, reminding her of the parking lot in front of the Sunrise Café. The way he pressed against her then. She didn't know if he was doing it on purpose or not, but when he dropped his voice that way, Toni couldn't stop her body from responding.

She tried to whirl around to face him, maybe even to put some distance between them, but he stopped her with a strong hand at her waist. She swallowed a groan at the casual control he used to turn her around slowly as if he was making sure that no part of her could help but touch him.

When they finally came face-to-face, Mike's face had turned red, and his pupils were dilated. When he pulled her closer, Toni could feel his response to her.

"Are you okay to get home?" he asked again.

"Stop doing that with your voice."

"Doing what?" He lifted an eyebrow, but the smile on his face was playful. Toni might not have known what he was doing, but there was no way Mike was accidentally making her wet with his voice. This was a calculated attack.

"You know what," she said in a voice that felt as wobbly as her knees. She licked her lips, and Mike's gaze lingered on her mouth.

He shook his head. "I don't. If I did, I would stop, I promise."

That wasn't the response she'd expected, and somehow it made her wetter. There were so many things Toni was good at, but apparently, thinking when she was horny was not one of them.

Mike squeezed her waist and then loosened his grip on her by degrees. He stepped back and shoved his hands into his pockets. "Do you remember the outfit you wore to your teaching demonstration?"

"I... No."

"You had on this dress that..." He took his right hand from his pocket and moved it right and left across his chest with a small smile. "A wrap dress?"

Toni nodded. She remembered that dress. She'd *loved* that dress. It was the perfect shade of emerald green, and it made her brown skin look deeper and richer while lightly skimming her curves, just skirting the boundaries of professional. Toni had bought that dress in grad school and worn it until the hem was falling apart.

"Why do you remember that?" she asked in pure disbelief.

Mike shrugged and looked away as if he couldn't believe he was about to admit this. "I have had hundreds of fantasies about all the ways I could take that dress off you." He turned back to her.

Her breath hitched. "Mike," Toni whispered because that was all she could muster.

He stepped closer. "Antonia."

"That was so many years ago."

He bent forward, watching her as their faces — their mouths — inched closer and closer. "Don't worry, I'm going to fantasize about you in this outfit now. Let me walk you to your car."

TONI ALWAYS WORE a vanilla and musk perfume. It was earthy and lingered, and he might have once spent an hour in a department store smelling perfumes, trying to figure out which one she wore. It was embarrassing; even Alejandro didn't know how bad it had gotten. But he would do it again.

"Toni—"

She shook her head once, a sharp slash of her chin before she lifted her face. Her long eyelashes fluttered as she blinked before looking him in the eye with a pleading Mike could feel in his gut. "Say my...full name."

He had to swallow a groan and ball his hands into fists just to make it through the next few moments. "Antonia," he said slowly, enunciating every letter of her name, not just the syllables. "Let me walk you to your car. Please."

The right side of her mouth quirked up into a smile. "Okay," she whispered.

She somehow managed to press herself against him while also moving past him.

He'd had control of this moment for the briefest period of time, but now the reins were in her hands. Mike turned and let her walk away only so he could finally appreciate her from the back. He would never get sick of this view. There was always some new angle to see and some new fabric to accentuate her curves.

But Toni stopped and turned to look over her shoulder at him. "Are you walking me to my car or not?"

Mike loved some challenges, but none as much as Toni. "Yes, ma'am."

He followed her across the parking lot, but not too closely. At the sound of her car unlocking, Mike frowned. He wished the car had been further away, although now that the sun had set, Mike could see that Toni's car was actually sitting in the shade and shadow of a large oak. Before the event, it had been surrounded by cars, but right now, it stood all by itself.

"Well, thanks, I guess," she said, starting to turn around, but he stopped her by snaking his arm around her waist and pulling her back into him.

"What?" she yelped.

"Antonia," he whispered against her ear. He could smell her and taste her, but he was desperate now to touch her in ways he never had before. "I've wanted to make you come since the moment I first saw you."

"Fuck," she breathed.

He smiled and placed a soft kiss against her temple. "Not yet. But I can make you come without fucking you."

She whimpered.

His right hand flattened over her lower belly and pulled her back against his erection. "Is that a yes? Can I make you come, Toni?" He felt her shiver in his arms, and it was delicious; he would never get enough of that feeling. He pressed her forward with his hips, grinding himself into her ass.

She groaned and pressed her hands against the hood of her car, the only thing stopping their bodies from slamming against it.

"Is that a yes, Antonia?" he asked again.

She nodded her head and then finally said the word "yes," in the softest, filthiest moan Mike had ever heard.

He didn't hesitate. Years of desperate masturbatory fantasies came to life as his hand moved down her front and pulled up the front of her skirt.

She shivered as the cool night air hit her skin, and he warmed her up with the back of his knuckles grazing along her leg.

But when his palm flattened against her bare inner thigh...

"Oh god," Toni groaned.

"Mierda," he groaned against her ear before sucking her earlobe into his mouth. His hand pressed between her legs, warmed by the heat of her pussy. He pulled her thighs apart and then moved his fingers over the gusset of her underwear, enjoying her wetness on his fingers. She hadn't stopped trembling in so long. "Perfecta."

It took more energy than he could imagine to not rush this moment. To feel every dimple on her skin, the fuzz of her softest hair, the smooth bareness of her inner thigh, the damp cotton of her underwear as he pulled it aside, the short, curly hair over her mound, the clinging wetness of her lips, and then finally — after years of dreaming — the smooth, hot, silky depths of her pussy all around his digits as he pushed them inside her opening.

"Mike," she begged.

She begged!

Antonia Ward was begging him for more. Mike couldn't believe it, and he really couldn't believe what was next.

"Deeper," she groaned and then rolled her hips, pressing down on his hand and then back into his groin.

There might have come a point where he would have second-guessed himself, but there was no way now. Not when Toni was being very clear about what she wanted from him. And if there was anything he wanted, it was to fulfill her desires, to give her everything she deserved.

Antonia was begging him to finger-fuck her deeper, and he had never been happier to follow an order.

Antonia asked him to move "Harder," and so he brushed his thumb across her clit. He enjoyed the way her groan broke as it passed her lips and how her body shuddered as he hunched over her.

"More," she gasped, and he gave her another finger, pushing two and then quickly a third inside her.

She started riding his hand, and her ass was bumping against the erection that was so hard, it hurt. After a while, Toni's pussy started leaking down his fingers, and his already hard dick managed to stiffen more.

Words stopped mattering. The danger of being discovered disappeared. For the first time ever, Mike got to experience what it would be like to be lost in his own world with Toni.

And it was beautiful.

CHAPTER SIXTEEN

Toni hated mornings. If left to her own devices, she would lounge in bed for as long as possible with a good book, reading and napping and petting Paw until almost noon. Sometimes she made time for a good, lazy day with a carafe of coffee, a full water bottle, some snacks, and a bag of Paw Robeson's treats, and they would lounge in bed for the better part of the day, maybe even all day. But over the past two years, those days had become more and more rare.

She was more often than not up soon after the sun. It seemed as if every year, she had to wake up earlier and earlier just to have enough time to get through the basics; a gentle workout, a breakfast she didn't have to eat on the go, quality time with her cat, and a leisurely commute. Once upon a time, she could wake up at eight in the morning, but for the past year, she'd been crawling out of bed at five, sometimes earlier. And maybe that would have been okay if she didn't also have to stay up later to grade, for course prep, or to answer the student emails that always seemed to come in close to midnight. Toni had been burning the candle at both ends for far too long and, if nothing else, she hoped — no, needed — to get herself on a sleep schedule that didn't feel like a punishment. If that was all that came out of her sabbatical, it might be worth it.

But this morning, Toni woke up with the sun again. Although, this morning, there was a text message from Mike waiting for her.

Good morning. I hope you have a great day.

She stared at his message for a good long while. Toni had, of course, dated on and off over the years, but it had been a very long time since some man had sent her a text message just to say good morning. She'd forgotten how much she loved this part of a new situation. She'd forgotten how good it felt to see a man's words and remember the feeling of his hands on her body. It was impossible now to think of Mike without her gut tightening in needy remembrance of last night. And it was probably inevitable, once her brain started to work, that Toni's hand would move inside her panties. She wet her fingers with her own arousal and whimpered as they brushed over her clit. Her touch was practiced, knowledgeable, and welcome, but she was shocked to come up short.

Her fingers didn't make her feel quite as good as Mike's.

Maybe it was because she didn't usually prefer using her fingers to masturbate since it took so long. Well, normally, it took so long. This morning, with Mike's good morning message on her cell phone and the memory of his hand in her underwear and his mouth on her skin, in no time at all, her pussy was making wet, squelching sounds as she plunged two fingers inside her aching core. It made no sense, but it felt amazing.

And after she came, she drifted happily back to sleep.

She didn't text him back, though.

She wasn't ready for that just yet.

"THANKS FOR THE RIDE, HERMANO," Alejandro said as Mike pulled along the curb on the departures level.

"No problem. Just remind me of your itinerary a couple days before you come back."

"Will do." Alejandro pushed the passenger car door open and walked to the trunk.

Deja, however, launched herself between the two front seats.

Mike jumped back and frowned at her. "What the—"

"What's going on with you and Toni?"

"Are you serious?"

"Yes," she hissed. "And hurry up. Alejandro told me to leave you two alone, but I'm obviously not doing that. Spill."

Mike's eyes darted through the back windshield. On the one hand, he appreciated Alejandro trying to intervene on his and Toni's behalf. But on the other hand, he was as curious as Deja about this issue. "What'd she say?"

"Nothing!" Deja said. "But that's Toni. She wants to talk about everyone's problems but her own."

"I'm not...a problem. Am I?"

Deja shook her head impatiently. "No, I didn't mean it like that. I just mean that Toni is tight-lipped as hell."

"And I'm not?"

She frowned at him. "A closed mouth don't get fed, friend. If you want Toni, you're going to have to go after her."

"I—"

She shook her head quickly. "We don't have time for that cute, humble, timid shit." She leaned forward. "If you want Toni, you're going to have to *go after her*. Even if she knows what she wants, she'll do almost anything to stop from having to ask for it. For herself, I mean." She placed an arm on his shoulder. "But I saw the way she was looking at you last night."

"H-how was she looking at me?"

Just then, Alejandro pulled the passenger door open. "Deja, we agreed to leave them alone," he said, sounding equal parts exasperated and amused.

Deja smiled in his direction. "No, you said I should leave them alone, and I agreed to disagree. Besides, he's almost as clueless as we are, so I'm giving him some advice."

"And how's that going?"

"It was getting better until you interrupted," Mike said testily, shrugging the shoulder Deja was holding. "How does she look at me?" he asked again.

"Usually, she looks at you like she doesn't hate you, which for Toni is high praise," Deja said excitedly.

Mike sighed.

"But last night..." Alejandro added.

Deja nodded quickly at Alejandro before turning back to Mike. "Last night, she couldn't *stop* looking at you. And also like she couldn't wait to get you naked."

Mike's mouth fell open.

"Unless she already got you naked?" Alejandro asked.

Deja raised her eyes in her boyfriend's direction.

"If we're already all in his business..." Alejandro replied with a shrug.

"Get out of my car before you miss your flight."

"Seriously?" Deja whined.

"Definitely. Have a good summer."

Alejandro glared at him, not because he hadn't divulged the ins and outs of his and Toni's not-really-a-relationship but because he'd made Deja sad. He was so predictable. Mike stared back, unbothered.

"Come on, amor, I'll get you a glass of champagne as soon as we get on the plane."

"Okay!" Deja said, brightening immediately.

Alejandro helped her from the car.

"A closed mouth don't get fed, Mike," Deja repeated. "Remember that, pendejo."

Alejandro burst out laughing.

"You're teaching her how to curse in Spanish?" Mike yelled.

"I sure am," Alejandro laughed before slamming the car door.

Mike glared at his friends as they kissed on the curb, apparently not worried about missing their flight. He rolled his eyes but still waited for them to grab their suitcases and wheel them into the airport.

Once they'd disappeared, Mike snatched his cell phone from the center console and sent a text.

Just dropped A & D off at the airport. Have you had lunch yet?

She hadn't answered his text from this morning, but he hadn't really expected that she would. He and Toni didn't have a texting relationship, even though they'd been in a group chat with their friends for over a year. Other people might have taken this evolution in stride, but Mike knew Toni and knew that change was hard for her, even a good change. He also knew that Deja was right. Toni knew a scary amount of information about other people's lives, but when anyone tried to give her the same kind of attention, she balked.

He'd always thought the way to approach her was to wait patiently in the wings, but now he knew that had been the wrong tactic. Last night, all he'd had to do was ask for her to let him in, and she had, coming all over his hand. He couldn't even imagine what she might do if he asked for more.

He waited a few seconds after he sent the message before throwing his phone into the passenger seat with a sigh and pulling out into the flow of airport traffic. He was on the freeway when her text message popped up on the navigation screen.

Not yet, but I'm about to make something if you want to come over.

He hadn't expected that. In all honesty, he hadn't expected a reply.

"Yes. I'm on my way," he yelled, loud enough for his car to pick up the voice and send the text. "Holy shit," he mumbled under his breath in pure disbelief.

EVERY YEAR, Toni ended up at some faculty development program where someone droned on and on about work-life balance. She tended to consider those events to be a gigantic waste of time, but actually, sometimes she used the hour or so to catch up on her emails because the reality was that being a professor was in some ways entirely antithetical to even the idea of balance.

She didn't know anyone who didn't bring work home. She didn't know anyone who worked forty hours a week, not even on average. There was no balance for Toni; work ate up most of her life. The best she could do for herself was to carve out pockets of freedom like the rare quiet morning in bed or rushed battery-operated orgasms, or when she had just a little more time and a lot more energy, the afternoons she spent in her kitchen making some of her grandmother's old recipes.

Baking and cooking made Toni feel at peace, and she usually did them when she was all alone. She assuaged the need to feed people by giving away her muffins and cakes to friends, but the process of cooking was one of solitude; at least, that had been true since her grandparents died.

When she'd woken up from her morning nap, the plan had been to deep-clean her kitchen and then eat lunch while she went through some wallpaper samples. She had not expected to invite Mike over. Her thumbs had typed out that invitation and sent it before her brain could process what was happening. And once he'd accepted, she'd freaked out.

Suddenly, it wasn't just the kitchen that needed to be cleaned; it was the entire first floor of the house. And then she opened her refrigerator to find it shockingly bare. She'd dashed quickly to the grocery store and seriously considered texting him to cancel the invitation.

She thought about it but never did it.

She threw some chicken thighs and pre-chopped vegetables in a quick marinade and ran upstairs to shower. By the time she heard Mike's car pulling into her driveway, she had just thrown on a short summer dress, and her stomach felt like it was full of the biggest, most aggressive butterflies ever.

"No going back now," she said to herself as she walked down the stairs to the front door.

He rang the doorbell, and Paw Robeson suddenly jumped from the couch and ran toward the door.

"What the hell?" Toni grumbled, following him to the foyer. The cat stopped at the top of the stair, forcing her to step over him to open the door.

Mike looked as he always did. Maybe dressed more casually than normal — in a plain white t-shirt, black khaki shorts, and the most pristine Jordans Toni had ever seen — but nothing else stood out. Still, she looked him over from head to toe to make sure.

What was not the same was the way she felt about him. A soft rumble of pleasure moved through the back of her brain like the best white noise ever, hitting all her erogenous zones. The wind picked up, and the scent of his cologne brought an actual smile to her face.

"Hi," he said gently, his own smile spreading across his lips.

"Hi." Her face flushed, and she backed away from the door. "Um, come in."

Apparently, Paw took that as a sign to step into the foyer. "No!" she screamed, her heart racing. She instinctively moved to shut the door, but Mike stepped inside. And instead of running through the open door, Paw sauntered up to Mike's legs, meowing loudly and then sitting back on his haunches.

Mike eased the door closed behind him and squatted down. He placed the paper bag in his hand — which Toni had not noticed until this moment — on the floor next to him. She watched as he extended a hand slowly to Paw's head and started scratching him behind his ears.

Her mouth gaped as her absolute whore of a cat melted under Mike's touch, pushing up onto his claws and walking in a circle to evenly distribute the pleasure. After a while, he wound his way around the man's legs, sniffing at his shoes, the bag, and then his hand before leaning in for more affection.

"You have got to be kidding me," Toni hissed. "I had you for a full week before you let me touch you!"

Mike laughed. "Cats love me."

"What the hell does that mean?"

He smiled up at her. "My mom's a vet. We always had dogs and cats and bunnies, you name it, in the house. She even used to take care of the strays in our neighborhood. I guess cats can tell I'm a fan."

"Oh," Toni said, but she was thinking that this was a very odd thing to be turning her on. "Um, what's in the bag?"

"Oh," he said, scratching Paw one more time and then standing, grabbing the bag in both hands. "I brought some... stuff. I don't like showing up empty-handed. And I don't know about you, but whenever the semester ends, I realize that there's barely anything in the house to eat, so I picked up some things. You know...just in case."

His gaze was darting between her face and whatever was inside the bag. His face was turning red, and he was rambling nervously.

Toni found all of this ridiculously endearing. "Yeah, I realized there wasn't much in there, so I had to run to the grocery store before you got here," she said.

"Oh." His face fell. "I could have done that for you."

She shook her head. "What kind of sense would that make? Then you'd have gotten here, and we wouldn't have eaten for another hour."

"I'm fine with that," he said eagerly.

She bit back a smile and then froze. "Shit, are you allergic to anything? I didn't even think to ask." She glanced toward the kitchen, trying to think if there was anything in the marinade that might cause a problem.

"Penicillin," he said quickly. "I'm allergic to penicillin, that's it. So whatever you made is fine. I'm sure it'll be great. Deja and Marie always said you were a great cook."

"They did?"

He nodded. "And you bake."

She squinted up at him. "You've tasted my baking, though, right?"

He pursed his lips and shook his head.

"Seriously? I bake for everyone. It's my stress relief. I usually just give all my muffins and cookies away." Her mouth fell open when she realized what she'd said.

Mike huffed out a small laugh. "I would have remembered if you gave me your cookies. Believe me."

Their eyes locked for the first time since he arrived, and those aggressive ass butterflies had a field day with the way he was looking at her.

"Um," she said, breaking eye contact and looking away. She wiped the back of her hand over her damp forehead. "My kitchen gets hot as hell in the spring and summer, so I barbecue as much as I can. Is that okay?"

"Absolutely," he said. "Is the kitchen on your renovation plan?"

"Yeah, but not until next spring. I've got a long list of things to do before then."

"Oh, okay," Mike said. "Is that what you said in your sabbatical application?"

She grinned. "Nah, I said what we all say." She put on the voice she used when speaking to the Provost; crisp and intellectually distant. "I said I have a robust research plan for a groundbreaking new study that will revolutionize my field. Or something like that. It wasn't a complete lie."

"No?"

"First thing on my list this summer is a full renovation of the spare bedroom upstairs. I want to use it as an office. I have a team coming to redo the floors soon, actually. Once I have an office, that will be groundbreaking and revolutionary for me."

He smiled and stepped forward. "So...technically not a lie," he said. "I love a woman who's good with her words."

Toni exhaled a shuddering breath.

CHAPTER SEVENTEEN

"Ignore my backyard," Toni said as soon as Mike stepped through the back door.

He smiled and was just about to tell her that her yard wasn't nearly as bad as she was making it out to be, but then his eyes took in what he was seeing. They stepped from the house onto a brick patio that had seen better days — maybe in the last century or the one before that. He took one step, and a loose brick wobbled under his weight. He looked around the yard, and his gaze caught on a tangle of vines hanging from the far fence. Everywhere he looked, the view was somehow worse than before. The fence was almost entirely covered by an overgrowth of ivy, some of which was very likely poisonous. What wasn't covered with plant life featured chipped white paint that made him think of a derelict house. The grass in the spacious yard was overgrown but also patchy. Mike couldn't believe his eyes.

"Um..."

"I said ignore it," Toni sighed.

"How?" he replied without thinking. "How?" He aimed that second question not at Toni but at her yard.

"It was like this when I bought the place," she said, wrenching the lid of her impeccable grill up with more force than was probably necessary. She grabbed a pair of tongs from a table next to the barbecue and began to lay pieces of chicken on the grill.

He sighed in relief that the food smelled like it would be great, even if the view was not. As she spoke, he moved carefully across the brick patio toward her.

"The last owners were an older couple. They completely redid the front but never got around to the back, and they couldn't take care of the place by the end anyway, so it all just... went to hell. I knew when I bought it that I would have a lot of work to do, but I underestimated how much. I just don't..." She sighed. "I barely have the time to keep the inside together. The backyard is too much."

Over the years, Mike had spent a lot of time listening to Toni closely in meetings and at other university events. He expended so much time noting the exact words she used — and didn't — paying attention to the tone of her voice, trying to discern what all of the small details meant. And that was why her sigh sounded poignant as hell.

"I get it," he said, placing his hand on the small of her back.

"Do you?" she asked, poking at the chicken. But her voice was a wry laugh, maybe even self-deprecating.

Mike hated to hear her sound this way. "I do, actually."

He'd spent so many years pretending to Toni that he was just another colleague; someone who didn't hoard information about her like precious jewels. But that was not what this moment called for. "How many days a week do you spend fixing other people's problems?"

The heat of the grill and the muggy air was oppressive, but

it was hard for Mike to feel anything but light and free when he was close enough to touch Toni and could. Both hands moved up and down her sides.

"Answer the question, Antonia."

There was a sliver of space between their bodies, but not enough to hide her shiver.

"I don't... I don't know."

"I do," he said again, whispering those words against her ears. "You teach two days a week and then spend the other three putting out fires. Fires you never even start. So, of course, you're spending your sabbatical getting your home in order. You deserve that. You deserve so much more than that."

It was only because Mike was so close and so used to watching her closely that he saw the way her body reacted to his words. Her back muscles went stiff, her shoulders lifted toward her ears, and the rest of her body froze as he spoke.

He inhaled deeply, and he didn't smell roasting chicken or grass. Somehow, all he could smell was the heady vanilla scent of her perfume in the moment and the phantom scent of her pussy as she shuddered around his fingers. His salivary glands started to weep as he remembered the greedy way he'd shoved his fingers into his mouth that night, desperate just to taste her.

"I don't..." she breathed.

"You do. Our sabbaticals should be our own, not one more way the university can keep us productive."

Toni nodded and turned her head. Her inky eyelashes fluttered before she lifted her gaze to look him in the eye. She looked vulnerable in a way he'd never seen before. He couldn't help but pull her against his chest and let her lean on him.

"You deserve to rest, Toni."

"You keep saying that."

"Has it sunk in yet?"

She smiled softly. "Maybe a little bit."

He dipped his head to brush his mouth against the top of her cheek. "I can say it again. I have time."

"Do you?" She shifted her head, bringing her mouth closer to his, tempting him.

He smiled. "Like I said, I believe in taking a summer break. I have nothing but time. And I don't mind using some of it to help you figure out what the word 'rest' means."

"I *know* what the word 'rest' means," she said, turning back to the grill.

He moved his mouth to her ear. "Do you?"

She licked her lips at his words before turning to the grill. "Lunch is almost done," she said in a shaky voice.

"Perfect timing."

THEY SAT down to eat lunch at the reclaimed picnic table Toni bought at a nearby estate sale. It was awkward for her, but Mike seemed perfectly at ease. Every time she tried to talk, Mike focused his entire attention on her and made her tongue feel heavy and thick. After a while, she just gave up and let him lead the conversation while she tried to figure out how she could have spent so much time around him over the years and never felt *this* before.

It wasn't until he stood from the table that she started to get it. The bottom of his shirt didn't fall immediately, and Toni saw a peek of his stomach covered in dark hair before he turned toward the grill for seconds. She fanned herself while she stared at his ass, and he told her something incredibly technical about his research that she didn't understand anyway.

"Uh-huh," she said, just to have something to say.

She might not have been paying attention to his words, but she noticed everything else. His dark beard, which reminded her of the way it had felt against her skin. The single curl of black hair that flopped over his forehead. The way his shoulders and chest filled out the t-shirt. The curve of his lips. The heat of his gaze on her.

He set his plate back on the table and swung his leg over the seat, spreading his legs obscenely as he sat.

Toni pressed her thighs together and shoved a piece of grilled zucchini into her mouth to stop from saying or doing something embarrassing.

"So, if you think about the way we teach the sciences, physics is always different because..." Mike continued, cutting into a piece of chicken. Unfortunately, he started using language Toni didn't understand or care to have him translate.

"Interesting," she mumbled.

"It is, right?" he said excitedly before launching into another monologue.

And that's when she got it. She'd seen Mike like this before — when he and Alejandro used to laugh together at the Faculty Senate meetings, whenever she happened to pass him teaching in the Oval, his students trailing behind him eagerly, notebooks and calculators clutched in their hands. But he'd never been like that with her. In Toni's presence, Mike was...muted was the word that came to mind. She realized now that it had been purposeful; Mike had been shrinking into the periphery of her presence, waiting patiently for her to finally see him.

It was kind of romantic but mostly annoying. She cut him off mid-sentence. "So what exactly are your intentions this summer? With me," she clarified.

Mike placed his cutlery on his plate, grabbed his napkin and wiped his face and hands, and then sat back easily in his chair, a small smile playing on his lips. "How well did you sleep after the union meeting?"

Toni's mouth went dry. "I—"

"After I made you come that hard?"

"Yep, I got it. I remember."

"Good. So do I."

"And my question is—"

"If I want to do more of that?"

Toni nodded and swallowed the lump in her throat. That question hung between them, but she could see the changes in him now. He'd been opening himself up to her by degrees for the past couple of weeks, and as he did, he seemed to loosen up as well. His clothing and posture relaxed, his smiles came easier, and the touches...

She sat back in her own chair and fanned her face.

"I think you can answer that question for yourself, Antonia."

She pressed her thighs together again. "Yes," she breathed.

"Absolutely," he corrected. "But the question is what you want from me."

"It's hot out here," she mumbled.

"Sure," he said with a snarky smile on his face. "What do you want from me, Antonia?"

"What do you want to give me?"

That word made him pause.

Mike's mouth bunched to the side, and he nodded to himself before leaning forward over the table. He pushed their plates to the side and extended his right hand to her, palm up. He waited patiently until she placed her hand in his. "I want to make you happy."

"And what exactly do you mean by that?"

He seemed to think about that for a second before not answering her question. "Let's just spend a little time together," he offered.

"Have you been waiting all these years for that?" she asked

and then shook her head. "God, the Black Feminist Futures Club is going to fire me as their advisor."

Mike chuckled and squeezed her hand. "I won't tell on you. And just so we're clear, you're worth the wait."

"Was I?"

"You *are*," he said, squeezing her hand again. "I'd still be waiting if I hadn't gotten impatient."

"Is that what happened?"

He nodded.

"Why now? Was it Steve Titjens?"

He laughed and sat back in his chair. Toni watched as he smoothed the hand that had held hers over his lips. "You're beautiful," he said with a shrug.

"Had that changed?"

"No," he said. "You've always been gorgeous. You're even more beautiful every time I see you."

"Oh, that's smooth." Toni laughed, and Mike joined her. "Are you always this smooth?"

"Absolutely not. We don't have to plan anything, Toni. We can just spend time together. No expectations."

"I'm not good at unstructured time," she said.

"Neither am I, actually." He leaned forward and reached for her hand again. She reached for him faster this time. "Maybe we can learn how to give our calendars a rest together."

She smiled. "That sounds nice."

"And without our friends all in our business."

"That sounds fantastic," she laughed.

Mike squeezed her hand, too overcome with a hope he was trying to hide to do more than that.

TONI DIDN'T KNOW what to do with herself.

Mike was at her sink handwashing her dishes — because a dishwasher was a hope and a dream for after the renovation — humming a song she didn't recognize, seeming perfectly at ease in her home. It was disconcerting, but not as much as she would have expected.

Toni didn't usually invite people over, especially not people from work. This was just another way to enforce the separation between her work and home life. But when she did invite people over, she so rarely let them help cook or clean because Toni's mother and grandmother had raised her to be a gracious host. Unfortunately, Mike breezed past all that training, taking control of the cleanup because she'd cooked. It was a fair trade that she mostly accepted because she was tired, not just from the school year but from the past few school years combined. In the end, she simply slumped against the doorway and tried not to spend too much time staring at his ass while he cleaned.

When the dish rack was nearly full, Paw Robeson slid his soft body against her ankles and then walked into the kitchen with a loud meow.

Mike turned at the sound and hummed the same tune he'd been singing to her cat. Paw Robeson meowed again and then slid against the back of Mike's legs with a big stretch.

Toni rolled her eyes. "Traitor," she muttered, although happy she now had something to do. She eased across the kitchen to the corner she'd ceded to her cat and all his necessities. She bent over the airtight tub of Paw's expensive specialty cat food and dumped a small cup into his bowl. Paw rubbed his body against Mike's legs one more time before sauntering across the kitchen to eat.

"That's what I thought," Toni muttered triumphantly. While he ducked his entire face into his bowl, Toni grabbed the base of his tail softly and smoothed her palm along its fluffy length.

"What's his name?" Mike asked.

She looked up to find him leaning against the counter, drying his hands on a dish towel. Her gut clenched. "Paw Robeson," she said and then licked her lips.

He bunched his eyebrows in confusion.

"He's named after *Paul* Robeson."

Mike shook his head again to indicate that he didn't know that name.

"Black athlete, actor, singer, and famous communist. He was blackballed during the McCarthy Era. They took his passport for 'un-American activities,' which included criticizing the US government for Jim Crow racism and praising the Soviet Union for its lack of racial bias."

"Shocking," Mike deadpanned.

Toni smiled. "I adopted this fluffy monster when I was co-teaching a class on McCarthyism with my advisor, and she named him. She died a few years later."

"Oh," Mike breathed. "I'm sorry."

Toni nodded and focused her attention on smoothing the fur down Paw's back, blinking away tears. She hadn't thought about Dr. Little in years.

"You were close?" Mike asked.

"Very. She was like a surrogate aunt in grad school on top of being my advisor. She didn't have to be all that, but I appreciated it. I wouldn't have made it through grad school or gotten my first job without her. I wouldn't show up to work the way I do if I hadn't been trained by her. The only good thing about losing her the way I did is she never got to see how shitty that first job turned out. She never got to see me here, though, either."

"I have a hard time thinking she didn't know this is who you would be," Mike said.

"You think?" Toni's voice cracked, a wave of sadness washing through her.

Mike squinted. "You have no idea how people see you, do you?"

"Of course, I do," Toni laughed sadly. "I'm the bitch they call in when the administration is getting out of hand, and they want someone with tenure and brown skin to yell at them. Someone with far more annoyance than good sense."

"Sorry, I should be more precise. You have no idea how people who admire you see you."

Toni pressed her lips together and shook her head, hating to admit that she was her own blind spot.

"Once they scheduled your job talk, it was like a bulletin went out around the College. Everyone I knew — and some people I didn't — basically told me to clear my schedule to come see you. And then, after you left, you were the talk of every meeting I went to. It was my third year here, so I thought everyone was just *that* excited about every job applicant, but we're not. You know we're not. It was just you."

Toni was speechless, a rare feeling for her, and she felt too shy to look him in the eyes. But she could feel him watching her for a few minutes.

"I think I'm going to go," he said after a while.

Toni's stomach clenched, but she didn't want to process that, so she stood and brushed Paw's fur from her hands. "Okay," she breathed in a tight voice. "I'll walk you out."

Mike nodded as he folded the dishtowel neatly and then looped it over the oven door handle. He walked through the kitchen door, and Toni followed, somehow nervously, in his wake, the sound of Paw's crunching receding as she moved toward the front door.

"Thanks for lunch," he said back in the foyer. Toni watched

him sit on the bench she'd placed against one wall and pull his shoes back on.

"You're welcome. Anytime." Toni hadn't meant to say that, and her eyes went wide with shock.

Mike stopped, and he turned to look at her.

She braced herself for whatever he would say next, preparing herself for something that would, no doubt, make her take back that dangerous slip of the tongue.

But he only looked at her for a few silent moments and then went back to tying up his laces. He stood and reached for the door handle, but then stopped and turned fully toward her, opening his arms.

"Do you want to come and give me a hug?"

"W-what?"

Toni's shock only seemed to amuse Mike. In fact, she watched as he transformed, as a tension in his shoulders eased and a smile spread across his mouth.

"Come give me a hug, Antonia," he said in a heated whisper.

IT WAS ONLY because Mike had years of watching Toni under his belt that he could see the changes in her. The way her mouth fell open in a tense smile. Her widening eyes. The way her shoulders lifted to her ears, her tongue darting to either corner of her mouth as she resisted the urge to nervously lick her lips. These were Toni's tells, and it had taken Mike years to pick up on them. Years of careful, surreptitious observation.

"What?" Toni spluttered again.

"You heard me. You can always say no, and I'll go." His hands dropped to his sides.

She shook her head once, and the knot in the center of

Mike's chest loosened. He could see before she decided that Toni was going to come to him, after all these years.

He could wait. The impatience of the last few weeks was one thing, but he meant what he'd said earlier; Toni was worth every second she made him wait.

She twisted her fingers together and took a deep breath, and then finally took that step down into the foyer.

Mike's heart was pounding against his chest. He was light-headed as she walked toward him without an ounce of urgency.

When she was standing in front of him, he still didn't move. Her eyes were on his chest, and he watched as she took a deep breath before lifting her gaze to his.

"Do you only want a hug?" she asked in a shockingly husky voice he'd never heard before.

Mike shook his head slowly but then sighed. "Absolutely not. But for today, a hug will be enough."

She raised an eyebrow. "Enough?"

He dipped his head and was elated when she lifted onto the balls of her feet. Their lips brushed together softly, and he let himself go.

Mike grabbed Toni around her waist and pulled her against him before dragging her up his body.

"I didn't think so," she groaned before pressing her mouth fully against his.

Mike moaned into Toni's mouth as she wrapped her arms and legs around him, holding onto him as tight as he was holding onto her.

But their kiss was soft, tentative; this was all so new. They began to learn one another through this kiss.

Toni sucked Mike's tongue into her mouth. She smiled at his grunting approval.

Mike trapped her bottom lip between his and scraped his teeth on the sensitive flesh.

She thanked him by pressing her hips forward into his stomach.

They lost track of time in that kiss, which was, in and of itself, a gift. They didn't have an early morning meeting tomorrow or a lecture to rewrite for class. At least for the next couple of months, they had nothing but time to spend exactly like this if they wanted.

And for his part, Mike was absolutely open to the idea.

CHAPTER EIGHTEEN

Mike had stumbled out of Toni's house on unsteady legs. Evening was settling in, and the arc of light from Toni's foyer illuminated the path to his car door. He'd driven home in a daze and then jumped into a cold shower, not that it worked. Mike had stroked himself to a release that barely took the edge off his lust. After years of masturbating to images of Toni, suddenly, his imagination and his own hand wouldn't do.

He'd been too close to the real thing. His own touch would never be enough again, but at the very least, he'd been able to fall asleep. The sun had barely sunk below the horizon by the time he was dead to the world. He was too tired to care.

The next morning, he jumped out of bed feeling more rested and alive than before spring semester started. He threw on a pair of basketball shorts and a t-shirt and took the stairs down to the gym in his condo complex. He preferred the gym across town where there was little to no chance he'd run into any of his neighbors and very few of his colleagues, but he only wanted a quick run on the treadmill; just enough to burn up some endorphins and calm him down, but that was a double-edged sword.

When he was back in his shower — a hot one this time — the doubts started to creep in. His last few encounters with Toni all felt too good to be true, and Mike was far too cautious to just go with the flow. If anything, the closer he'd gotten to her physically, the less sure of himself he felt. He washed his hair with far more intensity than was necessary, honestly hoping that he could knock a couple of brain cells loose so he could enjoy whatever time he had left with Toni in ignorant bliss.

It didn't work.

After his shower, he stared at his reflection in the bathroom mirror for a few seconds before his gaze took in the sight behind him. Maybe it was a result of nearly twelve hours of sleep. Or he was overthinking everything. Or maybe it was just because Toni's renovation plans were fresh on his mind, but suddenly he saw his bathroom in a new light, and he wasn't pleased.

He turned from the mirror and took in just how outdated everything was. He'd owned this condo for almost three years and had somehow never noticed the basic mirrored medicine cabinet, the ugly off-white walls, the builder-grade fixtures, or the basic vinyl floor. Maybe he'd thought about making changes when he'd bought the place, but just like Toni, he'd never had time.

And that gave him an idea.

He strolled down the short hallway to his bedroom. This room needed more work than his bathroom, but he ignored that and sat heavily on his bed, snatching his cell phone from the bedside table.

His hands were shaking as he typed the text message. After a long minute, he deleted the whole thing because it was full of typos, took a deep breath, and then retyped the ridiculously simple message carefully.

Do you have plans today?

He wasn't expecting a quick response. Hoping for it, definitely. Expecting it, absolutely not. So, when the blue bubble appeared next to her name, his eyes went wide.

Nothing I can't move.

Mike tried to bite back his smile and then remembered that he was home alone. There was no need to hide how he felt.

Want to spend the day with me?

He pressed send before he realized that that was not the question to ask, but he could always count on Toni to get specific.

And do what? If you want me to change my plans, you're going to have to make it worth my while.

MIKE DIDN'T NEED the smirking emoji to catch on to Toni's tone, but it helped. His smile practically overtook his face as he typed out a reply.

I could tell you or you could let me surprise you.

He didn't technically mean for that to sound like a double entendre, but he didn't not mean it.

Intriguing.

That was her only reply. Just one word. Mike laughed at how utterly perfect she was.

Intriguing enough for you to clear your day?

He held his breath for the minute it took her to respond.

Sure. Why not? I need to hop in the shower. Give me an hour?

He exhaled in loud relief.

Of course.

Sure, Mike would have preferred to see Toni sooner rather than later, but when he read the word 'shower,' he suddenly imagined her there and undid the towel around his waist, reaching for his hardening shaft.

See you in an hour, Toni.

She sent a brown thumbs-up emoji in reply.

———

"STOP LOOKING AT ME LIKE THAT," Toni said, glaring down at her cat.

Toni was in a stare-off in the middle of her walk-in closet with Paw Robeson.

"You're not even supposed to be in here," she muttered to him. For his part, Paw only blinked up at her because they both knew Toni was full of shit.

Technically, Paw had the run of the house. The only place that was supposed to be off-limits to him was her closet. There was nothing she hated more than trying to brush cat hair off her clothes. But, considering all the fur she vacuumed up from the carpet each week, clearly, she was the only one who acknowledged this boundary.

"So, exactly when should I decide that you talking to your cat like he's a whole damn person is a problem? Do you have, like, a guide for me? Or do you want me to play it by ear?"

Toni squinted at her cat for a few seconds more before she stomped back into her bedroom.

Her tablet was propped up on the top of her dresser, where her aunt Toya was looking at her in dismay. Toya was only five years older than Toni and the family's uncomfortable reminder that, apparently, Toya's parents — Toni's grandparents — had been having sex until the end. Toni's mother also used Toya as an example that God had a sense of humor. But for Toni, Toya was the sister she'd never had — and also an annoying mirror for her own behavior.

"He's my pet, okay? Of course, I talk to him," Toni tried to defend herself.

"I talk to my dog like a dog. *You*," Toya said, pointing at Toni through their tablets and putting heavy emphasis on that word, "talk to your cat like he's about to talk back."

"I fail to see the distinction you're making," Toni deadpanned.

"I know you're lying when you use your professor voice." Toya laughed. "Anyway, wanna see the pasta I just made?"

"Obviously," Toni replied. She moved closer to the dresser. On the other end of their connection, Toya moved away from her camera, giving Toni a view of the kitchen that made her sigh every time she saw it. The marble countertops and modern cabinets were broken up with decorative open shelving styled to perfection. Sometimes Toni imagined herself in that kitchen making a sandwich. It was the calming scene she used to meditate on when she was in a meeting that was getting on her nerves. The stainless steel appliances weren't Toni's style, but they were big and brand-new, and Toni couldn't help but be jealous.

Toya didn't have paint swatches on odd walls. Toya didn't pray every time she washed clothes and took a shower, hoping against hope that this wasn't the day her ancient plumbing finally gave out. Toya didn't have loose carpeting in all her bedrooms — carpeting she'd pried up, hoping for hardwood underneath and finding anything but.

"I hate you," Toni said breezily.

"Jealousy's a sin, Antonia," Toya said, sounding more like her aunt than normal. "Look at them!" Her face lit up as she tipped a sheet pan with small mounds of flour-covered linguine toward the camera for Toni to see.

"Oooh, they look good!" Toni exclaimed. "Send me some."

"You're joking, but I've been looking at small blast freezers and overnight shipping rates."

"Oh my god, I can't believe you're really doing this!"

Six months ago, Toya had called Toni sounding relieved if a bit manic. She'd quit her job as an in-house lawyer at a tech startup to become a chef out of the blue. Well, not completely out of the blue. She hated her job and everyone she worked with, so quitting to become a chef had always been her pipe dream until one day, it was her reality.

Sporadic jealousy aside, it had been easy for Toni to support Toya. She had enough money saved and solid investments to survive for at least a year, and most importantly, she could cook — she'd learned everything from her mother before she passed. When Toni missed the comfort of her grandmother's kitchen, she hopped on a plane and showed up at Toya's front door with an empty stomach and let her aunt cook her food that reminded her of rural Virginia — of home.

"What are you going to use the pasta for?" Toni asked.

Toya set the pan down and leaned back into frame. "I'm going to freeze most of it, honestly, but I got some fresh lobster today. I might just have a glass of wine and see where inspiration takes me."

"God, I hate you."

"Still a sin. Guess I don't need to ask if you've been reading your Bible."

"What Bible? Girl, if you don't shut up." They burst into giggles, both leaning close to their tablets. It had been decades since Toni and Toya had lived in the same state, but sometimes, when they video chatted like this, it was like they were still little girls sitting on Toya's bed, whispering their secrets after bedtime. And sometimes, the wave of homesickness was too much for Toni to bear.

"So, what's his name?" Toya asked out of the blue.

Toni's laughter died on her tongue. Her gaze lifted to the corner of her screen to check the time. "I don't know what you're talking about."

"Lying's a sin," Toya teased.

Toni rolled her eyes. "How did you know?"

"Oh, girl, first of all," she started, the tip of one finger just edging into view at the bottom of Toni's screen. "You're wearing your good bra."

"How the hell do you know that?"

"'Cause your girls are sitting up and at attention. I noticed, and he for damn sure is gonna notice too. Also, you look... happy!" Toya managed to say that with a mixture of glee and shock vying for supremacy in her voice.

"Ouch," Toni said, standing up straight.

"Don't get all butthurt. You know what I mean."

Unfortunately, Toni knew exactly what she meant. "I'm officially on sabbatical. That's what you're seeing."

"It's not, but if you wanna keep lying to me, that's alright. You'll tell me eventually."

"There's nothing to tell," Toni said just as the sound of her doorbell rang out in her quiet home. Out of the corner of her eye, she saw Paw dart through her bedroom door.

Toya laughed. "Yep, nothing to tell. Use protection," she trilled and then hung up without even saying a proper goodbye.

Toni locked the screen on her tablet and put it face down on the dresser even though Toya was long gone, anything to stop her from having to think about her words. She stepped to the side and checked her reflection in the full-length mirror next to her dresser. Unfortunately, Toya was correct. Toni was wearing one of her good bras, and her breasts were damn near jumping out of the v-neck baseball tee she'd thrown on. Since she didn't know where Mike was taking her, she'd dressed casually. She spent most of the year in suits and slacks and heels, running from one professional event to another. But it was summer, and Toni didn't have any classes to teach, no meetings on her calendar, and no one to impress but herself. Except she'd clearly been thinking about impressing Mike because her khaki shorts were very short and tight, and the sliver of skin peeking out between the bottom of her shirt and the top of her pants was a lot when one considered that Toni never showed much skin on campus.

She second-guessed herself for a moment, but it was too late to change. The doorbell rang again, and she shrugged. They were both grown.

As she jogged down the stairs, Paw's shrill howl greeted her. Once again, he was sitting at the mouth of the foyer, staring at the front door.

"I know you're fucking lying," she muttered. He howled again.

Toni shook her head and grabbed her purse from the

credenza as she passed. She pushed him gently aside with her foot and slid her feet into her sandals before slipping through the front door as fast as she could.

On her crowded front step, she collided with Mike, accidentally pressing herself into him.

She pulled the door closed and looked up into his shocked face.

"What?" he breathed.

Toni smiled at his cool, minty breath. "I don't want the cat to run out," she explained.

"Does he do that a lot?" Mike's brows creased in concern.

"No, but I think he knows you're here. My cat definitely likes you more than me," she said.

"Oh." A boyish grin bloomed on Mike's face. "That's okay. I still prefer you to him."

"Oh," Toni breathed, smiling shyly at him.

Although it was hard to be shy when she was sandwiched between her unyielding front door and Mike's tall, hard body. As she took stock of her predicament, Mike's eyes moved down to her chest briefly before lifting and settling on her mouth.

His fingers wrapped loosely around Toni's left wrist and then trailed up her arm, leaving goosebumps over her skin.

Toni shivered against him and lifted her chin just as Mike dipped his head forward.

Their mouths inched closer and closer. Their breaths mingled. Toni felt Mike's smile just before their lips finally touched. She smiled in return as she welcomed his tongue inside her mouth with a soft moan.

CHAPTER NINETEEN

"So, where are we going?"

Mike sighed dramatically. She'd been aiming that question at him like clockwork every other block or so since he'd pulled out of her driveway. A different man might have been annoyed by it, but Mike would have been worried if Toni hadn't been curious. He'd learned that Toni's indifference was the kiss of death, and he'd never seen anyone come back from that. Besides, he'd so rarely seen her giddily excited, and he'd never been the cause of it. As far as he was concerned, she could pester him for the entire drive — every block, if she wanted — and he would still have no complaints.

Besides, the tradeoff for letting her pester him was that every time he looked in her direction, all he could see was miles and miles of smooth brown skin. Toni wasn't particularly tall, but she seemed all legs today in those impossibly short shorts. He'd nearly had a heart attack when she lowered herself into the passenger seat. And when she crossed her legs, he'd had to lay his right arm casually across his lap to hide his growing erection.

"We're here," he finally said, easing his car into a parking spot and putting it in park.

Toni turned toward the front windshield while he turned to her. This was a risk, but when she broke into a shocked, loud laugh, he knew he'd made the right decision.

This was how he wanted to see her every day.

"You brought me to a hardware store?" she laughed.

"I did," Mike said smugly. He pressed the ignition button to turn the car off and unbuckled his seatbelt, turning his torso in her direction.

"I swear I'm here most weekends."

"So this is where you hang out?"

"Don't judge."

Mike put his hands up. "I'd never. I can't. I spend most weekends in the library."

"On campus?" Toni asked, her smile drooping to a frown while her voice dripped with disapproval.

He shook his head. "Public library by my house. The librarians all like me, so they let me use one of the empty offices like a carrel for a few hours every weekend. I wrote my last two articles there."

"Damn, that's smart."

Mike shrugged. "It's not free, though."

"They're charging you?"

He nodded. "Last year, their regular Santa had a family emergency, and I had to stand in."

Toni started laughing again. She laughed so hard tears leaked from the corners of her eyes.

Mike was unprepared to feel pride swelling in his chest. He watched her and marveled at the fact that he'd done that. Not Deja or Marie or as an offshoot of his playful banter with Alejandro. Just him.

"What about Easter?" she asked, still laughing, using her

knuckles to brush the tears from her cheeks. "Please tell me you were the Easter Bunny."

"I haven't been yet," Mike said, his gaze focused on a teardrop forming in the corner of her left eye. It had barely started to run down her face before he smoothed it away with the pad of his thumb. "But there's always next year."

Toni stopped laughing, but her face was still bright with joy. "You better call me if that happens," she gasped, leaning into his touch.

He cupped her face. "Do you want to come support me?"

"Wouldn't you like that," she whispered.

"I would, actually," he replied in earnest while moving his thumb over the tips of her eyelashes.

"You're good at this," she admitted.

"I'm good at a lot of things."

"You should have told me that the first time we met," she said before brushing her lips against the heel of his hand.

Mike's eyes widened as Toni pushed the car door open and bounced up in the warm afternoon. He blinked in shock at her empty seat.

"Come on," she called. "I want to see if they have this paint color I've been stalking."

AS DATES GO, Toni had experienced worse. It was hard for anyone to top the disaster that was the single, not-quite-divorced dad of three who brought his kids to a Michelin-star restaurant. Toni had only endured that date long enough to call a cab, but still, a four-year-old asking her if she was trying to take his mommy's place left an indelible mark on her memory.

The real question was if she'd ever been on a better date. She and Mike were closing their second circuit around the store when Toni realized that her cheeks hurt from smiling, her abs were sore from laughing, and the goosebumps on her arms and legs might be permanent because every time they started to go away, he touched her again and they were back in full force. It wasn't a fancy dinner or an impromptu vacation, but she also wasn't in her twenties anymore. She wasn't wearing a stitch of makeup and was in her most comfortable pair of sandals, but every time Toni made eye contact with Mike, she felt sexy.

"How much paint is too much paint?" he asked, eyeing the samples in their cart. He was strolling behind her, pushing the shopping cart filled with their purchases. She'd caught him watching her ass more than once.

They left the air conditioning of the main store and stepped into the heat and humidity of the garden center. Toni glared at him over her shoulder. "Be careful," she whispered in warning. "Keep playing with me and you might fuck around and tease yourself out of..." Toni snapped her mouth shut as a man strolled from an aisle. They smiled and nodded at him as he walked back into the main building.

Mike leaned forward, resting his forearms on the handle of the cart. "Talk myself out of what, Toni?"

Instead of answering him, Toni ducked down the closest aisle, finally breathing easily once she was free from the heat of his gaze. But it was only a momentary reprieve. She whipped around at the sound of their cart colliding into a tall metal shelf full of fertilizer and soil.

Mike abandoned the cart and started stalking toward Toni with a slow, deliberate stroll. "What, Toni?" he asked again. "Tell me what I might talk myself out of?"

She hadn't realized how much cover the cart provided, the way it kept them apart and allowed Toni to tease him — and herself — without the fear that he might get his hands on her for real. She could have backed away — maybe even run away

— but she didn't. Toni stood in the middle of the aisle and let him advance on her. She let Mike crowd into her space and press his body against her front.

She was wet for him.

He brushed his lips over her cheek until his mouth was at her ear, reminding her of their encounter at The Stax. Toni tried and failed to swallow the moan at his touch.

"What am I about to talk myself out of, Antonia?" His voice had gone deeper again.

She couldn't help but shiver every time he aimed that voice at her. "You know what," she whispered, feeling his mouth curving into a smile before he grabbed her ass in a firm, deliberate, almost possessive grip. She yelped and then moaned.

"I want to hear you say it. You've never had a problem making threats." His lips grazed her ear with every word, and his hand had started to roam over her ass, mapping every curve.

It wasn't just what he said or how he said it but that he was touching her as if he'd been thinking about it for years because, apparently, he had.

There was a certain beauty to being wanted this way, to feeling Mike's desire for her in his touch, hearing it in his voice, and reciprocating his need deep in her core. Once again, Toni was at a loss for words. All she could do was moan.

"Shhh," he whispered and then pressed a light kiss to the side of her mouth. "Shhh," he whispered again as his tongue tasted the corner of her mouth, and she parted her lips to let the tip inside.

Toni had been holding onto the fear that the Mike who had been seducing her over the last few days would disappear, and he would turn back into the man she'd known all these years. But as his tongue made its way between her lips, his hands gripped her ass, and his fingers pressed between her legs, Toni let that fear go. *This* was not the Michael

Hernandez Toni had known for so long. The man who some-times showed up to the faculty of color support group in t-shirts with dorky science puns or equations printed on the front. The Mike who played soccer on the lawn with the Latinx Student Association at least once a year — and only once a year because he was getting old and Toni had seen him limp off the lawn a couple of months ago. The Mike Hernandez who'd raised his voice only once, as far as Toni knew, two years ago during a march in support of undocu-mented students and only because their megaphone had stopped working. But also he was. Mike had been right — apparently, the only thing that had changed between them was that she was just now learning that there were other facets to the man she'd thought she knew.

He moved his mouth back to her ear and began to lick the outer shell while his free hand settled on her stomach, rubbing slow circles just under her t-shirt.

Blood was racing through Toni's veins. Her mouth had gone dry. Her nipples were so hard they hurt. Her pussy was dripping wet. She grabbed his wrist, seriously considering spreading her legs and inviting his fingers to meet at her opening.

"Do you need help?"

Mike and Toni jumped apart like guilty teenagers, but his arms still gripped her around her waist, and he pulled her into his side. Apparently, he wasn't that guilty.

It took a few sluggish moments for Toni to recall Linda's name. She'd come to know the older woman who owned the hardware shop relatively well over the years. Linda was always on hand to give her advice on home improvement projects and special-order tools or paint samples. So, it was very strange to be smiling at her with a light head, pounding heart, and Mike's fingers trapped between her thighs.

"Um," Toni started to say, but it sounded a little too much like a moan to her ears.

Thankfully, Mike stepped in. "Actually, yes," he said. "We think we're going to get some of these bags of fertilizer."

Linda's face lit up. "Wonderful. Our supplier sent us double our order for some reason. It's buy two, get a bag of soil free. How many bags do you want?"

Toni could just barely follow the train of this conversation; she was too busy trying to grind her pussy down on Mike's fingers.

"How about six bags?" Mike said cheerily.

"Excellent. Would you like us to deliver that?"

"You deliver?" they asked at the same time. Toni's brain cleared for a quick second because, just last month, she'd had a hell of a time trying to fit a big ass ladder in her car.

"We do," Linda exclaimed obliviously. "My nephew just moved back to town, and he's doing deliveries for some of our loyal customers a couple of days a week. We can schedule your delivery before you go."

"Wonderful. We'll be right up."

Linda nodded happily and then turned away, apparently having forgotten whatever drew her back here.

As soon as she was out of sight, Mike turned to Toni and pulled her up his body. She wrapped herself around him again and sucked his tongue into her mouth. They kissed one another desperately as if they'd been separated for weeks. Mike's hands roamed over Toni's body, rubbing her back, squeezing her ass, even pinching her nipples. All she could do was moan into his mouth and rub her pussy against his stomach. She couldn't remember the last time she'd been this horny.

But at the sound of a loud metal crash, Toni hopped down from Mike's body and pushed him away, playfully slapping his chest.

Mike burst into amused chuckles.

"You're..." Toni exhaled loudly, using both hands to fan her overheated face. But she didn't have enough brain power to finish that sentence.

Mike grabbed her around the waist and pulled her against him. "I'm what, Toni? Hard?"

It really wasn't a question because he ground his erection into her lower belly as he asked it.

She groaned and shook her head, even as she wrapped her arms around his waist. "That too."

He bent forward and pecked her on the lips. "Is this okay?" he asked in a whisper that betrayed a note of wariness.

"This is more than okay," she whispered back. "I like you like this."

Mike's smile was like the sun. "I like *you* like this," he echoed.

"You better," she teased, and he kissed the hell out of her again.

CHAPTER TWENTY

Mike pushed the cart with their purchases out to his car. Toni tried to help him load his trunk, but he'd refused her help, so she leaned against his car and watched his muscles flex as he worked. And then he'd jogged to the hardware store to return the cart, and she'd watched him with a dreamy smirk on her face. He jogged back, and she enjoyed this view as well.

"Like what you see?" he asked, opening the passenger door.

"It's alright," she teased.

He rolled his eyes and motioned for her to get inside the car.

She folded her arms over the top of the door. "So, is this the end of our day?"

"Do you want it to be?" he asked and then swallowed, betraying his nerves.

"Did you have anything else planned?"

"Are we only going to talk in questions?"

Toni scrunched her face together in a frown as Mike moved close and wrapped his arm around her waist. His fingers danced along her lower back.

"Trying to think of another question?" he asked.

"Can you shut up?"

"Are you hungry?"

Her eyebrows lifted. "What are you thinking?"

His eyes went to her mouth, and he licked his lips. "I'll tell you after lunch."

"No, I'm listening now. I'm not even that hungry."

Mike swooped in and kissed her quickly. "Bullshit."

A COUPLE OF YEARS AGO, her therapist asked Toni what she wanted out of her personal and professional lives, and it had reduced her to tears. She'd cried for nearly the entire hour, but it took a few more weeks of sessions to get to the heart of the issue.

Unlike a lot of her friends and colleagues, Toni didn't hate her job; it would have made her life so much easier if she had. The fact that she loved her work but hated the way it cannibalized all the other parts of her life made disentangling her personal self from her professional life all the more difficult. She'd hoped buying a home would provide that boundary, but it did not. Her best friends were work colleagues, her neighbors were retired staff and faculty, and now, there was Mike.

"Where are you taking me?" she asked.

He drove with his left hand because he held onto Toni's with his right, their fingers laced together. It had been a long time since she let a man drive her around. She'd forgotten how sexy this view could be.

"We're almost there," he said, easing the car to a stop. He looked both ways, his eyes darting to her legs when he looked right.

"Almost where?" she asked as he turned left, using the heel

of his left hand to control the wheel. Toni's pussy throbbed at the sight.

"You know where we are," he said.

"Do I?" To be honest, she hadn't been paying attention to where they were going, she was too distracted by him. So, when she turned to see the familiar street and then the strip mall at the edge of town, she smiled. Yes, she did know where they were.

Alejandro had started calling this shopping area Seasoning Street almost as soon as he arrived, and it had just stuck. The university town where they lived was so white Toni's dad had bought her a gun when she moved there, "just in case." Toni had never used it, but she dutifully and carefully cleaned it each month and made sure that no one knew about the gun safe in her walk-in closet but her and her parents because she could never be too cautious.

But as the number of students, faculty, and staff of color had risen, so had the businesses catering to their needs, and they all found a home on Seasoning Street. Black barbershops and beauty supply stores, a pan-Asian supermarket that had even started stocking some African foods in a specialty section, and a small corner of ethnic restaurants that faculty and staff, as year-round residents in town, refused to let close.

"What are you in the mood for?" Mike asked.

"Vietnamese," Toni said without hesitation.

He nodded once and aimed his car in that direction.

"But can we get our food to-go?"

Mike's foot eased off the ignition, and he nodded again, glancing in Toni's direction. "Y-yeah. Of course."

"Good. Then you can tell me what you're really hungry for on the way to your place."

Instead of answering, Mike lifted their joined hands and

kissed his way across each of her knuckles while he eased his car into a parking space.

"I'VE NEVER BEEN on this side of town," Toni said, switching her gaze from the front windshield to the windows on either side of the car.

Mike eased his foot off the gas. He wasn't in a rush and wanted to savor every moment with her. If she wanted to drive through every street in his neighborhood, he'd do that. Hell, if she wanted to walk down every street, he'd do that too.

"Do a lot of students live over here?"

"There's an apartment complex that's about fifty percent instructors and fifty percent grad students, but otherwise, it's mostly retirees and families."

"Huh. Interesting."

Mike looked at Toni out of the corner of his eye and then pressed his foot on the gas.

Toni noticed the accelerating speed and turned to him in confusion.

"You're thinking about work," he said, navigating the familiar streets of his neighborhood. He passed the park that butted up against the back of his condo complex.

"What makes you say that?" she asked, turning to him, abandoning her perusal of his neighborhood.

"I know you," was the only answer he offered.

The car was silent as Mike pulled into his complex and aimed it toward his assigned parking spot. He also had a covered garage storage unit that he didn't bother to use outside of winter. He eased his car in place and turned it off, and then Toni spoke.

"So, tell me what I'm thinking."

Toni's voice had always been a kaleidoscope of emotion. He'd once heard someone describe her as either flat or aggressive and had spent an infuriating twenty minutes explaining how deeply ignorant that assessment was because Mike had tuned his ears to the subtle shifts of her inflection. Like right now, he could hear the gentle challenge and disbelief.

Mike turned toward her, his seatbelt dug into his left shoulder, and they made eye contact. "Every year, new hires get a packet of information that includes neighborhoods where they might want to buy a home."

Toni's mouth turned down, and she rolled her eyes. Mike couldn't help but smile. "No one ever asks if the new hires want to stay here long enough to buy a whole house, if they want to live in this place." Toni hummed her assent at this. "Or if they can afford a down payment."

"Exactly," she cried.

"But for the past two years, I've noticed a supplementary packet for people who want to rent everything from a room in someone else's house to places that offer short-term leases."

Toni's lips pursed, but Mike could tell that she was trying not to smile.

"No one seems to know who puts that supplementary packet together."

"Oh, yeah?"

Mike leaned over the center console. "The apartment complex is called the Garden Village, doesn't rent to undergrads, and has six- and nine-month lease options."

"That would be good to know," she said, "assuming I put that list together."

"Yeah. Assuming." Mike cupped the back of her head and pulled her mouth to his. It was better than he could have imagined to have Toni smile against him before her tongue licked the seam of his lips.

TONI WAS A NOSY BITCH.

Normally she had time to warn the men she dated that she would be snooping. Nothing too invasive, but she would for sure take notice of any pictures in frames, art hanging on the wall, and whatever was laying out on their bathroom sink. Okay, and also in their medicine cabinet. But she would not open any drawers or closed doors. She wasn't interested in judging; she just loved information. Although, she always made it clear that if she opened a bedroom door and found a mattress on the bare floor, she would grab her purse and leave. No questions asked, no comments.

Everyone deserved boundaries.

She didn't get to give Mike that heads up, but apparently, he didn't need it. He let her into his apartment and closed the door behind them. "I'll plate the food. Feel free to look around."

She lifted her eyebrows.

"Bathroom's there," he said, pointing toward a small hallway. "My bedroom's to the left. Spare bedroom slash office to the right. And here's the rest," he said, gesturing toward the partially open-plan living, dining, and kitchen area.

She squinted at him as he kicked his tennis shoes off at the door and then walked toward the kitchen. "Um," she said.

He glanced over his shoulder at her. "It's fine. I don't have anything to hide. Although, listening to you talk about your renovation plans has made me think about updating this place."

Toni opened her mouth, but he cut her off with a sharp shake of his head. "Let's just stay focused on your house for right now. We can renovate my place after." With that, he turned back to the kitchen.

Toni watched him for a few minutes more. She thought about telling him that the renovations she had planned would take about two years if she was lucky, but she wasn't ready to think that far ahead for things that didn't involve flooring and paint or updates to her syllabi. So, she kept her mouth shut, toed off her sandals, and created a mental list of things Mike's condo needed; top of the list was a shoe rack for his entryway.

He was humming to himself as he pulled bowls and plates down from cabinets. She didn't think there was a chance that he'd forgotten about her, but he was kind enough to give her the space of his inattention. Toni made a quick rotation around the living room. There wasn't much to see in this space besides the pictures of his family on the mantelpiece above his faux fireplace.

"You have a sister?" she said. She didn't actually speak loud enough for him to hear; it was just an observation that slipped past her lips.

Mike heard her anyway. "I do. Her name's Patricia," he said, pronouncing the name in Spanish.

Toni walked to where she could see him over the breakfast bar. "Younger?"

He nodded as he placed their egg rolls into the air fryer to warm them up. "Four years younger. She was born about a year after we moved to the States."

"I didn't realize you were born in El Salvador," she said, trying not to betray the surprise at all the things she didn't know about Mike and how that made her feel when he knew so much about her.

"I was. My parents started their immigration applications right after they found out my mom was pregnant, and we moved here when I was three."

"Wow."

"Yeah. I'll be done in about five minutes. If you want to snoop in my bedroom, you still have time." He glanced at her and winked before turning back to their vermicelli.

"Why are you so chill about this?" she finally asked, a shocked smile spreading over her face.

He shrugged and carefully tipped some noodles into a large bowl. "I'm really not interesting enough to need to hide anything." He lifted his gaze to her, and half his mouth tipped up into an almost-smile. "And I want you to want me for who I am, not someone who makes their bed every day."

Toni exhaled loudly. "But you have a bed? Like a bedframe?"

Mike's smile took over his full mouth now, and it was adorable. "Not to toot my own horn, but I have a headboard and a frame with under-bed storage."

Toni tipped her head to the side and smiled in shock and awe. "Oh, someone is an *adult*."

He frowned. "And I have the heating pad to prove it."

Toni barked out a sharp laugh and turned toward the hall-way. "What brand? Because I have a heated weighted blanket that is to die for."

"Weighted? They make them weighted?"

Toni smiled at him over her shoulder.

***

TONI HAD PROMISED herself in grad school not to mess with someone she worked with again, and she'd managed it for over a decade. That had been a surprisingly easy promise to keep, actually. Eligible, attractive single men of color who were not trifling were a rarity in academia, especially the 'not trifling' part. She'd had lots of opportunities to date men she worked with who were 'kind of' married, 'in an open relationship' that their wives did not realize were open or were just...not to Toni's aesthetic tastes. Those were easy offers to decline.

Mike was not.

In the blink of an afternoon, that decade-long streak came to an end without Toni even noticing.

They were sitting on his couch watching a romcom that neither of them found romantic or funny, but both of them enjoyed dissecting scene by scene. They weren't cuddled together, and Toni felt a way about that, but she didn't know how to admit it to herself, let alone to Mike. So, they'd spent the hour since they finished their lunch sitting next to one another, close enough that their sides touched whenever they shifted, but not a purposeful touching. Not the purposeful touching she wanted. When the 'hero' burst into his love interest's very important work meeting, Toni's brain wanted to implode. She gave up on the movie entirely.

"What are we doing?" she asked. "Together?"

Mike turned to her with wide eyes. "Huh?"

"Like, are we dating or...?"

Somehow, his eyes got wider.

"Don't freak out."

"Too late. Because I'm worried I'll be too honest, and you'll freak out and leave."

"If you think I'm walking home, you're very mistaken. Besides, you have all my paint samples."

He seemed to remember that and nodded. "Good point."

"So you can be honest with me," she said.

Mike turned to her and laid his arm across the back of the couch.

For her part, Toni turned to him, bending her knee and resting her leg against his thigh, touching him deliberately for the first time in hours.

"I have spent years just wanting this," Mike said slowly. "Just wanting to spend a little bit of time with you. I want to enjoy spending time with you. Is that okay?"

Mike had told her he didn't lie, but she could see that he

could be creative with the truth if he wanted. She heard him say "a little bit of time" and understood that was only half-true at best.

Normally, when men lied to Toni, she left; no conversation, no negotiation, no second chances. But in this moment, she had to reconsider that hard line. Mike didn't lie to her outright; he just hid his full desires from her as he had been for so long. And she didn't hate him for it. On the contrary, Toni didn't think she had long-term in her anymore. All she wanted was right now.

She smiled at Mike, nodding happily. "Yeah, that's okay. I want that too."

SUMMER

CHAPTER TWENTY-ONE

"Sure thing, Charles, just let me know when you're free next week. We can talk more then."

This was the second time Mike had said this in the fifteen minutes he'd been trying to get off this call. Fifteen minutes that he'd been sitting in Toni's driveway, looking wistfully at her front door, listening to the director of his program try and talk him into a role he'd already agreed to accept.

"So, do you have any ideas about contract negotiations?" Charles asked.

Mike closed his eyes and pressed the back of his head into his seat rest with increasing pressure. "Not yet. I'll have a better idea *next week.*"

"Okay, as long as you remember the timeline on this is pretty tight."

"I understand," Mike said, letting a slight, frustrated sigh invade his words.

"Great. Well, I've gotta run."

Mike excitedly pushed his car door open. "So do I. Have a great day." He didn't wait for a response just in case Charles tried to reinvigorate their conversation yet again. Mike turned the phone off, silenced it and shoved it into his pocket, and then jogged up the stone pathway to Toni's house.

He pressed the doorbell, and Toni pulled the front door open.

"Oh, you decided to get out of the car?" she said, grinning up at him.

"I got stuck on the phone with my director," he said, his eyes traveling down her body and focusing on her legs. She was wearing another pair of very short shorts again, and he liked it. But then he realized what she'd said, and his eyes shot up to her face. "Wait, were you watching me?"

Her grin disappeared. "Is everything alright?"

Mike was sad to watch her playfulness melt into serious consideration. He knew this tone of her voice, knew that it meant she was ready to put on her cape and save everyone else but herself. That was not the Toni he wanted. "I'm fine. Everything's fine. It was just a phone call."

"About what?" She rolled her eyes. "You all always say that."

Mike stepped forward. "Who is you all?"

"You," she started to say as he crowded her space. She backed into the foyer, her eyes settling on his arms exposed by the muscle tee he'd worn in a desperate hope that she would look at him exactly like this. "You...all," she gulped, letting go of the side of the door as she backed further into her home, "whenever someone on that campus needs help, they always say everything's fine at first."

Mike pushed the door closed behind him while he shook his head. "I don't need help," he said. "I'd use damn near any reason to spend time with you. If I needed your help, I would have shown up here at dawn. But I don't need your help, Toni. I'm here to help you, remember?"

That pulled her out of her stupor, and she glared up at him. "There you are," he whispered.

Her cat meowed and slid between their legs.

"And there *you* are," he said, bending forward to pick up his new friend.

"Whore," Toni said, tossing her braids as she turned away.

If her cat understood her disdain, he didn't care. He was too busy rubbing his head along Mike's chin and purring.

"Whenever you two are done, I'll be upstairs. Take off your shoes," she said with a dismissive wave.

He laughed and toed off his sneakers. "We can do both," Mike said in a gentle voice. He followed Toni upstairs to her spare bedroom while he held her cat against his chest. On the second-floor landing, he turned around in a circle, taking it all in. "Oh, I see," he said. "This is your sabbatical project."

"Yeah. It's livable, but most of it needs a lot of damn help. You sure you wanna do this? You can always back out."

When Mike had offered to help Toni with her renovations, all he'd really wanted was to spend time with her, and that hadn't changed. "I'm sure," he said, bending over to put her cat on the floor. "What do you need me to do?"

She eyed him warily for a few seconds and then shrugged before turning and leading him down the hall. She didn't tell him to follow, but they both knew he would.

Still, Mike took in everything he could see. There was more artwork on the walls up here, paint swatches across from a hall window, and then a glimpse through her open bedroom door. His gait slowed all the way down as he stared wide-eyed at her unmade bed, flowers on her dresser, and something, maybe a nightgown, thrown over the end of her bed.

"Don't be nosy," she called down the hall.

He turned and found her standing at the end of the hall,

arms crossed but that grin back on her face. He gestured toward her bedroom. "Need any help in there?"

She looked away as that grin turned into a smile.

And even though he wanted to stay right where he was, Toni was so adorable that Mike felt as if she was pulling him toward her.

"I don't need any help in there, thanks."

"You sure?"

She bit her bottom lip and ducked into the room. "Here's the office," she said, changing the subject. "I don't need to do a lot of work in here, but I do have a team coming in to pull up this carpet and change the flooring."

"To more carpet?"

"Yeah. I was hoping there would be hardwood under here, but that was wishful thinking. Besides, this room is already so cold in the winter that it probably needs carpet, especially if I really plan to work in here."

Mike nodded and looked around. "It's a great space."

She nodded. "I went back and forth about which spare room to make into my office. There's one downstairs."

"Why'd you choose this one?"

She smiled. "My parents are getting older. My dad has a cane. I'd feel better if he didn't have to bother with any stairs."

"Makes total sense. So what do we need to do today?"

She clapped her hands together. "I've basically been using this room as storage. Extra clothes, boxes of books, whatever. All we need to do is clear everything out. The carpet people get here tomorrow. They said it'll take three days to pull this all up and lay down my new ridiculously expensive carpet." Toni cringed as if she didn't believe that.

"And after?"

"Once they're gone, I'm going to paint, and then my favorite part."

Mike had drifted close as she spoke, and he looked down at her now with a raised eyebrow and his heart beating hard and fast in his chest.

"Shopping," she said. "I have a whole set of new office furniture in the garage, but it's all about the details. There's a new interior design store in the city that I've been stalking online, and once the walls are painted, I'll be there."

"*We'll* be there," Mike corrected. "Where do you want me to take these boxes?"

"Uh...the garage," she said.

He stacked one small box on top of a medium-sized one and bent to pick them up together. "Let's get to work."

Toni had planned for this to take all day, but that's mostly because she'd thought she'd have to do it all alone. Mike hadn't been any part of the equation. With his help, her soon-to-be office was clear by lunch.

When the room was empty, she stood in the middle and tried to imagine how it would look in a month. She closed her eyes and transformed the room in her mind. She turned in a circle and imagined the marble desk she'd spent a fortune on in shipping alone in the far corner — it was big enough for two people and all hers — the mirror she wanted on one wall to reflect the light coming in from the window on the opposite wall. She imagined the reading nook she could create in the corner of the room behind the doorframe. And most importantly, she imagined the joy of being able to close this door at the end of a workday and leave all her work-related stress right here.

When Toni opened her eyes, she found Mike leaning against the doorframe with his hands in his pockets, watching her.

"Don't mind me," he said. "Keep going."

She smirked. "Thanks for your help today."

"You're welcome. What's next?"

She shrugged. "Nothing for today. I thought this would take longer, but with your help, it didn't. So, thank you."

"It was my pleasure. But are you sure there's nothing else I can do for you?"

Toni gulped as Mike stepped inside the room. As soon as he crossed the threshold, the air between them changed. Before he'd arrived, Toni had been wondering what would happen with Mike in her home, but the answer was mostly nothing.

Or the answer *had been* nothing. All morning, they'd been squeezing past one another in the hallway, their arms brushing, handing off boxes and bags, their fingers tangling for brief moments, and Toni had felt normal — just small shots of electricity that settled over her skin. Those touches kept her aware of him — and her own body — for hours, but not enough to distract her from the task at hand.

Toni had talked to her therapist about Mike more than once over the last few weeks, hoping the other woman would help her get some clarity on the situation, and finally, it had arrived. She didn't know what spending all this time with Mike would bring, but she resolved to welcome whatever came next, no pressure or expectations. Just joy.

Mike kept his distance physically, walking around the now-empty room with a casual grace she wouldn't have expected from a man as tall and thick as him. Still, he filled the space with his presence, all that silence suddenly crowded in close. And then there were his eyes. She could feel his gaze all over her skin, slipping underneath her clothes, circling her nipples, teasing the juncture of her legs.

Not for the first time, she wondered how she could have spent so much time with him and never known how he felt about her. How he could have hidden so much of himself. Some days, Toni could hardly hide her hunger, but Mike had spent years hiding the fact that he could look at her and make her wet. It was unbelievable, but a parlor trick that wouldn't work on her again.

Ever since Multicultural Graduation, Mike had been steadily moving from the periphery of her thoughts toward the center. If this continued, in a month, she might be well on her way to developing an infatuation that rivaled his.

"Antonia."

She'd been lost in her own thoughts and hadn't noticed as he rounded back into her peripheral vision. She turned to look at him full-on. "Michael." She hadn't meant to, but she said his name in a gasping whisper she'd never heard from her own mouth. "Let me walk you out."

If she hadn't been watching him so closely, she would have missed the slow blink and the quick glance away that betrayed his disappointment. But through it all, his smile never faltered. "After you," he said, nodding toward the door.

It took a few seconds for Toni's feet to listen to her brain. The first couple of steps were halting, awkward, but Mike fell into step behind her. She imagined that she could feel the heat of him at her back and his gaze on her ass, his attention reminding her that there was no need to rush him out of her home.

As they descended the stairs, Paw passed them on his way up but made sure to rub his body along Mike's leg in farewell.

At the foyer, Toni turned and leaned against the wall.

"Thanks again," she said.

He ran a hand through his hair. "Anytime."

They stared at one another in silence.

Mike looked like he wanted to say something, and Toni waited patiently, feeling very sure that this was the moment he would fuck it all up because this morning — and the past few weeks — had been far too good to be true. She braced herself for it — steeled her back, clenched her abs, held her breath, and got ready to lower her expectations for other people once again.

"Call me if you need anything else," Mike said breezily before stepping down into the foyer.

Toni blinked in shock.

She watched as he slipped his shoes back on, but when he reached for the door handle, Toni made a decision.

THE PROBLEM WITH MIKE, according to Alejandro, was that he was too cautious.

Mike hadn't thought that was a character flaw until this moment.

It had made so much sense to hang back with Toni. When they met, she was busy applying for a job, and then she needed to acclimate to the new university, but after that, he wasn't sure what he'd been waiting for anymore. He was certain that it had made sense at the time, but as he put his tennis shoes on — much slower than was necessary — he couldn't make his reticence curl all the way over.

He reached for the doorknob and started to turn back to get one more glimpse of her when the sound of her footsteps shuffling in his direction caught his attention.

"Seriously?" she breathed, and that was all the warning he got before she was rushing toward him, her arms reaching up for his neck.

Mike let go of the handle and reached out to her, picking her up by the waist. He smiled just as her mouth crushed into his. He tasted the curve of her bottom lip before invading her mouth with his eager tongue. The groan she let out tasted like lemon water, mint, and sweat. Her fingernails scratched at the back of his neck and scalp. The sting of that touch went straight from his head down to his dick.

His back hit the door, and he groaned. Toni suckled on his tongue as she started to grind her pussy into his stomach.

He moved his hands under her ass and squeezed, helping her get herself off on him.

"Fuck," she breathed against his mouth.

He grunted, jutting his own hips forward. He'd been fighting an erection all morning, but with Toni writhing against him, he happily surrendered. His dick was hardening in his basketball shorts, and all he wanted was to bury himself inside her.

His fingers moved between her legs, feeling the warmth radiating through her clothes. He groaned into her mouth.

She pulled away from their kiss, pressed her forehead to his, and started to grind onto his fingers and against his stomach in earnest.

He pressed his head back against the door and closed his eyes, cursing under his breath in Spanish as he helped her chase an orgasm, already worried he wouldn't make it home in time to jack off, but that was a problem for later.

Right now, he just wanted to make sure Toni got what she needed from him.

***

TONI COULD FEEL the orgasm coming, and she closed her eyes to concentrate.

This would be her third of the day. She'd woken up nervous, excited, and wet at the prospect of seeing Mike again. She'd had to use her fingers and a vibrating bullet to get herself off twice before she could muster enough energy to crawl out of bed.

But this release would be better than both of those orgasms. Mike's fingers pressing against her clit and squeezing her ass, his abs giving her the friction she needed, were doing work she hadn't had the time to replicate this morning when she was all alone.

She was so close to coming nothing could have stopped her except herself, and she did.

Mike's stomach twitched as he pressed his hips forward mindlessly, pumping into nothing but air.

She opened her eyes to find his closed, his brows knit together in concentration. On her. Her body. Her pleasure. Her release. Just as he had been at The Stax.

She was starting to understand him now, little by little, with each interaction. She stopped grinding.

His eyes flew open. "What's wrong?"

She was panting and shook her head as she climbed from his body. One foot hit the floor and then another, but she kept leaning into him and felt the rigid length of him against her stomach and breasts as she lowered herself to the floor.

"What—" he started to ask and then stopped, his eyes widening as she settled on her knees. "Toni?"

Their gazes locked as she pushed his shirt over his stomach.

It took a second for him to catch on and help her, tucking his shirt under his chin.

She let her hands glide over his stomach, feeling the downy hair the closer she got to his groin. Toni curled her fingers inside the waist of his basketball shorts and pulled.

Mike's lips burst open on a loud, needy pant. "Are you sure?" he asked, lust and worry warring in his gaze.

Toni smiled, excited to show him that there were so many things he didn't know about her yet.

His dick sprang free from his clothes, bobbing next to her

cheek. The shaft brushed her chin, leaving a spot of wetness there.

He closed his eyes on a groan.

Toni could feel his body straining not to press his hips at her again, and she silently promised to help him lose that war. She wrapped her palm around his dick.

"Fuck," he breathed, tilting his head back for a moment, but only a moment. When his face came back into view, his eyes were wide open with excitement, ready to watch her break him down to his most basic elements the way he had broken her down at The Stax.

She stroked him once, so slowly he started wheezing, as she lifted up onto her knees to press a single kiss into the hair above his shaft and breathe him in. He smelled like soap, sweat, and something she could only guess was his natural scent. It made her pussy weep.

Her palm moved over the mushroom head of his shaft, and she used the wetness to ease the path of her grip. She watched him for as long as she could as she kissed her way through the neatly trimmed hair and then down the length of his dick. Her hand lightly cupped his balls before moving to the base just as her mouth opened.

Time slowed for the next few minutes. Toni looked up Mike's body, capturing his gaze again. Her free hand settled on his right thigh for stability. She opened her mouth even more to comfortably accommodate the size of him. And then she lowered her face as her hand moved up his shaft in a tight grip.

By the time her lips met her fist, Mike had stopped breathing. She tightened the suction of her cheeks on him until he let out the air in his lungs in a loud gust.

"My god," he groaned.

Her head moved back just as slowly and then forward again. Each time her hand moved, she twisted it left and right at a pace that matched her mouth. She spread her saliva along his length, using her tongue as much as her lips and hand to get him off.

Mike's face was beet-red, his muscles were clenching, and precome was pouring from the tip of his dick. Not that it was a competition, but Toni planned to show Mike that he wasn't the only one who knew how to make an impression.

As it happened, Toni loved giving head.

Some people did it as a matter of course, a tit-for-tat exchange on a sexual checklist that was nice but always lay bare when the passion wasn't there.

But the passion was here in this moment.

It was in her mouth and tongue, caressing every inch of his shaft.

In her wet palm, rubbing and squeezing his balls.

It was in his fingers twirling in her braids.

It was in every groan he couldn't stop now.

It was in her losing herself in the moment, closing her eyes, and concentrating on getting just a little more of him into her mouth.

It was in the way they both groaned when the tip of him tapped her throat and the moment they took, bodies stilled, to commemorate it.

The passion was in the way they let go as her mouth started to move again, faster now, his hips jutting forward, trying to meet her lips.

It was in her own hand leaving his thigh to get inside her shorts and panties, slipping through her wetness and teasing her clit.

It was in the way Mike bent forward not just because she felt so good but because he wanted to get his free hand inside her bra to pinch her nipple.

It was in the way he whispered filthy encouragements to

her while he fucked her face. She didn't need them, but they were very appreciated.

"That's right. Suck me. How does your pussy feel, Antonia? Are you wet from sucking me? Are you wet for me? You're going to feel so good around my dick."

And that was when Toni lost it. When she pushed her fingers into her pussy, ground the heel of her hand on her clit, and came with a surprised shout that his dick muffled.

Apparently, that's when Mike lost it as well. He squeezed her tit and came in a thick, salty rush inside her mouth. Her fingers played over her clit to extend the life of her own orgasm. And finally, on instinct, Toni hollowed her cheeks as the rush of his ejaculation slowed. She wanted to savor every drop from him.

Mike moaned pathetically as her mouth and fist pulled away from his shaft one last time.

She wiped her mouth with the back of her hand before reaching up for him.

He helped her stand and looked about to say something until she shoved the fingers wet from her pussy into his mouth.

She didn't know how he managed one more spurt of release, but it hit her on her thigh. She smiled and watched him lick the taste of her pussy from her hand.

All in all, Toni thought this was a great first renovation day.

CHAPTER TWENTY-TWO

Come over

When Mike woke up to that text message from Toni, he thought he was still dreaming. In fact, he'd been so certain that something was wrong he'd turned his cell phone off, counted to thirty, and turned it on again.

The text message was still there.

Did you mean this for me?

Toni sent an eye-rolling emoji.

Unless I sucked the life out of someone else's dick yesterday. Can you forward this message to him?

THAT GOT him out of bed.

On my way

He hoped she didn't take that literally because he needed to hop in the shower, jack off, clean himself, jack off again, clean himself again, and then get dressed. Still, he was out the door in record time.

He didn't want to show up at her house empty-handed, though, so he stopped at Toni's favorite bakery on the way to pick up breakfast. He knew her favorite coffee order — vanilla latte — but not her favorite pastry, so he ordered one of everything just to be safe.

When he pulled his car along the curb in front of her house, he was in a great mood. He'd gotten the best blowjob of his life, went home, immediately passed out, woke up in the middle of the night hungry as fuck, made a sandwich, gone back to bed, and immediately passed out again. If he hadn't woken up to Toni's text, he'd have been in a great mood, but being back at her house less than twenty-four hours after he left was best-case scenario times twelve.

But then she stomped out of the front door. "Get back," she hissed at her cat, using one foot to push him back inside before closing the door. She crossed her arms and glared at him as he walked toward her, wary but never slowing his steps.

"Good morning," he said happily, but maybe not as cheerily as before. "I brought breakfast."

She rolled her eyes. "Follow me."

She turned right and led him down another stone path he hadn't noticed before. This one led to a gate that she unlocked before leading him down the side of her home into her backyard. The view of her yard here was only slightly less wild than what he'd seen during his first visit, but when they rounded the house, Mike finally understood the annoyed look on her face.

"Shit," he hissed.

"Exactly. What the fuck am I supposed to do with all this goddamn soil and fertilizer?" she asked, throwing her hands in the air.

THEY ATE breakfast at the picnic table in the yard.

Toni sipped her latte and ate a cruller and a chocolate mousse-filled donut while glaring at the bags of soil and fertilizer stacked neatly in the middle of her jungle. Er, backyard. She clearly didn't want to talk, but Mike noticed the way she nodded happily when she spied the chocolate center of her donut. She was pissed off but not too pissed off to enjoy it. He enjoyed the hell out of it himself.

He watched her while polishing off a cinnamon twist and a croissant. He even squirmed uncomfortably in his seat as she licked the chocolate from the middle of the donut in long, deep, seductive swipes of her tongue. He normally had a glass of water and a piece of fruit in the morning before a workout, so in every way possible, this was the best breakfast of Mike's life.

"What?" she asked when she found him staring at her.

"Nothing. I have an idea."

She squinted, and he nodded toward her yard. She turned to glare at it again. "Don't take this the wrong way, but I thought about blocking your number when Linda's nephew showed up with all this. 'Cause what the fuck?"

"All I heard is that you thought about blocking me but didn't."

"Are you always this optimistic?"

"No. Have another donut, and let me tell you my plans."

"Wanna share this cinnamon roll?" she asked, breaking off a piece and holding it into the air.

"Sure," he said, bending over the table to close his mouth

over her fingers. He took the cinnamon roll and then sucked the sugar from both of her digits.

That made her smile.

He sat back down and took a sip of his coffee while she broke off another piece of the pastry and put it in her mouth, watching him as she licked them clean again. "I'm listening," she said.

WHEN LINDA'S nephew had banged on her front door, waking her out of a dead sleep to deliver the fertilizer and soil Mike bought, Toni had thought her brain was broken and she'd lost the ability to count because Mike had only bought six bags. But either Linda had assumed he meant six bags of each, or she had finessed them, and they'd been too horny at the time to catch the mistake. Either way, Toni blamed Mike.

She'd invited him over, prepared to cuss him out and send him on his way. But then he'd shown up at her house with pastries and coffee, and his jet-black hair had still been wet from a shower, and next thing she knew, her nipples were hard, her pussy was wet, and they were spending a lovely, calm morning watching the sun rise together.

There were far worse ways to start a day.

"I think we should fix your backyard together."

"Excuse me?"

"You heard me."

"And do you hear me? The disbelief in my voice?"

"I don't," he said with a casual shrug. He reached into his back pocket and pulled his cell phone out, tapping until he turned his screen to Toni and scrolled down on a cache of pictures that only made her feel worse about her yard. She tossed pieces of the cinnamon roll into her mouth while he showed her what her yard could never be. "I know you're busy and probably think you can't take care of this."

"Because I can't," Toni said. "It's taken me two years to plan the renovations inside the house. And I just water the front yard every now and then. Whenever I remember, actually." Admitting this somehow made her feel like a failure.

He nodded. "Exactly. You need something back here that's low-maintenance but still looks good."

"And non-lethal for my asshole cat," she interjected. Her eyes were riveted to the screen. "Wait, stop," she said, pressing a clean finger to the back of his hand. There was a picture so pretty she wanted to look at it again. The garden seemed as if it was bursting with every color of wildflower. She shoved a piece of cinnamon roll in her mouth and imagined what that kind of yard would be like to come home to.

"One of the librarians I work with has a yard full of perennials and raised beds for decorative plants and vegetables."

Toni scoffed.

"You don't have to do the vegetables, but I thought we could plant stuff that can freeze over in winter and bloom in spring but wouldn't take a lot of work to maintain. And we can ask my friend about cat-friendly plants."

"Hmm," Toni hummed, taking her hand from his and nodding for him to keep scrolling. "But these pictures are a continent away from..." She glanced toward her yard.

"Your forest?" he offered.

She smiled and nodded.

"I know. I did a little research, and I think mostly what we need to do is clear out all the weeds."

"The whole yard is weeds," she said sadly.

"Then it's a good thing we have all summer."

Toni rolled her eyes.

"Just imagine it," he said. "You can be in your office

working and then look out the window onto a yard that doesn't look like nature is retaking the land."

She looked up at him, a shot of hope in her gaze.

"And we can sit out here and barbecue without pretending not to be afraid of what's in that bush."

"We?"

"If you think I'm about to pull up a whole yard of weeds and not benefit from it, you're beautiful but delusional."

Toni turned to look at the yard, staring at it in silent contemplation for a few moments. When she looked back at him, his face was full of longing and hope. She tore off another piece of cinnamon roll. "Okay," she said softly and offered the treat to him.

He smiled and bent forward, letting his mouth wrap around her fingers, his tongue bathing every inch of her skin. "Sweet," he said.

And they both pretended he was talking about the cinnamon roll.

CHAPTER TWENTY-THREE

"I really think you'll be great in this position, Mike. This isn't exactly how I planned to lure you into the role, but I'm happy, nonetheless. I hope you can be as well."

"I knew I'd do this eventually," Mike offered diplomatically. "Now is just as good a time as any other."

He was taking a stroll around the north oval with Provost Greene. When the director of his program decided abruptly to step down a couple of weeks ago, he created a logistical nightmare for the unit, not least of which was that their faculty was scattered across the world. One of his colleagues was in Hawai'i, another in Texas, and one more in Seoul. Deciding what to do with the position normally took months of soliciting new candidates, inviting faculty feedback, meetings with deans and the provost, and then a vote. It wasn't impossible to do those things over email, but it certainly wasn't ideal. But when the outgoing director had suggested Mike for the interim position of one year, it had seemed like the best solution to their problem, and everyone had agreed. Negotiations were easy for the things that only sort of mattered; course load, change in pay, etc. The only thing he'd asked for that was non-negotiable was the summer. Thankfully, his outgoing director had agreed.

"Good. Good. So, what are your plans for the rest of the break?"

Mike couldn't have stopped the smile if he wanted to, but as it happened, he wasn't interested in hiding the depth of his happiness from anyone but Toni. And hopefully, he wouldn't have to hide anything from her for much longer.

"I'm just relaxing, actually. Helping a friend and not thinking about work."

Provost Greene smiled. "I should try that one day. It sounds nice."

"It's better than nice," Mike breathed.

"Well, enjoy it," the other man said as the path in front of them split. He headed off toward his office, and Mike turned left toward the faculty parking lot.

"I plan to. Believe me," he said with a wave.

"DID YOU EVEN TASTE IT?" Toni laughed, reaching for Mike's plate. She realized what she said and how it sounded just as she locked eyes with Mike.

His face turned red, and he grinned, handing her his empty plate. "Not yet," he muttered.

She had to turn away, not because she wasn't very interested in letting him taste it, but she did not feel sexy at this exact moment. As soon as Mike had appeared at her door with his work clothes in a duffel bag, they'd started pulling out weeds and worked non-stop for hours. Actually, they'd been working non-stop for weeks and had settled into a kind of routine.

Mike showed up on her doorstep every morning, just a little bit earlier each day, as if he was racing the sunrise to get to her. Yesterday, she'd let him inside and fallen back to sleep on the couch while he made omelets. Once she was fed, fully awake, showered, and dressed, they tackled some new project around her house. While the flooring crew worked on her office, they'd put a harness on Paw and took him outside. He enjoyed the sun and bugs while they tackled her overgrown flowerbeds. They pulled weeds, read articles on the state of soil to one another over lunch, and tried to imagine what the yard would look like in a year's time.

Mike tried to convince her they were making great progress, but besides learning exactly what poison ivy looked like, she didn't think they'd even made a dent in her mess of a yard. It still looked like a jungle back there. But she found herself enjoying Mike's enthusiasm nonetheless.

When the flooring crew had finished in her office — in a week and a half, not three days — Toni took the weekend off from renovations to mourn the price of that one job. Instead of leaving her to her financial anxieties, Mike had shown up with Greek takeout and a bottle of wine. They got tipsy and made out on the couch for a couple of hours. That eased some of the pain.

For the past couple of weeks, they'd been alternating between painting her office and pulling up more weeds from the bottomless yard of weeds. It would have been more than a little disheartening if not for the fact that every hour Toni spent with Mike made her want two more.

"Behave," she whispered.

"Believe me, I am," he said, following her from the back-yard into her kitchen.

It was sweltering outside, but somehow it was even hotter in here even though they'd barbecued once again. She kicked off her shoes just inside the back door, and her shoulders slumped.

She placed their dishes in the sink with a weary groan.

"I've got it," Mike said. He wrapped an arm around her waist and moved Toni to the doorway between the kitchen and dining room, where it was cooler.

Now, Toni was a feminist, and she did not *need* a man for much of anything, but her time with Mike had been a reminder that need and want were not the same things. She didn't need Mike to pick her up like she weighed nothing at the drop of a hat, but she damn sure loved it. She didn't need a man to open doors for her, but it sure as hell made her feel good when he did. She didn't need anyone to make out with her after a long day of physical labor, but it sure as hell felt good to have Mike's big body between her legs.

He filled the left sink with steamy water and started to scrub, neatly stacking the clean dishes on the right. She watched the muscles in his back through his dark blue shirt as she had nearly every evening this week and tried to picture what those muscles looked like naked.

"When are we going to have sex?"

Mike nearly dropped a dinner plate on the rest of her dishes. He didn't, which was the only reason Toni found it funny. Once he'd rinsed the plate and gently placed it in the dishrack, he turned to glare at her over his shoulder. "Behave."

Toni smiled. But it wasn't just any smile. For weeks, she'd realized, Mike had been making her smile in ways she so rarely did, showing as many of her teeth as possible, big enough to make her cheeks hurt, deep enough that she felt joyful deep down in her soul.

This was something she wanted, something she deserved, but maybe, she wondered as she walked across the kitchen and wrapped her arms around his waist, maybe this was also something she needed.

A not-small part of her hoped that it was not.

"You want to take a shower?"

He turned the water off.

Since he'd spent most of every day at her house, Toni had practically surrendered the guest bedroom and bathroom to Mike. Once they were done working for the day, they usually retreated to separate bathrooms to clean up and change. Upstairs in her en suite, Toni usually touched herself while thinking about Mike and wondered if he was doing the same.

But that wasn't the offer she was making him today, and she could feel he knew that in the tension of his back, his stomach, and when her hand moved down, the firmness of his shaft.

He groaned and grabbed her hands, getting water all over the front of his clothes. He turned around with a nervous smile on his face and stared at her for a few heated seconds before leaning forward to give her a peck on the lips.

It was the first time he'd kissed her since yesterday. This, too, had become an uncharacteristic part of their routine, the way it seemed as if each day reset their intimacy. Even though Toni knew they would end up on her couch dry humping and kissing, the how and the why were always the mystery. Always the delicious unknown.

"Is that what you want, Toni?" He whispered that question against the corner of her mouth.

"Yes," she moaned.

"Are you sure? You can always tell me to stop or leave."

That made her laugh. "Obviously. If I didn't want you in my house, you wouldn't even know where I live, let alone be running through here damn near every day."

He kissed her bottom lip. "But the question is, do you want me in your pussy?"

She sucked in a sharp breath, tasting him on her lips and tongue.

He backed away, smiling down at her. "I've been waiting a long time for you, Antonia. I'll never rush you. I want this to be right."

Toni blinked up at him. "You mean that, don't you?" Mike's eyebrows furrowed. "About waiting."

"What's a few more days?"

"Months?"

His eyes widened, and his smile froze in place. "Or months," he wheezed.

She wanted to laugh. She wanted to call him out on his lie, but even behind the shock, she could see sincerity written all over his face. For a brief, unconscious moment, he accidentally let her see him and get a glimpse of his feelings for her — the depth and the complexity. She reached up to cup his face, not knowing if she had it in her to reciprocate but still wanting to revel in what she saw in his gaze.

"Michael," she whispered.

His thumb brushed across her cheek. "Antonia."

"Fuck me."

CHAPTER TWENTY-FOUR

"Fuck me," Toni said, and Mike thought he could feel colors and taste sounds, and he didn't need to be told twice. He scooped Toni into his arms; she wrapped her arms and legs around him and started placing butterfly kisses all over his face.

He'd spent so much of the last few weeks here that he didn't need to look to know where he was going. Still, he watched where he stepped over her shoulder and walked carefully. If anything could convince Toni to change her mind in this moment, it would be if he dropped her.

Also, he wanted to see her bedroom for real, more than just the glimpse he got as he walked down the hallway to her office. At the threshold, he stopped, peering inside, nervous to take the next step just in case this all went away. Blessedly, Toni was much less sentimental.

She crawled from his arms and stepped into the room, flicking the light switch on her way. "I'll give you a tour after you make me come."

Mike didn't need a challenge to make her come — hell, he

would have done that anyway, anywhere, whenever she wanted — but he did want the tour. He followed her, craning his neck left and right to see art on walls he hadn't been able to check out from the hallway, inside her closet, and then her bathroom.

He'd imagined it different — modern, already renovated, and smaller, actually. "Why is this bathroom so damn big?" he asked before he could stop himself.

"Right?!" she cried knowingly. "My realtor thinks the previous owners made the master suite by cannibalizing a closet and the only bathroom up here to combine it with the bedroom, but we're not sure." Toni walked to her shower and reached inside the curtain to turn it on.

Mike turned in a circle. "Maybe, but damn."

She nodded. "Basically. It's gonna be a bitch to renovate." She pulled her t-shirt over her head.

Mike's eyes went wide as he took her in — the dark gray sports bra, the fleur-de-lis tattooed on her front left shoulder, the curve of her breasts, her hard nipples as she pulled the bra up and off.

"I showed you mine, you show me yours," she teased.

He pulled his shirt over his head. Their hands went to their shorts at the same time. They smiled as they pushed the rest of their clothing to the floor. And then they stood there drinking in their nakedness as the temperature of the room rose from the steaming shower.

"Is it everything you hoped it would be?" she asked in a shaky voice.

"Better," he said because it was true but also because he never wanted her to question how beautiful she was or how he felt.

"Are you nervous?" she asked.

"Very. But mostly, I'm excited. Are you..." He swallowed slowly. "Are you excited?" he asked hesitantly.

"I am, actually. Really excited. Do you want to feel how much?"

Mike groaned and took a step toward her.

She turned and pushed the shower curtain open. They stepped carefully inside together. It was a tight fit.

"I don't think I thought this through," she said, ducking away from the shower spray.

It took some maneuvering to shuffle their positions. Once Mike's body had blocked the water from her hair, she sighed in relief. He watched as she pulled her long braids up and worked them into a knot. "Okay?" he asked.

She nodded and reached up to steady the wobbly bun atop her head.

"I can run downstairs, and we can—"

"Do you touch yourself in the shower thinking about me?" she asked.

"You're on one today," he said, his face heating from the steam and her question.

"I know, but do you?"

"All the time," he admitted. He couldn't look her in the face.

"I think about you too. And touch myself."

Mike felt like he was floating.

"If we do it together, we can save water."

They laughed. "That's a great point, actually."

There was a metal pole running up the back of the shower with triangular baskets jutting out at regular intervals, holding a dizzying amount of bath products. Toni reached for her loofah and pumped a body wash that smelled like coconuts onto the sponge. "I'm a fount of good ideas."

"I know."

Mike had dreamed of moments like this, tender moments where Toni touched him, and he touched her in the unhurried way of people who had all the time in the world. As he waited for her over the years, he'd reminded himself that he could only control himself. In those few moments when he had the chance, he touched her without an ounce of pressure, never asking, only giving. It had never been enough, but he couldn't say that a chance to touch Toni — even if only an accidental brush of their bodies — was anything less than lovely.

And to be fair, they'd been touching one another so much since the semester ended, but this shower was the stuff of dreams.

They stared lovingly into one another's eyes as they soaped their bodies from necks to feet, first with her loofah and then with their wet, soapy hands. They gave each other soft pecks on the lips, the cheeks, the center of his back, behind her ear. He was speechless as she used too much body wash and both her hands to stroke him until he came in a wet spatter that landed on her stomach. And then she sang her approval as he turned her toward the back of the tub and used three fingers in her pussy and one in her ass to return the favor.

But the best moment was when she leaned against him on weak legs for their final rinse. "Once I can breathe again, I'm going to ride you into the sun."

"That's the corniest thing I've ever heard you say," he said, bending forward to kiss her. "But I approve."

TONI THOUGHT she'd bit off more than she could chew in the parking lot of The Stax. Every day since had just reaffirmed her assessment that Mike Hernandez could give her a run for her money sexually. Still, she could not stop herself from wanting more of him. Even though she shouldn't. Even though she didn't have the time. Even though her sabbatical was supposed to be focused on herself. She wanted Mike in a way that was almost unholy. Because some things, she realized, had no substitute. Because there was a difference between being alone and lonely.

She pushed Mike onto her bed. He stacked the pillows under his head and got comfortable. "I don't want to miss anything," he said in that deep voice that made her pussy wet near constantly these days. He looked at her with a boyish grin on his face and a deep, penetrating glare in his eyes.

Her knees went weak.

Toni happily spent a small fortune on sex toys because she believed it was good self-care to invest in her own pleasure. But no toy she had in her bedside table had gotten her off quite as good as Mike's hands. Nothing felt like the molten pleasure in her guts as she crawled between his legs and rolled a condom down his shaft. Nothing made her feel quite as safe as when he held her steady with their hands pressed palm to palm. They used their free hands to get his shaft at her opening, and she slowly sank down the length. Her toys had given her so many orgasms, so much joy, but when Mike's thick length bottomed out inside her pussy and his thighs lifted under her ass for more support, Toni accepted that she had been missing something in her celibacy.

"You can set the pace, querida." She believed him, but she could also hear the strain in his voice. And when she bent forward to place her hands on his chest, she could feel his heart racing.

He grabbed her hips and gave her an encouraging squeeze.

A part of her wished he would push her, flip her over onto her back, and fuck into her until she was gasping for breath and screaming nonsense. But Toni had been in those relationships;

she'd dated those men. Over the years, they'd broken her heart and her spirit, stolen her will to care or try again, and that one time, her dissertation topic. She stared into Mike's face and realized that he was not the man who would take control, and the woman she was today preferred it that way.

She started to circle her hips, lifting onto her knees and back down.

Mike grunted and dropped his legs, but he tightened his grip on her, helping her ride him, giving her a bit of his strength. And he never looked away.

Toni moved on top of him with increasing speed. No matter how loud they moaned or how hard their bodies slapped together, not even when she got too excited and bounced too high and he slipped out of her, Mike's eyes never left her — not even when they changed positions and moved to their sides. Mike pushed into her from behind. His big hand held her left leg in the air, but his right hand cupped her neck and turned her face so they could stare into one another's depths while he pounded into her in long, strong strokes.

The only time he broke contact was late in the middle of the night when they were covered in sweat, muscles sore, throats dry and raw. They should have stopped but couldn't; the need from these past few weeks for her — years for him — was too great. So, they raided her toy drawer for more condoms, lubrication, and for the very last time, her favorite bullet toy.

Toni was back on top, riding him slowly with the last of her energy.

"Just one more," she moaned. Begged. "I just want to make you come one more time."

"I don't know," he groaned, squeezing her ass and lifting his hips. "Holy shit."

Mike's abs jumped at the soft buzzing sound of her vibrator. She moaned when it touched her clit.

He groaned when it grazed the base of his dick.

And then she bent forward, holding the toy between their bodies, ripping that very last orgasm from them both.

They slept most of the next day.

CHAPTER TWENTY-FIVE

Toni woke up for the first time in a month without Mike.

He'd been there when she fell asleep, his face pressed into the crook of her neck, his arm wrapped around her waist. But she woke up alone, and she loved it; her queen-sized bed was big enough for her and Paw, but adding Mike made her comfortable bed a tight squeeze. So tight that last week she'd found herself reconsidering that king-sized bed all over again. She'd closed her laptop and told herself that she was just exploring options for the future — whenever she got around to renovating her bedroom. She knew it was a lie, but as long as she didn't pull out the measuring tape, she rationalized, everything would be okay.

When she woke up alone this morning, she starfished on the bed and smiled for a few moments before pressing her face into his pillow. The pillowcase smelled like the spicy shampoo he used, a bottle of which was sitting in her bathroom right now. And then she curled her body around his pillow and drifted back to sleep for a few minutes more.

Toni had no appointments, no meetings, no deadlines; nothing to do but rest.

The next time she woke up, she got out of bed and walked right into the shower. The scent of his shampoo was stronger in here; his presence was stronger here. There was his shampoo and conditioner on the shower shelf she'd cleared out for him, not consciously, just as a matter of course. And then his electric toothbrush, toothpaste, and deodorant in her medicine cabinet. Under the sink, she'd even consolidated some space for his beard trimmer, shave gel, and hair products. There were so many damn hair products he had to keep the overflow in the bathroom downstairs.

The rest of her bedroom looked the same but also didn't. Most of Mike's clothes were downstairs in the spare bedroom, but when she opened her underwear drawer, a few pairs of his boxers were neatly rolled in the corner. His cologne was nested neatly on her perfume stand. The floor next to her bed was littered with condom wrappers, and her face flushed as she collected them and threw them in the bathroom trash can.

Toni got dressed in a pair of biker shorts, a bralette, and a vintage Janet Jackson concert tee she'd cut into a crop top and then spent a serene couple of hours setting her room back to rights. She changed the sheets on the bed, cleaned the tub, and washed her sex toys, but even those chores were shaped by Mike. Normally, Paw woke her up first thing in the morning for his food and attention, but with Mike, her asshole cat climbed over her to sit on his hip until his actual favorite human woke up. Toni endured the disrespect because it gave her another half an hour of sleep each morning, and that was a luxury she couldn't have fathomed a month ago.

When she finally made it downstairs, she found Paw asleep on his cat tower and a handwritten note from Mike on the kitchen counter in front of the coffee machine, somewhere he knew she'd find it.

Text me what you want for lunch. Be back by 2.

She read the two lines over and over with a smile on her face. He could have texted her that, but there was something about seeing his handwriting that made it more personal; intimate. It wasn't beautiful script, just neat and clear, the kind of writing that was easily legible to students.

But it was his.

She read the note one last time and realized what had been snagging her brain all morning. Toni's plan for her sabbatical of renovations was to finally make her house a home for her and Paw. But in just over a month, Mike had worked his way through the cracks. He didn't fill a room when he walked in or command it with his presence like Alejandro, but he was far from invisible. Mike, Toni now realized, found a corner to himself and made it his own, and then he made that corner so attractive that you couldn't bear to look away.

She realized now that if she wasn't careful, her and Paw's home would have Mike built into the foundation. Paw would love that. But would she?

That question was heavy. It made her muscles ache and her head hurt. It made that knot in the center of her back begin to tighten again. That question required focus, introspection, honesty, and caffeine. But this stress was not how she wanted to spend her sabbatical.

She turned away from the coffee pot and strode across the living room to the downstairs bathroom. She avoided all of Mike's hair stuff and pulled the basket of her own haircare products from the wicker shelving unit behind the door.

There was no better way to avoid thinking than for her to finally take these braids out.

MIKE NORMALLY TRIED NOT to overschedule summer break. His semesters were always jam-packed, and summer was his time to reset.

Sometimes he packed a suitcase and spent the summer at home, sleeping in his childhood bed, doing puzzles with his father, helping his mom at her veterinary office. Sometimes he traveled home to La Union alone or with his family for a real vacation. The only real constant in his summers was that he usually couldn't wait to get out of this small town.

Early in the spring semester, in the middle of a particularly brutal winter, he'd been planning to spend the break at his parents' house. A few weeks in the dry desert heat sounded like heaven in comparison to the gray, icy winter. But one day, right after midterms, he ran into Toni at an undergraduate symposium. She was sitting in the front row, staring intently at the schedule, probably hoping for a few moments of peace before the event started.

Mike slid into a seat, an empty chair between them, surprised to catch her without the entourage of graduate students and young faculty who usually followed her around. He'd cleared his throat, and when she looked up, there was a small smile on her lips for him.

He was speechless. They'd stared at one another for a few moments, and for him, there was only the two of them in that room, if not the entire campus.

Mike didn't know exactly how long that moment lasted, but it lingered long enough to make an impression. Eventually, Alejandro slid into the seat between them and immediately started talking to Mike about a scholarship committee they were on together. Marie and Deja had quickly snagged the seats on Toni's other side, and then the event started. Toni's eyes had never locked on Mike's again. But the warmth of that moment had made the rest of winter bearable, so he'd decided to stay in town this summer.

Just in case.

It was supposed to be a long shot. He'd only wanted to stay close on the off chance that maybe... Every moment with Toni had always been full of maybes, but even he couldn't believe the last month and a half of his life. He hadn't planned to do quite so much manual labor, but she was worth every sore muscle.

Still, he didn't mind a morning in his element.

"What's up, Doctor Hernandez?" Rickey said, knocking on his open office door.

Mike looked up with a smile and sat back in his chair. "You tell me, doctoral candidate Chávez."

Rickey ducked his head, walked into Mike's office, and sat in the chair on the other side of the desk. "I still can't believe it."

"I just signed the electronic paperwork. Believe it."

There were few things that could have gotten Mike to leave the bubble he'd been in with Toni — especially not first thing in the morning when she was naked and pressed against his side — but Rickey's qualifying exams were worth it.

"So, what now?" Rickey asked.

Mike sighed audibly.

"Okay, hear me out," Rickey started.

"No. I told you the plan is to take a break. Go visit your girlfriend."

"I am! I'm driving out at the end of the week, but I can do some research and start some grant applications while I'm there."

"Sounds great," Mike said blandly.

"And what else?"

Mike stared back in silence.

"Seriously?"

"Seriously. I'd rather you rest for the rest of the summer. It'll go faster than you think. But I'd also prefer you to rest instead of come to me mid-semester burned out."

"Again," Rickey said. Mike hadn't planned to point that out, but it was true.

"Again," Mike echoed. "Learn how to pace yourself. You'll thank me later."

"I guess," Rickey admitted, deflating in his chair.

Mike leaned forward. "And learn how to celebrate your wins."

Rickey's smile returned, and he nodded. "Alright. So what about you? What are you up to? 'Cause word around Schlessinger Hall is we're about to get a new Director."

"We're not announcing that until the beginning of the semester," Mike said.

Rickey laughed. "All the grad students know already. But I'll pretend to be surprised. Congratulations."

Mike stood, and Rickey followed suit. "Thanks."

"So maybe I'll be the one telling you to pace yourself in a few months."

"Good. I'll probably need the reminder." Mike slipped his laptop into his messenger bag. "Drive safe, alright?"

Rickey picked up his backpack and headed toward the bed. "I will. Enjoy the rest of the summer, Doctor H."

"You too."

Once Rickey was gone, Mike pulled his phone from the charger on the corner of his desk. He'd been waiting for a text message from Toni all morning, and he tried not to freak out when her name wasn't in any of his message notifications.

Alejandro had sent him a bunch of photos of him and Deja on the beach. Pictures he didn't ask for that were mostly just meant to rub salt in the wound of Mike's failure with Toni. They didn't hit the way they would have a month ago, and that at least made Mike smile. He liked a nice picture of Deja sipping from a frozen cocktail that was bigger than her head and then sent his friend an emoji flipping him off.

His sister, Patricia, planned to visit him in the fall and was spamming him with possible dates. He rolled his eyes and chose a date range at random; they were all in the middle of the semester, so it didn't matter. All he wanted was to see her and maybe, possibly, introduce her to Toni.

Speaking of, she still hadn't texted him, and he was debating calling. He didn't want to overwhelm her, but he couldn't help but be nervous that a morning apart could undo the fragile relationship they'd been building.

He knew she was awake, but since she hadn't messaged him, he started to wonder if maybe she needed a break from him. It was so easy for the doubts to set in. When it came to Toni, the doubts were more familiar than these past few weeks of happiness.

He was just considering heading home to hide and pick up his mail when his phone vibrated in his hands.

Empanada Towne?

Toni ended her message with the big eyes emoji.

Mike's chest had been tightening all morning each time he glanced at his phone, but it was like a balloon burst when he saw her message.

Sounds great. Tell me what you want?

It took a while for Toni's response to arrive, and when it did, it was in the form of a voice note. Mike listened to her overly detailed order, saved the message, sent her a thumbs-up emoji, and rushed out of his office before anyone could try to rope him into more work.

A morning away from Toni was enough.

BY THE TIME MIKE ARRIVED, Toni had undone barely a quarter of her braids. She was annoyed at herself, uncaffeinated, and hungry as hell. Somehow, she'd decided that this was all Mike's fault.

She opened the door in a huff and spun around before he could even say hello.

"Uh, Toni, you okay?"

"Yes," she called, even though she was stomping to the downstairs bathroom to wash her hands.

"Um...you sure?" he called from the living room.

Toni rolled her eyes at the sound of Paw's excited meow. In the bathroom, she pulled the towel from her shoulders and dumped it into the wicker hamper full of Mike's clothes. She sighed and started dragging the hamper back down the hallway.

Mike was standing in the living room watching her warily.

She sighed at the sight of him.

He was wearing a light gray summer suit without a tie or shoes. His brown skin was a darker shade of golden brown, which made his dark hair seem a deeper black. He was holding her annoying ass cat in the crook of his left arm and a large bag of empanadas in the other.

"What's wrong?" he asked, swallowing nervously. "Did...I... do something?"

Once again, Toni knew she was in over her head. She'd been worried about letting Mike get too comfortable in her house when she should have been worried about letting him get too comfortable in her heart. And based on the way it skipped a beat at the sight of him looking perfectly at home in *her* home, all that worrying was too late.

She gestured toward the hair she'd undone. "I decided to take out my braids, and now my arms hurt, and I'm hungry, and I didn't drink any coffee today. I'm pissed."

A month and a half of sleep, great sex, and hard work couldn't erase the burnout; she knew that. But she'd felt so good and normal for so long that feeling unhinged just because her day hadn't gone exactly as she'd expected reminded her of just how exhausted she really was. But it was seeing Mike looking put together and at ease that tipped her over the edge because she wanted that. She wanted that with him, and instead of saying it, she'd let herself come undone.

She waited for the look of disgust on his face. She'd been here before when a man who was certain he wanted to date her was confronted with the reality of her — rather than his fantasy — and ran away. It was inevitable, and yet she thought it would hurt more with Mike, which was ridiculous but true.

"Why didn't you wait for me?" he said gently.

"What?"

"Come on. Let's eat lunch, and we can finish your hair together."

"*We?*"

"Have you eaten?" he asked Paw, turning toward the kitchen as if the matter was settled.

"Excuse me, what do you mean, we? Do you know how to do my hair?"

Mike scoffed at her, but he aimed the sound at her cat. Her cat! "I have an entire PhD, Antonia. I'm sure I can learn." He raised the pitch of his voice and bent down so Paw knew this next bit was for him. "She can teach me, but she just had to do it herself."

"Not you talking about me to my cat," Toni said, picking up the hamper and following him.

When she made it to the kitchen, Mike was kneeling down to scoop some food into Paw's bowl while the cat wound his way through Mike's legs.

Toni rolled her eyes at them and walked through the door into the utility room. She sorted his clothes into the hampers she kept back there. She had enough clothes to start a load of darks and did so before heading back into the kitchen.

Just like her bed, the kitchen felt smaller with Mike in it, but not unwelcome. Here, too, she found his presence overwhelming as he washed his hands and started to load their empanadas into her air fryer.

"You want some wine?" she asked in a hard tone.

"Sure," he said.

She squeezed behind him to get to the fridge. She pulled the first bottle of white wine she laid eyes on and turned to find Mike watching her, and she startled.

"You can ask me for help, Toni."

"With my hair, Mike?" she asked sarcastically.

"Yes," he responded, his voice serious but warm. "With anything."

CHAPTER TWENTY-SIX

"Just use the pads of your fingers. *Not* your fingernails."

"Yes, I heard you the other three times you said that."

Toni was sitting in a dining room chair she'd pushed against the kitchen counter in front of the sink. She'd talked him through the process in excruciating detail — how to carefully undo the twists she'd put in after detangling her hair, how much product to use, and how to gently cleanse her scalp.

Mike could tell she was nervous. He wanted to be understanding, but he was also exhausted, and it was late. "Toni, please. Just let me wash your hair so we can go to bed. My neck and back are killing me."

"How do you think I feel?"

"Then do it for both of us," he practically begged.

She chewed on her bottom lip for a few moments, trying to hide the vulnerability just underneath the surface. "Okay." That one word was such a delicate whisper that his gut clenched.

He bent forward and kissed her on the lips. "I won't fuck it up."

She laughed, and it tasted like everything. "I have faith in you."

"Liar," he said, kissing her one more time. "Alright, sit back and relax the best you can." He flexed his fingers in the air. "I'm about to make magic."

"Oh, lord," Toni mumbled.

ALL THEIR LIVES, Toni and Toya had tried to dissect the things they liked in a man. Toya had a thing for a man who could make things. Anything. She'd gotten her heart broken a time or two by a few artists and a couple of guys who worked construction.

Toni was agnostic on a Bob the Builder ass man, to be honest. She could put together flat-pack furniture just as well as anyone else. But as Mike gently, carefully, and by the end, expertly washed her hair, she realized she should have been asking for a man like this. He handled each twist as if it was precious, unraveling them delicately until he had a large enough section to wash. At some point, every time he massaged her scalp, a moan slipped from her throat, different than all the other moans he'd pulled from her. She couldn't rank them, but having this man clean and caress her scalp was almost as good as when he touched her pussy.

When she washed her own hair, she was very conscious of time. How long it took to detangle. How long until her hot water heater gave out. But she lost track of time while Mike cleaned her hair and conditioned it and then smoothed her deep conditioner into the sections.

She fell asleep under his touch, and his soft voice pulled her awake.

"Okay, I'm done," he said. "How did I do?"

She yawned and arched her back. "Great. Let's go to bed."

Mike shook his head. "The label says to keep the deep conditioner in for thirty minutes." He picked up the small tub and reread the directions. "Leave in hair for fifteen to thirty minutes. Rinse thoroughly."

"God, you're adorable," she yawned. "I'll wash it out in the shower in the morning. Can you put the chair back, and I'll throw all that back in my basket?"

"Are you...sure?"

She grabbed the bottles from the counter and snatched the conditioner from his hands. "Very sure," she called, already walking away. "I'll clean the kitchen tomorrow."

She could hear Mike following her. She rushed to put away the detritus of hair washing, desperate to crawl into bed. When she walked back into the living room, she found Mike waiting for her at the bottom of the stairs with a tired smile on his face.

"You sure I did alright?" he asked innocently.

She swallowed the lump in her throat and nodded. "Ready for bed?"

He nodded and offered her his hand, leading her up to the second floor. They crowded into the bathroom as they had so many nights. While Mike washed his face, Toni put a shower cap over her head and then tied a satin scarf over that. She bumped him with her hip so she could get to the sink and brush her teeth. He squeezed her waist when he needed to rinse his face. She rinsed her mouth, and he moved behind her to reach for his toothbrush.

They switched back and forth, crowding the small pedestal sink, easily and happily sharing this tight space.

At some point, she stood up to see him standing behind her in the mirror, gargling his mouthwash. They locked eyes, and he lifted his eyebrows at her. "Childish," she laughed around her toothbrush.

He kissed her cheek before leaving the bathroom to change for bed.

Toni rinsed her mouth and followed him into the bedroom.

Mike crawled into bed and reclined on his side, watching her.

She undressed and threw on a thin t-shirt that came to her thighs. "I bet you've never seen anyone this sexy," she joked, walking to the light switch.

"I haven't," he said in all seriousness.

She turned around, and they locked eyes one more time before she turned off the light. Toni knew the way to her bed in the dark. She could navigate it with her eyes closed and so often had after a long day of teaching. But this time, she imagined that it was Mike's eyes drawing her to him. When she made it to the bed, he pulled the covers back and gathered her into his side.

This was their first night just sleeping in her bed.

She wished it didn't feel so good.

MIKE WOKE up in the middle of the night to Toni rubbing her face on his chest.

She'd wrapped both of her legs around one of his and snuggled as close to him as it was possible to get, as she did most nights.

But what woke Mike up was the feeling of her damp hair on his chest. It took a while for his eyes to adjust, but once he could see her silhouette almost clearly, he saw that her cap and scarf had shifted out of place. It took a while to convince her to release him and turn on her other side without waking her.

He inched her scarf back into place before he placed her

head on a pillow. He wrapped his body around her back and pushed his knee between the juncture of her legs.

Once all was right with Toni, Mike drifted back to sleep.

CHAPTER TWENTY-SEVEN

Toni should have known today would be terrible the minute she opened her eyes.

It was late July, and this was about the time that the end of summer break usually started to weigh heavy on her spirit. It didn't matter that she was on sabbatical and had no classes to prepare or committee assignments to accept; her body had over a decade of hardwiring for what this time of year meant.

Also, it was raining.

They'd planned to keep working on the backyard today — Mike was still trying to convince her that they were so close to... something — but the sound of rain hitting the roof meant that plans would have to change, and something about that made a pit open in Toni's stomach.

Surely it had rained at some point this summer, but Toni couldn't remember those days suddenly. In her mind, every day had been nothing but clear blue skies and low humidity. She lay in bed listening to the rain with one ear and Mike's heartbeat with the other, certain that this was the first rain since the spring.

"You're thinking too loud," Mike said before kicking the blankets off them while he stretched.

She shifted away from him and then laughed as he rolled on top of her. She could only admit it to herself, but Toni loved when he gave her all of his weight. She loved the way his body fit perfectly between her legs, giving her inner thighs the tiniest bit of burning stretch.

"I'm not thinking," she lied.

He grunted into the crook of her neck, and it made her smile.

"You're judging me loudly," she sighed. "So let's just say we're even."

His mouth moved to her ear. "No."

She started to reply, but then he started kissing his way down her neck and her chest. He gripped her right breast in his hand and licked her nipple through her nightshirt.

"God," she moaned as he gave the same attention to her other breast.

His fingers played with her nipples as he kept moving back down her body. She spread her legs for him.

Suddenly the rain was peaceful, a calming soundtrack to Mike pushing her shirt up her stomach, grabbing her behind her thighs, and pulling her down the bed with a sharp tug, a playful smile on his face.

"Childish," she whispered, but that word fell apart on a groan as Mike lowered his mouth to her pussy.

He licked her from her opening up to her clit and back again and again. His nose bumped her clit as he buried his face in her sex.

Toni pushed her own hands under her shirt to tease her nipples, but she kept her gaze on the top of Mike's head as he licked at her folds, tasting every inch.

And then his hands smoothed up the backs of her thighs,

lifting her legs before spreading them wide. He looked up briefly when she whimpered.

She could feel his smile against her pussy as he really got to work.

Mike held Toni open with his big hands behind her knees as he settled his lips over her clit.

"Oh, shit." Toni pressed her head back on the pillow and shut her eyes tight. She didn't want to come too fast, but also she did, and Mike knew it.

He sucked at her clit until she was on the verge of coming and then pulled back to use his tongue again. Her legs started to shake, so he tightened his hold.

She moved her hands over his, and they both managed to spread her thighs wider.

He looked at her again, pulling back so she could watch him swipe the flat of his tongue up and then circle her clit. The tip of his nose and lips were wet.

She closed her eyes on a shocked gasp. She couldn't imagine lasting much longer.

And so, of course, that's when Mike pulled away. "Get a condom, Antonia." He wiped his mouth and then used that same wet hand to stroke himself.

She blinked up at him, her gaze darting from the fire in his eyes to the head of his dick.

She was practically vibrating when she reached for the bedside table.

She stretched out her arm to him, but he shook his head. She frowned.

"Put it on me."

She rolled her eyes in annoyance but also lust. She couldn't understand how he could do this to her every time. How he understood her so well in just a few weeks.

"Thinking too loud," he groaned.

Toni sat and ripped open the condom wrapper. "Good point."

He smiled, but his gaze was focused on her hands. She heard him suck in a sharp breath in anticipation.

Toni wished she had the restraint to tease him the way he'd been teasing her. Maybe next time. This time, she aimed the condom at the tip of his dick, and her fingers tangled with his. He only let go of his shaft and the air in his lungs as she started to roll the condom down his length.

She barely got to feel the triumph before he reached for her knees again and gave her another sharp tug.

Toni flopped on her back with a loud yelp followed by a deep groan as Mike moved the tip of his dick between her lips, bumped her clit, and then made his way back to her opening.

They groaned together as he pushed inside and retreated, leaving her gasping and her aching hole clenching, begging for more.

"Please," she whispered.

"Tell me," he whispered back.

"Tell you what? Goddamn."

She loved looking at him from this vantage point, the curve of his stomach, the angle of his nose, the way that one piece of hair flopped forward, his beautiful brown gaze hot on her.

"Tell me what you were thinking about," he said in a voice rough with need.

Toni's body was writhing, but her brain started throwing up alarms. "It's raining," she said because that was the beginning. Unfortunately, they both knew it wasn't the end.

He pressed the head at her opening again. She was ready to beg.

"And what else?"

"I—"

He pushed the head inside and stilled. Toni shivered at the lovely pressure of him stretching her open, but she frowned as he pulled out.

"We only have a little time left," she whimpered.

His face fell.

Toni wished he hadn't pushed. She wanted to take it back, but she couldn't. They'd spent the entire summer in a bubble. Many bubbles, actually. There was the fictional town where they never ran into their students or other faculty at the grocery store. There was the fantasy of their lives without their friends or work. And then there was the ultimate alternate universe in her house. They'd been pretending for so long that they were just spending a little time together, avoiding the fact that Mike had practically moved in. But once they were back on contract and their friends returned, fantasy would meet reality, and this would all end because it had to.

Because Toni didn't shit where she ate.

Because Toni didn't want to be one of those HR memos.

Because Toni did not plan to spend her sabbatical navigating a new relationship unless it was her relationship with herself.

"We're back on contract in a couple of weeks," she said.

He took a deep breath before he spoke. "I am. Your sabbatical starts in two weeks."

"I— Holy shit!" she screamed as he pressed forward, entering her in one long, beautifully agonizing invasion. She curled her body forward — curving her back, lifting her legs — and reached for his hips, not wanting to guide him, just needing to feel his muscles move while he fucked into her.

Apparently, their conversation had come to an end, and Toni was somehow both heartbroken and relieved.

Mike pushed her legs open, gripping her inner thighs with

a hold that hurt so good as he stroked into her with increasing force.

Toni's body tried to lie to her as the orgasm built. The pleasure told her that they had all the time in the world.

The rain didn't matter.

The end of summer meant nothing.

This was a beginning, not an end.

And she was grateful.

MIKE HAD ALWAYS BEEN ATTUNED to Toni's moods, even when he only saw her a couple of times a week. He could always tell when something wasn't right. Usually, he had to watch her in frustration, trying to figure out by the set of her frown or annoyed glances what was bothering her, wishing they were close enough for her to confide in him.

Now that they were close enough, he almost wished for ignorance again.

They'd been working at her house all summer — one small project here, another there — and one more sign that summer was more than half over was the fact that the list of projects was dwindling. Her office was practically finished — new floors, fresh paint, very expensive furniture. The backyard needed one or two more days of turned soil and a few more stones for the paths from the fence and patio to the weed-free flower beds. They hadn't finalized plans for what to plant, but they still had time.

Mike hoped they still had time.

He was trying not to let her fear infect him, but it was difficult because her fear was valid. It wasn't as if he hadn't known it was coming, but when Toni said fall semester was looming, it all became more real than he was ready to accept.

All day he'd been trying to distract them from what was coming, but no matter what he said, it was as gray and gloomy inside as outside in the rain.

Thankfully, they didn't need to talk much to paint the spare bedroom.

They'd spent the late morning and early afternoon working their way around the small room; Mike used the paint roller, and Toni swiped the paintbrush around the edges to get the details. It was a partnership they'd figured out while painting her office. They worked so well together that he'd had to bite his tongue not to point it out. He was desperate to convince her that this was just an example of all the things they could do together, but he couldn't push her like that.

"That's it. We're done?"

He looked in confusion around the room, surprised at how quickly they'd completed this task.

Toni swiped her paintbrush carefully through a corner. She stepped back and looked at the wall in front of them. "That's it."

The tone of her voice broke his heart. "Toni."

His phone rang with a text message, and Mike grunted in frustration. He turned to glare at the phone briefly, but when he turned back, Toni was shifting away.

"You should get that," she said, looking everywhere but at him.

He didn't care. Whoever was texting him, he didn't care. But she turned away from him and started pouring the excess paint into the open can. There was something about her cleaning up their last project that hurt in a way it was hard to define.

He needed a moment to process, so he did as she said.

He immediately wished he hadn't.

"Alejandro, Deja, and Marie are back."

It was only because he had oriented in her direction that he saw the way she froze, the way her back tensed. "Great," she said dispassionately. "When do you pick them up from the airport?"

He swallowed the painful lump in his throat. "No, they're back."

She turned sharply, looking at him with bunched eyebrows over her left shoulder.

"Their flights arrived this morning, and they split a shuttle from town." The words tasted like ash in his mouth.

"Oh." The word was nothing but smoke from her lips.

"Yeah," he said, feeling like that breath hollowed him out.

"I'm gonna put this in the garage." She picked up the can of paint and clutched it to her chest.

She walked from the room with even strides while Mike's heart shattered.

THEY BOTH KNEW it was the last time.

They acknowledged the end of it all by touching one another softly, kissing each other deeply, and moving against each other slowly. It was unplanned and unhurried, and so goddamn sad.

Mike followed her to the garage. He took the paint from her hands and placed it on the shelving he'd built. And then he wrapped himself around her back, kissing the curve of her ear.

She wanted him to tell her that it didn't have to end. That whatever they'd said in the spring didn't have to hold in the summer. She wanted him to give her a reason to break her deals with herself.

She wanted him to give her a reason. One more reason.

In truth, he'd given her a summer of reasons, so many moments just begging her to reconsider, to ask herself what she wanted now versus what she'd wanted in the spring. To ask herself what her brain said after a little rest and a lot of happiness. It would have been so easy to convince herself to change her mind, and that was the problem in the end.

No one could gaslight Toni like herself. When she wanted something — someone — she could make any excuse. She could ignore every red flag. She could tell herself everything was good as the world burned around her. She'd done it in grad school with her ex. She'd done it at her last job, wanting to keep it even though she hated it more each day. But she just couldn't do that to herself again.

So she let Mike wrap her in his arms. She let him push his hands under her shirt and caress her breasts the way he'd learned she liked. She pulled her leggings down and kicked them over her feet. She groaned when he pushed his shorts down and his bare dick pressed into her ass. She spread her legs and grabbed him by the head. She cherished the sound of his moan and guided him inside her one more time.

She ignored the alarm that he was bare and reveled in the feeling of him skin-to-skin, the feeling she'd been trying not to think about all summer.

She covered his arms with hers and squeezed because the tight hold tricked her into thinking there was more.

She swallowed all the things she wanted to say but couldn't find the words.

She came not once but twice, just from the perfection of his thrusts and her own desire.

She forced herself not to cry until he was gone.

And for the first time in weeks, Paw Robeson curled his body into Toni's stomach as they fell asleep together.

MIKE SLEPT in his own bed for the first time in nearly two months.

It didn't feel like home.

CHAPTER TWENTY-EIGHT

Toni was emptying the last of the bags of soil Mike bought into a decorative planter she'd picked up on her last visit to the hardware store. Decorative planters weren't part of her plan for the yard, but as soon as Linda had started asking about "that nice young man who'd been with her all summer," Toni had just started adding things to her order to avoid her questions. Of all the things Toni did not want to talk about, Mike was top of the list.

"My god, please tell me this isn't how you spent the entire summer."

Toni turned at the sound of Deja's voice to see her and Marie strolling down the stone path she and Mike had laid without a care in the world.

"Someone got a tan," Toni called.

Deja twirled in a circle. She was wearing a sky-blue dress, fitted at the bust and hanging loose around her thighs, but it billowed out around her in an almost-perfect circle.

Almost. Marie swatted Deja's dress with an annoyed flick

of her hand. "Can you stop doing that? You're not in Brazil anymore?"

Deja frowned and came to a wobbly standstill. Her shoulders slumped forward. "Believe me, I know. Swear to god, America has a smell," she whispered to them.

"Duh," Toni said.

"Big time," Marie said before turning to Toni. "What about me? Do I have a tan?"

Toni looked her over. "A trucker's tan." Toni pointed a finger covered in soil at Marie's arm and the harsh tan line on her bicep. "What the hell were you doing during that professional development retreat? I thought you were in Milwaukee?"

Marie smiled. "I was. And mostly, I was bored as shit. But after that, I went to visit a friend at South Dakota State—"

"Damn, girl, why?" Deja asked playfully.

Marie rolled her eyes with a smile. "Because I have other friends. And I like to go camping."

"God, why?" Toni asked, her voice dripping in shock and disbelief.

"*Anyway*," Marie stressed, "I was visiting my friend to catch up, but also because her school just unionized."

"Good for them," Deja said while Toni nodded.

"For sure. And get this, they were able to make provisions in their CBA for instructors and even adjuncts," Marie said.

Toni crossed her arms over her chest. "Now, how the hell did they do that?"

Marie smiled smugly. "That's what I wanted to know. So I basically spent the summer interning with their union."

Deja threw her arm over Marie's shoulders. "Well, look at you! I don't know how that explains the tan, but I'm proud of you."

Marie smiled shyly. "I'm good for some things."

Toni frowned and snapped her fingers. "You're good for a

lot. Stop talking like that."

"Oh, there's the Toni I know. I thought there was a chance you'd changed while we were gone."

"Why?" Toni asked, thinking of Mike immediately.

Deja shrugged. "You basically went radio silent all summer, and then we show up to find your yard looking barren but manicured."

"I kinda liked the haunted house vibe," Marie said.

"Wow," Toni breathed.

"And you dug those overalls up from 1998."

"Wow," Toni said again. "If you must know, I was resting."

It wasn't a complete lie. She'd never slept so good as she had in Mike's arms.

"That's what Alejandro said." Deja rolled her eyes affectionately. She hated being forced to admit that her boyfriend was sometimes right.

Toni smiled nervously. "What made Alejandro think I was resting?"

Her friends squinted at her, which was the first sign Toni had that her question hadn't made any damn sense. It sounded right in her head.

"Girl, your undereye bags had undereye bags when we left," Marie said.

"Goddamn, did you two come over here just to roast me?"

"No, that's a bonus. We missed you, bitch! We wanted to see how your sabbatical is going since you aren't answering your phone."

"Huh?" Toni's hands flew to the breast pockets on her overalls and then every other pocket she could think of. "I must have left it inside. I didn't even realize."

"Look at you," Marie teased.

"Isn't it great? Alejandro and I had cell reception, but those data charges didn't make any sense to me, so we barely used our phones unless there was free Wi-Fi. And some of those hotels barely had Wi-Fi, so we just," Deja shrugged easily, "checked out. It was lovely."

Marie shrugged Deja's arm off her. "That's her way of saying they've been fucking all through South America. Anyway, I had cell reception, I just didn't want to talk to anyone from here. No offense."

"None taken," Toni laughed.

"Some offense taken," Deja added.

"So, what'd you get up to while we were gone?" Marie asked Toni.

Toni had been dreading that question for days. She'd trailed sadly behind Mike, helping him collect all the things he'd left at her house — things she hadn't even noticed because they had found a home — and wondered how she would explain her summer. How she would explain that there was an empty closet where his clothes had been, an entire drawer in her dresser for his underwear and socks, a laptop charger behind the couch that he'd forgotten, and a shelf in her shower she couldn't bear to use again because it was his.

"Um...just house stuff," Toni said, turning away and walking toward the back door.

"God, really?" Deja asked. "You didn't have any fun?"

Toni didn't answer. She didn't want to lie, but she was also too nervous to open her mouth, afraid of what might come out. But it wasn't the lie that had her worried; it was the thought that she might say Mike's name, that she might tell Deja and Marie about every second she'd spent with him in painful and filthy detail.

Or maybe she would just cry. It had been a week, and sometimes that was the only way to get to sleep.

"Nope," she forced herself to say. "No fun." A lie felt safer than sharing her pain.

"Told you," Marie muttered. "You can Venmo me my winnings."

Toni pushed the door open, smiling sadly that at least her pain had won Marie a probably trifling amount of cash. "I should lock you two assholes out," she called over her shoulder.

"Don't do that," Deja cried.

"You're lucky I want to show off all my renovations."

"Okay, but can a bitch get a glass of lemonade or ice water or something?"

"No," Toni said, but she was already laughing as she toed off the old tennis shoes she used for the garden.

MIKE HAD BEEN STARING at the baseball game for at least half an hour when the intercom in his condo buzzed. He walked toward the front door in a daze.

"Yeah?"

"It's me. Let me in," Alejandro grumbled.

"Did I invite you over and forget it?"

Alejandro's only answer was a loud sigh.

Mike made sure to press the intercom button so Alejandro could hear his own sigh and know that he felt the same way, and then he pressed the buzzer. He unlocked the door to his condo and went back to his seat.

He was supposed to be watching the game and finishing his syllabi for the upcoming semester, but it was hard to focus. All he could think about was Toni.

He'd gotten out of bed every day for the past week with Toni on his mind. No matter what he did or didn't do, the memory of her never let him rest. This morning, he'd gone for a long run that did nothing but aggravate his left knee. He was just as frustrated and annoyed after his shower.

Even masturbating didn't help clear his head. About the only thing he did regularly was unlock his phone on the off chance that Toni might have texted him, nurturing the small hope that she might have changed her mind.

She had not.

And if it wasn't Toni at his door, Mike just wanted to be left alone. But here was Alejandro coming to ruin his already ruined day.

Alejandro pushed the front door open with a flourish, but Mike didn't even look in his direction. "Damn, really?"

"This is what happens when you show up at people's homes unannounced."

"Hmm," Alejandro said. He closed the front door and kicked off his shoes. He walked into the living room and set a bottle of something on the coffee table before sitting on the farthest end of the couch.

Mike squinted at it.

"Brazilian Cachaça. Deja thought you would like it. The bow was my idea."

That pulled a huff of laughter from Mike's nose and put a faint smile on his lips. "I'll thank Deja when I see her."

"Cabrón. So did Toni break your heart, or are you mad at yourself for wasting another summer with her?"

Mike turned to look at his friend. He was trying for a blank expression, but whatever Alejandro saw in his eyes shocked him.

"No fucking way. Dime."

"No," Mike said like a petulant child.

"Are you—" Alejandro cut himself off in frustration. "You've been annoying me for years about her, even when I didn't ask."

"Like I ever asked about Deja."

"Exactly, but the minute I had a chance with Deja, I took it."

"Good for you."

"And I told you about it."

"Not that I asked."

Alejandro glared at Mike. "What did Deja say before we left?"

"What?"

"When you dropped us off at the airport, what did she say to you?"

It took a few seconds for Mike to remember, and then he rolled his eyes. "You mean when she called me a pendejo?"

Alejandro grinned. "Before that."

That took a few more seconds. "A closed mouth don't get fed."

"Exactly."

"That's not the problem. I opened my mouth. I got fed."

"Past tense," Alejandro observed and shook his head.

"What?" Mike asked, annoyed. He sat up, ready to escort Alejandro the hell out of his house.

"Since you won't tell me, let me guess."

"Or not."

Alejandro started speaking as if Mike hadn't. "I bet you spent the summer giving Toni whatever she wanted."

"Is that a bad thing, Mr. 'I don't know, let me check Deja's calendar to see if I'm free?'"

"It is if you didn't also tell her what *you* wanted. And knowing you, I bet you didn't."

Mike turned back toward the television, not that he could even pretend to be interested in the game anymore.

"Hit a little too close to home," Alejandro said triumphantly. "So, how are you going to fix this? Do you have a plan?"

"Are you moving into relationship counseling now?"

Alejandro recoiled with a frown, but then his features softened. "I mean, we could—"

"Is that why you came here?"

"No. Actually, I was assuming she'd be here or you'd be at her house. I'm disappointed in you."

Mike looked away. He was disappointed in himself.

"Do you have plans tonight?" Alejandro asked.

"Yup!" Mike almost managed to sound excited. "I'm gonna have a couple drinks, wallow in my own self-pity, and then pass out on the couch again."

"Jesus," Alejandro muttered in disgust. "Or you can have dinner with us tonight."

Mike started to shake his head.

"Deja and Marie are at Toni's."

He stilled.

"I made a reservation for all five of us at this new Brazilian place in town."

It took all Mike's energy to keep his body, well, not still but doing exactly what it should — breathing in through his nose, exhaling softly from his mouth, heart beating evenly in his chest.

The worst thing about Alejandro was that when he knew he was right, he was insufferable. While Mike tried to pretend that his brain wasn't shifting into overdrive at this new information, Alejandro sat back in his seat, crossed his legs, and had the nerve to watch the baseball game like this was no big deal.

Mike didn't know how much time had passed. He didn't care. "What's the restaurant called? What time?"

At those questions, Alejandro stood abruptly. Mike frowned up at him. "I'll send the group chat the info in a bit," he said, already walking toward the door.

Mike rolled his eyes.

"Maybe you should ask if Toni needs a ride."

"She doesn't," Mike said bitterly. "She can take care of herself."

Alejandro slipped his shoes on. "Of course, she can. But maybe you should tell her that taking care of her makes you happy."

"Get out," Mike mumbled.

Alejandro laughed and pulled the door open.

"Welcome back," he said before Alejandro could leave.

Alejandro laughed again. "Thanks. Do better," he said and then pulled the door closed.

"DO YOU NEED A ROOMMATE?" Marie asked.

Toni was showing them the spare bedroom. The last time they'd visited, it had been fine but uninspired, like almost every other room in the house. But now it was lovely. She and Mike had painted the walls a soft blue that looked white when the sun hit it full on. She put her whitest sheets on the bed — the bedding she couldn't use in her master bedroom because sometimes she was too tired to take off all her makeup and she definitely didn't have the energy to bleach her sheets every week. She'd found a sky-blue comforter that complemented all the other blues in the room. All she needed was some nice pieces of artwork — and to get them framed — and this room would be done. Unfortunately, the thought of finishing this room made a yawning pit open in her gut. And sometimes she felt the pressure of phantom tears at the back of her eyes when she came in here. That's why she decided to stand in the doorway while Marie looked around and Deja took pictures on her phone.

"Absolutely not," Toni replied.

"Okay, but you have a whole spare bedroom that looks like something out of an interior design magazine."

"For guests. For visitors. Temporary tenants," Toni corrected.

"That's rude," Marie deadpanned.

"Don't care," Toni said.

"So anyway," Deja cut in, "did you get the people who did the floors to move your furniture around?"

"No, I did it myself."

"How?" Marie and Toni asked at the same time.

"No way you moved this furniture by yourself," Deja said.

Toni ran a hand over the back of her neck. It was hot, wet, and she brushed the sweat up the nape of her neck into her hairline. She'd make an appointment to get a fresh set of braids in a few weeks, but until then, she would enjoy letting her hair rest in a soft, frizzy bun atop her head. The next year of her life would have so many days of unconstructed time that she could use at her leisure; she didn't want to waste that time worrying about her hair.

Unfortunately, the only way she wanted to use that time lay behind a door she'd closed.

"No, I had a little help," she said breezily. Thankfully she'd turned away so neither of them could see the way those words made her cringe. "Come see the office."

She led them down the short hallway past the living room, but when she turned toward the stairs, she came up short. Toni sighed.

"Aw, hey, honey," Deja cried, reaching out to Paw.

Toni grabbed her hand and shook her head just as the cat let out a loud wail.

"Is he okay?"

"He's fine, just give him a second."

Paw let out another cry and then descended the stairs,

walking around them before he crossed the living room and climbed into his tree.

"Um, I don't know anything about cats, but yours seems mad at you."

Toni sighed and continued up the stairs. "He is," she said simply in a flat tone to convey that she would not be entertaining any follow-up questions.

"Um...okay," Deja said awkwardly. "Hey, you two wanna have dinner tonight? Me and Alejandro found a Brazilian restaurant nearby and thought it might be cute for us all to get together before the semester starts."

"We still have a few weeks before that," Marie said.

"Yeah, but technically, we're back on contract in like two weeks. And we haven't seen you all in so long, and we want to catch up. Like, who even knows what Mike's been up to?"

Toni tripped on the last step and stumbled onto the second floor of her house.

"You okay?" Deja asked.

"Yep, I'm fine. What time were you thinking? For dinner, I mean?"

Deja stepped onto the landing and shrugged. "Seven."

"Yeah, I'm down," Marie said. "Can I catch a ride?"

"Sure," Deja replied. "What about you, Toni? You coming?"

"Um, yeah. Sure."

"You want to drive or..." Deja's phone beeped, and she looked down at her screen, a small smile on her face. "Mike's in."

Toni felt each of the dozens of goosebumps as they erupted over her skin at the sound of his name.

"Y'all wanna catch a ride with him?" Deja asked.

"No, I'm good. I'll drive myself," Toni replied quickly. Denying herself was second nature.

CHAPTER TWENTY-NINE

After Alejandro left, Mike went for another run. But he put on a knee brace and visited the treadmill in the condo building instead. This run was slow and easy but just as fruitless.

When he made it back to his apartment, he started pacing in tight, frustrated circles around the living room. He clutched his phone in his hand, alternating between opening his silent chat with Toni and almost pressing her contact to call. But he couldn't do it. Every time he failed, he pictured Alejandro's disappointed face in his head. And he hated that.

Eventually, he pressed call, but not on Toni's number.

"Wenas," Patricia trilled into the phone.

"Qué pasó," he whispered in greeting.

"Oh, you sound sad. Qué tal? Is it about Antonia?"

There weren't many people Mike could tell about Toni. It would have been one thing if they were dating, it would have been another thing if they'd even been friends, but in reality, Toni was just a woman he kind of knew. His crush on her didn't give him any ownership of her time or attention, which made it hard to admit the way he felt about her to anyone he didn't trust implicitly. Or Alejandro, but that was only because Alejandro had been in the same boat with Deja. Now Mike was alone.

"Do you think I'm too passive?" he asked his sister.

"Where's this coming from?"

"Nowhere. Just..."

"Alejandro." Patricia was barely five foot three, and a strong wind could blow her away, but Mike sometimes likened her to a chihuahua, yappy and bold for no reason. "You tell that char-rule that I said—"

"I'm not telling him anything," Mike said, cutting her off.

"Fine, I'll find him online."

"Can you answer the question?"

"No, because I don't like it. You're not passive, you're patient."

"Okay, but am I *too* patient?"

"Is this about Antonia?" she asked again.

"Yeah," he admitted begrudgingly.

"And is she why you didn't come home this summer?"

"Yeah," he whispered.

"Was staying there worth it?"

The question brought to mind a picture of Toni on one of the last nights they spent together. She'd been barefoot in her backyard with a glass of wine in her hand and a smile on her face. They were enjoying the cool night air, the smell of fresh soil, and the sound of crickets. He couldn't stop the smile from spreading along his mouth. "Yeah," he whispered. "She was worth it."

"Then no, you're not too passive," she said. "Hold on."

Patricia put him on hold, and Mike took the opportunity to check his messages. The chat with Toni was still silent, but Deja had sent a message to their friend group chat and tagged Toni.

Toni you sure you don't want a ride to dinner?

"I'm back," Patricia said. "But I've got an appointment in a couple of minutes. There's nothing wrong with you. Alejandro's a dick, stop listening to him. If you waited all this time for Toni and she was worth it, all that matters is that you don't fuck it up now. Please don't make me agree with Alejandro."

Mike laughed. "I can do that."

"Chivo! I would be so pissed."

"Que la vaya bien, Pati."

"Bye, Mike."

Mike disconnected the call and sat on his couch, his mind racing. His phone vibrated, and his heart skipped a beat when he saw Toni's name for the first time in over a week. It wasn't their personal chat, but he didn't care.

Yeah, I'm good. I'll probably have to leave dinner early to check on my cat anyway.

TONI WAS PROCRASTINATING.

She'd walked through the entire house twice, first to make sure that all the windows were closed — they were — and a second time to find her cat.

Paw Robeson hadn't hidden from her since they'd moved to this house, and he'd needed a few days to adjust to the size. But even then, he wasn't so much hiding from her as hiding from the house. She knew exactly where he was. He slunk into the closet in the downstairs spare room and forced her to bring his food and water there. He also had no problem meowing loudly when he wanted her attention.

Toni found him in the spare bedroom again, although this

time, he was hiding under the bed. She had to hike her dress up over her hips and carefully get on the floor, lift the bed skirt, and shine a light under the bed. It reflected off his yellow eyes, and she sighed.

"Come out from under there."

Paw blinked slowly.

"I just put food in your bowl."

He didn't even blink this time.

She dropped the bed skirt and then climbed to her feet slowly. "Jesus," she groaned when her left knee popped. She turned off the flashlight on her phone and walked back to the door where she'd placed a small table her mother had given her. She snatched up the bag of treats she'd left there and shook it.

The thing about Paw was that he was greedier than he was petty. It took a few shakes, but eventually, he crawled out from under the bed with a long, back-breaking stretch. But he didn't run to her the way he normally did. Instead, he sauntered across the room, followed her and the bag of treats down the hallway, and after a good, long while, into the kitchen, where she dumped a few of his favorite hard treats on the floor next to his food bowl.

She stroked his back while he gobbled up the treats. He'd been getting a lot of treats lately. They both knew they were a bribe to assuage her guilt that she wasn't Mike.

"I'm sorry, sir," she crooned to him.

He didn't respond, and Toni could understand. As it happened, she missed Mike too.

Maybe it would have been easier if they'd had more warning; if she could have weaned herself off of him over time. But instead, she felt as if the sudden reappearance of their friends had robbed her of something she hadn't been ready to let go, even though she'd known that she'd have to let it go eventually.

She'd spent every day since Mike left running from the

discomfort she felt at the loss. But the worst part of the past few nights, when she'd crawled into bed without him, was the nagging question in the back of her brain that couldn't help but wonder about things that felt too treacherous to say aloud. Like what, she wondered, would have happened if he'd asked to stay?

She ran her hand over Paw's back and up the length of his tail. "Have a good night, buddy." He moved to his food bowl. She washed her hands in the sink and considered doing one more circuit around the house but suppressed the urge. She had to leave now, or she might never.

Toni snatched her purse from the coffee table and walked on shaky legs to the front door because she was nervous. She hadn't seen Mike in a week and had no idea how she would react when she did. She could have stayed home, but the thought of missing a chance to see him — even if she would have to pretend not to know how good he felt inside her — wasn't an option.

She slipped her feet into her favorite tall pumps and checked her purse to make sure she had her cell phone, the tube of her favorite matte red lip stain to swipe on once she made it to the restaurant, and her keys.

"Don't tear up my couch," she called to her cat and then pulled the front door open.

Where she found Mike standing on her front doorstep, red-faced and surprised.

"The hell?" she breathed.

"I lied in the spring," he said. "I'm terrible at no-strings-attached relationships. Or I assume I would be because I've never actually done it before, and I definitely never wanted to do it with you. I should have said that."

"Why didn't you?"

"Because I thought you would say no. Was I right?"

Toni smiled sadly. "Yes."

That one word seemed to deflate him. She watched as Mike hung his head and nodded, his gaze drifting to the ground before them.

Just then, Paw meowed loudly and brushed past her left leg. She didn't freak out as he stepped on the threshold of the door because she knew he wasn't going to dart into the street. Instead, he rubbed his small black head against Mike's shin.

Mike kneeled to scratch her cat behind his ears and on top of his head. Paw closed his eyes and pressed into Mike's touch. She'd rarely seen him so happy. Toni wanted that for herself.

"Tell me now," she said in a voice rough with emotion.

Paw meowed when Mike stopped scratching him.

He looked up at Toni with a slack jaw but wide eyes. "What?"

"Tell me what you should have told me in the spring."

"Seriously?"

"Yes," she said. "We're going to be late for dinner."

***

MIKE HAD a hard time accepting when things were too easy, especially in this moment. He'd driven across town to Toni's house, trying to think of what he would say to her — assuming he would miss her — while also not running a red light.

When he saw her car parked in her driveway, he'd thought *that* was too good to be true. But when he looked up to find her looking down at him, her bottom lip trapped between her teeth, a nervous gleam in her eyes, he couldn't trust it. He stood slowly and then turned around in a circle.

"What?" Toni asked in a small, confused voice that was echoed by Paw's pitiful meow as he pressed his body against Mike's legs.

"Are Deja and Marie here? Is Alejandro going to jump out of a bush?"

"I don't have any bushes, Michael." Her voice had gone deep, husky. "You know I like to keep her cut low."

"I—" Mike's voice gave out at the memory. It hadn't even been two weeks since they'd been together, but Mike had spent every day they'd been apart romanticizing her, and still, he couldn't do her justice.

"Toni," he started.

"No," she whispered.

He ran his hands through his hair. He was starting to sweat. "Antonia," he said and then cursed when a sound escaped her lips that was almost exactly like the whimper she made the first time he eased his dick inside her. "Fuck."

She laughed and nodded.

"One week apart is enough," he said, feeling light and hopeful for the first time in days. "Antonia, will you date me in an exclusive, not temporary, probably going to lead to us meeting each other's parents and adopting another cat kind of way?"

This was not the speech Mike had planned. He'd wanted to sound smoother, more self-assured, and maybe even much less nervous, but it was probably better that he sounded exactly like himself. She already knew who he was. The only real question was if she wanted him exactly as he was for longer than a few weeks.

"What about renovating your condo?" she asked with raised eyebrows.

Mike took a deep breath, shook his head, and stepped off her front step. "Oh my god. Never mind."

Toni scooted Paw back into the house and closed the front door, talking to him as she locked it. "Okay, wait, hear me out."

"No," Mike barked over his shoulder.

Toni's heels clicked as she sidled up next to him and placed her hand in his.

He was smiling as their gazes touched, and she pressed her cheek to his shirt.

"But we're such a great team," she breathed.

He turned and smoothed his hand around the back of her neck and bent forward. She smiled and spread her lips, welcoming his tongue inside her mouth with a happy moan. She tasted like mint and sunshine and berry lip gloss. And when she wrapped an arm around his waist and pulled his body against hers, Mike felt like he was home.

"I'm glad you finally realized that."

She kissed his bottom lip. "As long as you're okay with the fact that I'll never love you as much as Paw does."

He smiled and kissed her again. "We'll see."

CHAPTER THIRTY

Girl where are you?
Have you heard from Mike?
Are you *with* Mike!?

That was the second text Deja had sent, and Toni still didn't have a good reply. The answer was that she and Mike were in the restaurant parking lot, just a few feet away from the front door. The full answer was that they had arrived nearly ten minutes before their reservation and thought they would make up the extra time they didn't expect to have by making out.

The answer she wouldn't be sharing was that making out had led to Mike pushing up her dress, peeling her panties aside, and slipping one, now two fingers inside her, and they'd lost track of time.

Toni's knees went weak every time Mike touched her, but when he used his fingers on her — especially after so many days apart — she felt as if nothing could keep all her body parts together. Certainly not her legs. He was stroking inside her with a firm pressure and then pulling out slowly, skimming the pads of his fingers along her g-spot, making her shiver every time. By the time his thumb started massaging her clit, he had her ready to ask him to move in. Thankfully, her mouth was busy sucking on his earlobe and groaning into his ear.

"I thought I'd never feel this again," he groaned, kissing his way down her chest, snaking his tongue inside her bra to tease her nipple.

"Oh god, we have to hurry up," Toni moaned. "We're late."

"Mmhmm," Mike hummed noncommittally as he kissed his way up her chest and neck. He planted a garden of soft pecks on her chin, and then their gazes met.

"Okay, a few more minutes," she panted, reaching for his zipper.

He nodded and kissed her deep and slow as she scooted down in the seat to spread her legs wider for him while unzipping his pants.

In the end, they were too excited to be *too* late. Once Toni wrapped her palm around his dick, everything sped up. Mike groaned into her mouth. Toni started riding his fingers. They missed the appetizers and feasted on the sounds of their pleasure instead. They stroked one another slow and then fast and then faster.

And when they came, they spent a few minutes feeling happy and loose-limbed at being back together again.

"I missed you," Toni whispered into the quiet of Mike's car.

"Let's not break up again, okay?"

"Deal."

"SORRY WE'RE LATE!" Toni trilled. "There was traffic on the highway. So weird. But we're here now. Did y'all already order appetizers?"

Mike pulled Toni's chair out and then sat in the empty one next to her. His arm brushed hers. Toni ignored the fact that even the feeling of the fine hair on his arms made her pussy clench. She needed to keep talking.

Toni's grandmother always said she had a knack for storytelling, and her mother translated that to mean that she was a fantastic liar. The trick, Toni had learned over the years, was to just keep talking. When a clingy man asked why she didn't want a second date, her students wondered when she'd finish grading their essays, or even when she had to look at herself in the mirror for a pep talk on a rough day, she got through all that by overwhelming the silence with the power of a good story.

Unfortunately, her friends were not a great audience for her storytelling.

Once they were seated, everyone's attention shifted from her to Mike, and he was *not* a skilled storyteller, a gift and a curse.

"I'm going to be the director of my program," Mike said confidently as a shy smile spread on his lips.

"What?" Toni screeched, turning to him.

He gazed deep into her eyes as if they were alone. "And we were making out in the car," he admitted. His words were so soft that the last couple were swallowed up by the table's reaction.

"Told you!" Deja cried around Alejandro to Marie. "I want the full bowling schedule."

"Bowling?" Toni asked, her head spinning.

"There's a lesbian bowling league in the winter, and she never told us."

"Wow," Toni said.

"Again, do neither of you two people with actual damn doctorates understand what the word 'lesbian' means?"

Meanwhile, Alejandro was signaling for their waiter.

"Yeah, can we get the champagne now, actually?" he said. "Apparently, we have some more good news."

"See what you did?" Toni said, turning to Mike.

"They were going to find out anyway," he said with a shrug that turned into him throwing his arm around her shoulders. He grazed her upper arm with his knuckles.

"Why didn't you tell me you were the new director?"

"Because you would have tried to talk me out of it."

Toni opened her mouth, and Mike rushed forward to kiss her quick, shaking his head.

"I want this job, Antonia. It's always been part of my plans. Besides, I don't need you to mother me. I can take care of myself on campus. And I can take care of you at home."

Toni cupped Mike's face in her hands and blinked back tears as full of happiness as relief. "I won't tell the Black Feminist Futures Club you said that or that I liked it."

"Deal."

"Ooooh," Marie and Deja sang because they were children.

Toni rolled her eyes before turning to glare at Alejandro across the table. "What do you mean, *more* good news?"

The sounds of celebration took a second to quiet. Toni moved her gaze from Alejandro to Deja.

"Oh my god," Marie said, echoing Toni's own thoughts.

Alejandro put his arm around Deja and pulled her into his side. They looked at one another in that sappy, lovesick way they'd all grown accustomed to. But then Deja stuck her left hand out for the table to see the diamond ring on her finger.

This time Toni and Mike joined Marie in celebration. But even as they stood from their chairs to congratulate Deja and Alejandro, Toni reached for Mike's hand and found him reaching for her in return.

FALL

EPILOGUE

He'd wanted this job. He'd asked for this position. This was part of his plan.

Mike didn't have to remind himself that he'd asked to be director of his program every day, but some days, he needed to close his office door and give himself this pep talk. When the tedious weight of his new position got to be too much, he needed to hear that this would all be worth it someday.

Not today, though.

He'd known the job wouldn't be easy. There were so many meetings, and Mike hated meetings. But he was still surprised that a shocking amount of his job involved mediating conflicts between his colleagues. It had only been a couple of months, but Mike thought he could understand why the previous director had stepped down.

And then there was the awkward position of being an Associate Director responsible for corralling full professors into doing more service than they wanted. Mike didn't have kids. He wasn't interested in telling grown people what to do.

He'd read the handbook for new chairs and directors, and it

hadn't been helpful for any of the things that were frustrating him, so he'd been channeling his stress into evening workouts with Alejandro. But in the middle of the day, the pep talk would have to do.

He turned to his desktop and navigated to his department's social media. He didn't really want to work, but handling the social media felt like the least work he could do. And when he saw all the tweets that ended with #DrWSpotted, he was truly happy for the first time since he left home.

He picked up his campus phone and called Anya, the department secretary.

"Hi, Mike! I'm almost done with the draft spring schedule."

"I'm not calling about that," Mike said easily. "Don't worry."

Anya sighed audibly.

"I'm gonna head to the library," he said. "If I get any calls, can you just forward them to my cell?"

"Absolutely. Um..." Her voice trailed off.

"What?"

"Are you going to see Dr. Ward?"

Mike couldn't help but smile. "Yes. So if it's not urgent—"

"I'll take a message," Anya said quickly. "Tell Toni I said hi."

Mike smiled against the phone receiver. "I'll definitely do that."

***

TONI WAS HAVING serious doubts about working on campus.

It had seemed like a good idea...at some point. She didn't have plans to do much research while she was on sabbatical, but after a few months of rest, her brain felt ready for a little intellectual stimulation, and her research projects were begging for some attention — not much, just a little. At first, she'd thought she'd work from home and put her newly renovated office to good use, but after her fourth trip to the library to pick up a book she needed, working entirely from home felt like a needless burden. So, she'd decided to go to campus one, no more than two days a week. The plan was to spend a few hours in her carrel, get a little reading done, and go home feeling accomplished. It had worked for a couple of weeks until word spread that she was back.

No one seemed to care that she was on sabbatical and had work to do. All that mattered was that everyone had a problem they thought Toni was uniquely qualified to fix.

She was not. What she was, much to her own chagrin, was a soft touch.

When someone knocked on the door to her carrel, she wanted to send them away, but she couldn't, so she did her best to solve their problem as quickly as possible. On a good day, her unofficial mentoring sessions ate up an hour or so of her time. On a bad day, there could be a line of junior faculty outside of her carrel trying to fit a meeting with her in between their classes. She was beginning to wonder if she would have to just go back to working at home and make do.

Three soft knocks on the door of her carrel made her back tense. She took a deep breath and steeled her nerves. She didn't need to smile to be helpful, and pretending would only exhaust her reserve of energy faster than not.

She turned slowly in her chair. "Good after— what are you doing here?"

Mike was leaning against the wall of her carrel with a smile on his face. "The question is, what are you doing here?"

"Trying to work, obviously."

He shook his head as he sat down sideways in the chair

next to her. He spread his legs obscenely, and she met his smile with her own. "How's the work going?"

"I picked up some books and just sat down, actually. You have great timing."

His left hand settled over her thigh and squeezed. "I wish I could take credit for that, but I heard you were here."

Toni's eyebrows bunched together. "From who?"

He pulled his phone from the pocket of his suit jacket and tapped the screen before turning it around for her to see.

"There's a hashtag?" she exclaimed, louder than she normally let her voice rise on this floor of the library.

"I figured you didn't know. I said I saw you in the Wellness Center."

"Why?"

"To buy us some time. Come on," he said and tipped his head to the right.

"Where are we going?"

Mike's eyes wrinkled at the corners when he smiled. He squeezed her thigh again and then stood. Toni's chin lifted to look up at him as he bent over her. They smiled as their mouths brushed and their breaths mingled. "You know I'm not going to tell you."

She gently bit his bottom lip. "But you'll make it worth my while?"

"Always."

He pressed his mouth to hers, and she nodded quickly before Mike pulled away.

Thankfully, Toni had barely unpacked her backpack. She hadn't even pulled her laptop out. She shoved her library books into the bag and tried to put it on her shoulder, but Mike easily grabbed it from her hand with an amused smile and a shake of his head.

She rolled her eyes even though they both knew that she

liked when he took care of her this way. Just like they both knew how much he loved it when he offered her his hand and she took it, entwining their fingers together.

Toni and Mike walked out of her library carrel hand-in-hand. She wondered if *this* would make it to her hashtag and made a mental note to send her friend in HR a quick but official email. She and Mike could worry about paperwork when her sabbatical was over.

They took the elevator down to the main floor and had almost made it out of the front door when someone called their names.

They turned to find Marie jogging in their direction.

"Did you use the hashtag to find me?" Toni asked.

"Obviously."

"You mean you knew there was a hashtag and didn't tell me?"

"You mean you didn't know? Aw, you're really taking this sabbatical seriously. Good for you."

Toni rolled her eyes and looked away.

Mike squeezed her hand. "What's up?"

Toni turned back as Marie handed them each a slip of green paper and stepped close. "Meeting tonight. We're voting officially on forming a union."

"Already?" Mike asked.

Marie nodded. "Administration found out we've been meeting. It's now or not for another twenty years."

"Wow," Toni said.

Marie's face had turned red with excitement. "I know. I'm going to go tell the library faculty while I'm here. Spread the word to your networks, okay?"

"Okay," Toni said automatically.

"Of course," Mike echoed.

They both watched Marie jog excitedly away.

"She doesn't remember that you're Director now," Toni said.

"Probably not. But that's alright. I'm not going to blow her cover."

Toni leaned into his side. "This is going to be chaotic as hell," she said.

"It sure is. Good thing you're on sabbatical." He kissed her temple.

Toni huffed out a laugh.

"Come on, let's get out of here. I've got a promise to keep."

He squeezed her hand one more time.

"EXCUSE ME, sir, what is this room?"

"*This* is my lab."

"Your lab? A whole damn lab just for you?"

"Calm down, it's for me and my grad students. I got an external grant and negotiated this space for us to work in. I didn't want to have to keep scheduling lab time around my colleagues."

"Well, ain't you fancy? You know this is everything that's wrong with—"

"The world," Mike said, cutting her off. "I agree. But I'd like to remind you that more than half of the grad students of color in the hard sciences work with me, and they were struggling to get adequate lab time. Now, they don't have to worry about that." As he spoke, Mike walked across the room and set Toni's backpack on a wide lab table nearest the large window.

He pulled out a chair for her and waited.

Toni meandered. "So you're gonna let me sneak into your lab—"

"No need to sneak," he said. "I set the schedule for access

to the lab every week. You let me know when you want to be on campus, and the lab is yours."

Toni stopped at the head of the table. "How much is an hour of lab time worth in your grant?"

"I haven't done the math, but I know it's not cheap."

"And you'll give some of that time up for me?"

"In a heartbeat. If I can give you a place to work in peace, it's a no-brainer."

Toni's cheeks hurt from trying not to smile. "And where will you be?"

Mike grinned happily. "Wherever you want me."

"Good to know," she said and then moved to sit in the chair.

Mike sat in the seat next to her, pulled out his cell phone, and threw his left arm casually over the back of her chair.

"What are you doing?" Toni asked as she unpacked her backpack.

"Looking at the Humane Society website. They just got some kittens in."

"A cat is a big commitment," Toni said, hiding her smile while she pulled out her newest library check-outs.

Mike's hand smoothed up her spine and caressed the back of her neck. "I know."

KEEP IN TOUCH

katrinajacksonauthor.com

Sign up for my newsletter

OTHER BOOKS BY KATRINA JACKSON

Welcome to Sea Port

From Scratch

Inheritance

Small Town Secrets

Her Christmas Cookie

The Spies Who Loved Her

Pink Slip

Private Eye

Bang & Burn

New Year, New We

His Only Valentine

Bright Lights

Erotic Accommodations

Room for Three?

Neighborly

Love At Last

Every New Year

One More Valentine

Heist Holidays

Grand Theft N.Y.E.

The Family

Beautiful and Dirty

The Hitman

The Enforcer

Dolci

The Don

Dolore

Bay Area Blues

Layover

Back in the Day

Curriculum Vitae

Office Hours

Sabbatical

Standalone stories

Encore

The Tenant

Sex Toy Soldier

Looking